Deadly variations

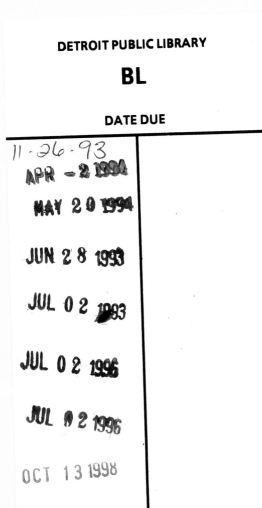

Paul Myers

Deadly variations

New York
The Vanguard Press

First American Edition 1986
Copyright © 1985 by Paul Myers
Published by Vanguard Press, Inc., 424 Madison Avenue, New York,
N.Y. 10017.

Library of Congress Cataloging-in-Publication Data
Myers, Paul.
    Deadly variations.

    I. Title.
PR6063.Y47D4   1986   823'.914   85-26294
ISBN 0-8149-0919-1

For Nicholas and John

Deadly variations

Geneva

The sound of the explosion probably awoke him. When he opened his eyes, he was conscious of a low rumble, echoing distantly, mingling with the hum of the early morning traffic. The digital clock on the bedside table blinked to 6.41. At his side, Anne-Marie was still sleeping, her head turned away, her long blonde hair sprawled across the pillow. In the half-light, her bare shoulders were immobile. 'She sleeps "anonymously",' he thought. Sometimes, on mornings when she left before he awoke, her side of the bed was hardly disturbed, with only a trace of her perfume to witness her presence.

Slipping quietly from the bed, he padded to the window, pulling the curtain to one side. Early morning mist hung over Lac Léman, masking the centre of Geneva until spring sunlight burned it away. There was not a ripple on the placid grey water, and the sailing boats in the small marina, still skeletal in their winter shrouds, hung motionless on their reflections. In the street below, a number of cars had stopped, their drivers peering through side windows at something out of view, farther down the road. Several of them had parked and were walking in that direction. Craning his head, he tried to see the cause of the disturbance, but could only make out a lazy veil of smoke drifting towards the mist on the lake. As he returned to bed, Anne-Marie stirred slightly.

'What is it?'

'Nothing, some sort of accident, I think.'

She sighed, and buried her head into the pillow. The air in the bedroom was cool, and he nestled against her back, fitting himself to the contours of her body, his arm encircling her. She wriggled slightly, closing the gulf where bare flesh did not meet and, almost instinctively, his hand moved over her,

1

stroking the firm skin. Her hand reached up to his, fingers intertwining, holding him close.

'What time is it?'

'Early.'

'Then sleep!'

'It seems a shame to waste the opportunity.'

He could feel her smile as she backed her body into his, flattening his palm against her stomach. He tried to free his hand, but she gave it a tightening grip. In the street below, a police car raced by, its siren sounding. Anne-Marie yawned.

'There's your accident.'

'Now we'll never get back to sleep.' He kissed her shoulder. She half turned towards him, smiling.

'I should go.'

'I told you, it's early.'

'I know, but I have to go to my apartment and change.'

'I can drop you off on the way to the office.' His lips traced the curve of her throat.

'No, I have other things to do. I haven't been home for days, it seems.'

Leaning his head on one hand, he looked down at her. 'If you'd marry me, this would be home.'

'Oh Mark, don't start again.'

'I mean it. Why won't you?'

'Because.'

'Because why?'

'Because it's better this way. You have no obligations, and I can be independent. You should be relieved.'

'It doesn't make sense. We spend most nights together, we're together all day in the office. Why don't we stop the charade and make it permanent?'

Anne-Marie released his hand and allowed his fingers to trace delicate patterns. She rested her face against his chest, turning closer towards him.

'If I marry you, you'll get bored. There will be no more mystery.' She pushed him gently on the chest. 'Go back to sleep!'

'That's nonsense. I'll want you more than ever.'

'No you won't. After a while, you'll want a sensible Swiss

wife to look after your sensible Swiss home. I like the way we live now. The music world intrigues me.' She stretched. 'It's so un-Swiss: all the daily changes and the little crises. It has temperament.'

'There's no reason why you should give it up. We could go on working together. There are plenty of husband and wife managements.'

She turned down the corners of her mouth, half in fun. 'You make it sound too ordinary. You didn't grow up here, Mark, doing all the correct things in a proper society. If I had wanted to get married, like all my schoolfriends, I would have done it years ago, and settled down with a reliable Genevois watchmaker.'

'You never know, he might have been a banker!'

'That would be worse. I'm not looking for security. We're having fun the way we are. Don't spoil it by being serious and settled. Go back to sleep.'

His fingers flattened against the smoothness of her body, warm with sleep. 'Getting married won't change anything. You won't notice the difference.'

'You won't, but I will. In a few months, you'll want a nice, plump *hausfrau*, cooking dinner and washing your underwear. After that, it will come down to dinner out once a week, love on Saturday nights, and "Where's my clean shirt?" on Monday mornings!'

'It doesn't have to be, and why would I stop sending my shirts to the laundry? They fold them better than you do.'

Anne-Marie sighed against his chest. Her breath felt warm and slightly moist. 'I'd better go. My dress needs ironing.'

'No, stay.'

'But I haven't cleaned up for days.'

'I still don't see why you bother to keep a separate apartment. Think what you could save in rent. There's a good reason in itself.' His hand continued to move, searching deeper and, although she made no response, he could feel her breath quickening. Her hand clasped his shoulder.

'You're just trying to save on my salary – Harpagon!'

'Harpagon?'

3

'You English never read anything. He is *L'Avare*, Molière's miser.' She had gently urged her leg across his.

'What would he know?' His mouth closed over hers, and her arms circled his neck, enfolding him.

The telephone, ringing insistently, awoke them a little after eight. A thin shaft of the promised sunlight was already streaming through a gap in the curtains, catching motes of dust in its beam. Watching Anne-Marie's body as she walked gracefully to the bathroom, Mark sighed contentedly. His life was, at last, moving in the right direction. In a while, he would persuade Anne-Marie, and the picture would be complete.

He lifted the receiver. 'Hello – *oui* – Mark Holland.'

There was a click at the other end, and he was about to hang up when a voice spoke. 'Well, dear boy, I would have thought that seven years amidst the industrious Swiss would have changed your sleeping habits by now. I take it you were sleeping?'

Mark sat up suddenly, swinging his legs to the floor. In the bathroom, he could hear Anne-Marie running the shower.

'What the hell are you doing, calling me?'

'Come, come, that's hardly a nice opening gambit when an old friend calls.'

'Friend?'

'Well, let's say past colleague. I always like to think of myself as a friend, too. Really, Mark, it's a little ungracious of you.'

Mark reached for his cigarette-case. To his irritation, his hand was shaking violently. His first reaction was to hang up, but he knew the telephone would ring again within minutes. He put the receiver down and lit a cigarette, waiting for his anger to recede. At length, he returned to the phone.

'What do you want?'

'Ah, there you are again. I hope you're not still smoking. So bad for you, and with that athletic body of yours . . .'

'All right, Willis, spare me your concern. Why are you calling me?'

'Oh, Willis are we? I can remember the days when it was

4

"HW". Of course, we were all copying the Americans and everything was first initials in those days. Horrid habit!'

'That was a long time ago. What are you doing, calling me here? I didn't know you had this number.'

'Oh, we try to keep up with our ex-employees. We never lose touch completely, you know.'

'As far as I'm concerned, you lost touch with me seven years ago, when I left. I'm not renewing any old acquaintances.'

'Come come, my dear, you are being churlish; it really doesn't suit you. A sullen pout doesn't fit the rugged type. Speaking of which, I suppose you've got half the young *demoiselles* of Geneva longing to run their fingers through those blond curls of yours? Am I making you blush?'

'For Christ's sake, spare me your prurient imagination!'

'Temper, temper!' He giggled. 'I thought you might enjoy the flattery. Tall, handsome men always take everything for granted.'

'Look, Willis, what the hell do you want, or is this your idea of a bad-taste joke?'

'There's no need to get nasty.' His elocution had slipped slightly, and a hint of Home Counties whine had crept in. 'I'm hardly likely to call you at this hour of the morning unless it was important.'

Mark paused before replying, taking time to grind his cigarette into the ashtray. In the bathroom, the shower had stopped, and Anne-Marie would return. He kept his voice low.

'There can't be anything of importance affecting me, Willis. I left a long time ago.'

'Nobody ever leaves the Department completely. I thought we made that clear at the time.' A hint of hardness had entered his voice.

'What are you getting at?'

'I really don't want to spell it out over the telephone.'

'You can say anything you like, as far as I'm concerned. Nobody's listening in at this end.'

'Well, you can't be too careful.' The accent had adjusted itself. 'You're too young to remember all those wartime signs about walls having ears. Let's see, you must be well into your forties by now . . .'

'My age has nothing to do with it. Besides, if I know you, you're sitting with my file in your pudgy little hand.'

'Not a file any more; it's done with computers. I type in a few letters, and it all comes up on a television screen in neat little green capitals. It's very different, these days. We're thoroughly modernised.'

'None of which is of the slightest interest to me. That finished when I walked out of your office seven years ago, thank God!'

'You didn't exactly walk out into a brave new world on your brave little own. I seem to remember an airline ticket, a nice new passport, and a not inconsiderable deposit in a Geneva bank, not to mention a word or two in the right quarter with some of our Swiss colleagues.'

'What do you mean?' Mark felt a tightening of the chest. Anne-Marie walked out of the bathroom, dressed in an old robe. She was drying her hair with a towel. Her eyebrows raised a question, but Mark motioned her to remain silent.

'What I mean, Mark, is that your decision to move to Geneva only came about with the concurrence and the assistance of this department. You were in such a hurry to sign all the papers at the time that you scarcely bothered to read them.'

'Do you blame me? I just wanted to get out.'

'Oh, quite, but there were one or two paragraphs covering possible future eventualities – the usual sort of Civil Service stuff. I'm surprised you never had a look through them later, but I suppose it happens all the time.'

'Get to the point.'

'Well, my dear, it appears that one of those eventualities has shown up, but we can't sit chatting like this all day.'

'And if I tell you to go and solve your problems without me?'

The voice remained silky. 'You wouldn't want to let your old friends down like that. I'm told the Swiss can be very sticky about residential permits these days. They really can't afford to have people with, shall we say, questionable pasts.'

'I see,'

'I thought you might.' His voice became brisk. 'Now, when can we meet?'

'I don't know. Any time, I suppose, if you give me warning. Why do you need me?'

'I'll tell you about it when I see you. What about tomorrow?'

'I suppose so. I haven't got my diary in front of me, but it should be possible, if you insist.'

Across the room, Anne-Marie nodded, mouthing 'Who is he?', but Mark returned to the phone.

'Where do you want to meet – my office?'

'In Geneva? Good gracious me, no! That would never do. Why don't we make it Vienna?'

'You're joking!'

'Not at all. After all, you're a musical agent, or manager, or whatever it is you call yourself. That must take you all over the place – very convenient, I would say. I seem to remember you look after that conductor Steigel.'

'Konstantin Steigel? What about him?'

'Well, if you bothered to look at your concert programmes from time to time, I think you'd find that he's conducting in Vienna this Thursday. Why don't you go to his concert?'

Mark sighed. Not for the first time, Willis was several moves ahead of him.

'I suppose I could be in Vienna tomorrow.'

'Of course you could. Only right and proper, I would have thought, considering he pays part of your salary. I hope he doesn't plan to do anything too heavy – such a bore!'

'Where will I find you?'

'I'll be there, don't worry. You'll probably sit in his box at the concert, won't you?'

'Probably.'

'Then we can find each other at the interval.'

'Can't you tell me what this is about?'

'Not really. We've been talking for hours already, and the Department only recently did a long memo about cutting down phone calls.'

'Bullshit!'

'Well, let's say I like to keep you guessing. It does concern a friend of yours if that's any consolation.'

'Who?'

'Do you remember a certain Eberhard Glantz?'

'Glantz? No.'

'Try a little harder, Mark. Berlin, 1969? There was that spot of trouble with Eberhard near Checkpoint Charlie. Does it ring a bell?'

For a moment, Mark recalled a night, many years earlier, by the Berlin Wall. There had been heavy rain, and the sound of gunfire. Conscious that Anne-Marie was watching him, he kept his voice impersonal.

'Was Glantz his name? I didn't remember.'

'Well, he remembers you. You saved his life.'

'That was a very long time ago. It has nothing to do with the present.'

'I'll explain it all when we meet. You really should be getting to the office, shouldn't you?' He paused for a moment. 'I'm surprised the bang didn't wake you up.'

'What bang?'

'A bomb went off in a block of flats just near you this morning. I believe it did quite a lot of damage. Didn't you hear it?'

'I thought I heard something. Is that why you're calling?'

'Sort of. Shall we say tomorrow evening, then?'

Before Mark could reply, the line went dead, and he remained with the receiver in his hand, staring into space. Anne-Marie sat by him on the bed.

'What has happened? You look terrible.'

'Nothing serious.' He lit another cigarette, and was glad to find that his hand was steady. 'Just a voice from the past. It was a surprise.'

A shadow crossed Anne-Marie's face. She stood and, allowing the robe to fall from her shoulders, began to dress. She did not look at him.

'Is this more of your secret past; the part you never talk about?'

'It's not secret. I don't talk about it because I didn't enjoy it. The memory depresses me.' She remained silent, buttoning a blouse, and he sensed her disapproval.

'I'm sorry. It was somebody I hadn't thought about for a long time.'

'But you're going to meet him in Vienna.' It was a statement rather than a question.

'It happens to fit with Konstantin's concert there. I can sort out his Japanese tour while I'm there.'

8

With her clothes on, Anne-Marie's personality seemed to change. A long, black skirt covered her slim, tapering legs, and a well-tailored jacket, broad at the waist, disguised the contours of her generous breasts. Her hair was drawn tightly back into a bun, and a large pair of sunglasses covered much of her face. Examining herself in the mirror, she frowned, smoothing a stray hair. Mark leaned back on his elbows and smiled.

'My God, with an expression like that, you'll frighten the postman!'

When she turned, her expression had softened.

'I warned you – a proper Swiss *hausfrau*! Maybe that's what you really want.' She motioned to the telephone. 'What did he want?'

'I don't know. He was being mysterious about it. He likes playing games like that. Apparently that commotion this morning was a bomb going off.'

'And he knew about it?'

'Yes.'

She looked at her watch. 'At eight-thirty in the morning? Where was he calling from?'

'London.'

'At seven-thirty, their time. You have some strange friends. Who is Glantz?'

'I hardly remember. We met in Germany a dozen years ago.'

'That was him calling you?'

'No, just a mutual friend.'

Putting on the robe discarded by Anne-Marie, Mark walked to her and took her in his arms. Her head rested for a moment on his shoulder.

'I think sometimes, Mark, that I would prefer not to know about you. I might not like what I learn.'

'There's not much to tell you that you don't know already. During the years I was in London, I worked for a part of the Civil Service, mostly attached to the Arts Council. It was boring and depressing, and there was a lot of office politics.'

'But your old friends call you about bombs at seven-thirty in the morning!'

'He must have heard about it on the radio, or he could have

been talking to somebody else in Geneva before he decided to call me. Anyway, he wasn't much of a friend.'

'I see.' He held her closer, but she did not respond.

'That was all that he said.'

'Was anyone hurt?'

'I don't know. He didn't mention anyone. I'm sure it will be on the news. All he said was that a bomb had gone off in Geneva and he wondered whether I knew about it.'

'You didn't seem very pleased to hear from him.'

'No, not really. I never liked him very much, and I was surprised that he should call.'

He opened the curtains, allowing the hot sunlight to stream into the room. The mist had vanished from the lake, and the waters now reflected the unending blue of the sky. A small door opened on to a narrow balcony, and he stepped into the fresh air, breathing deeply. Behind him, Anne-Marie called his name. He turned back to her.

'Its all right; I'm not going to stand out there.'

'The railing is too low; it worries me. I don't know why they build those things. They're dangerous.'

'I'll fix some flower-boxes along the top when I get back.'

Anne-Marie was putting things into her handbag.

'Why is it so necessary to meet this man in Vienna?'

'It isn't necessary, but it happens to fit in with my plans. I need to see Konstantin at some point. He gets nervous if I don't stay in touch with him.'

'It was not so important before he called.'

'I know, but putting off Vienna was laziness on my part. This way, I can get it all finished.'

'Shall I come with you?'

'No, I think I'd better look after this alone. It won't take more than a day or so, and the time will be taken up with a lot of boring people. Why don't we go away at the weekend, when I get back? We can go up to the mountains for a couple of days. There's plenty of snow left.'

'I suppose we could. You're supposed to have a meeting with La Suisse Romande tomorrow.'

'Can you look after it for me?'

'Yes, of course, and there are all the audition tapes you

10

promised to listen to. A pianist called Joachim Albrecht. He called twice.'

'If he calls again, ask him to wait for a day or two longer. I promise to listen to them when I get back. Have you ever heard of Albrecht?'

'No.'

'Well, tell him I want a few days more.'

'Yes.'

'What's the matter?'

She turned her head away. 'I don't know. I worry about you.'

'Then come and look after me all the time, and you'll see there's nothing to worry about.'

He walked over to her, taking her in his arms. She seemed to resist, but he held her tightly.

Her eyes searched his face. 'Could you promise me that?'

He kissed her. 'I promise. Will you think about it?'

'Yes.' She looked very serious, her head lowered. 'I'll think about it.'

Walking her to the door, he held her shoulder tightly.

'There's nothing more to it. Everyone has the odd skeleton in the closet. I'll see you in an hour.'

She kissed him briefly, but with sudden passion, then quickly opened the door.

'In an hour.'

The traffic was flowing freely again along the Quai du Mont Blanc but, as he passed a side street just before the Hilton, a barrier cordoned off the road. Two firemen were about to remove it under the watchful eye of a policeman. Mark walked over to a spot where a number of onlookers were standing. A man in white overalls was staring at the top floor of one of the buildings. Two of its windows were missing, and there were burn marks on the plaster.

'What happened?'

The man shrugged. 'Who knows? Some sort of an explosion on the top floor of that old building. Lucky it didn't take out every window in the street.'

'Was anyone hurt?'

'Not that I know of. The place was empty, or so I heard. The old girl in the apartment below got a nasty shock. A chandelier fell off the ceiling and landed on her bed.'

'What caused the explosion? Somebody said it was a bomb.'

The man looked surprised. 'A bomb? I doubt it. More likely a gas leak. Some of those old buildings are death traps; should have been pulled down years ago. Where did you hear it was a bomb?'

'I don't know. I thought I heard it on the morning news.'

The man grunted. 'You could be right. This town's full of bloody foreigners these days. They should kick 'em all out, the lot of them!'

Mark nodded, and moved on. 'Spoken like a true Swiss,' he thought. 'But what the hell's going on, in Geneva, of all places? And why should it affect me?' He frowned, and headed towards the footbridge crossing the lake to the centre of the town. Willis, the Department, the shadowy, half-remembered Eberhard Glantz were part of a past he had long since tried to erase from his mind. His pace quickened, and he wondered wryly whether it was because he was late, or because the adrenalin seemed to be flowing in his system.

Vienna

Over six feet three, with the permanent stoop of a tall man, his narrow head illuminated by a silver-white tonsure of hair, a pair of half-spectacles balancing precariously at the tip of a bulbous nose, Konstantin Steigel looked more like a benign Anglican parson than a distinguished conductor. Dressed in an old cardigan and a pair of shapeless slacks, he rose to his full height, dominating the living room of one of the smaller suites in the Imperial Hotel.

'Well, young man, so you've decided to give the old boy a few minutes of your precious time?'

'No, Maestro, I think it's the other way round.'

Steigel's Austrian wife, Heidi, bustled round Mark, relieving him of raincoat and briefcase with the efficiency of a well-trained servant, and Mark always had the impression that this was her chief function. In contrast to her husband, she was a small, apple-cheeked woman who must, he thought, be somewhere in her middle sixties, but with the sprightly cheerfulness that made her ageless. He could picture her in a dirndl and embroidered blouse, serving armloads of tankards in some Grinzing *biergarten*.

'*Grüss Gott*, Mark, how handsome you are looking! Tino has been asking for you all morning. You know how impatient he gets!'

'I have only just arrived from the airport.'

'Yes, of course you did, my dear, but it's no use explaining things like that to a conductor. He couldn't have seen you earlier; he's only just returned from the morning's general rehearsal.'

Long training had inured Heidi to her husband's well-known fits of temperament, and the major part of her time was given to smoothing over situations as they arose. She was also

13

aware that his legendary temper tantrums were usually carefully orchestrated and conducted with professional skill, as the occasion demanded. He was, by nature, a mild, scholarly man, who felt that his chosen profession required certain histrionic displays.

'How is it going?' Mark whispered, watching Steigel striding across to the window.

Heidi shrugged. 'How does it ever go in Vienna, my dear?'

He nodded gravely. The city of Mozart and Johann Strauss had long been famous for its ruthless musicians and orchestral politics. Even a veteran like Steigel had to be steered through the endless maze of petty intrigues, and he could not have had a better pilot than Heidi. He recalled that there had only been one delightful faux pas on her part, when she had foolishly undertaken a press interview with one of the more sensational German magazines. The interviewer had, somewhat impertinently, inquired about her sex life, to which she had replied: 'Well, he won't before a concert; he can't, after a concert; and he gives three concerts a week!'

Beaming genially, Steigel indicated a chair for Mark.

'So, my dear Mark, welcome to Vienna. You'd like some coffee?'

'No, thank you. How was the rehearsal?'

Steigel's face darkened. 'That's never a good question in this town. After the concert, when I see which of the musicians from the morning's rehearsal actually decided to play, then I can tell you how it was. At least I don't have that drrreadful young pianist to contend with.' He rolled his 'r's with Teutonic relish.

'Did he cancel?'

'At the last minute, I am happy to report. We had one meeting here, during which he explained to me that he was "into" Mozart and cocaine, I am not sure in which order, and proceeded to play Köchel 595 as though it was a transcription for xylophone solo. When I suggested to him that he might study some of the phrasing in the new Bärenreiter edition, he looked extremely puzzled and asked what that might be. I hope he was referring to the edition, but I have the feeling that "phrasing" may have been the problem word.'

14

Mark smiled. The old man was obviously enjoying himself. He had probably been preparing the speech all morning.

'I'm sorry to hear that. He has very good fingers...'

'Then I suggest, my dear, that he should put them to good use as a motor mechanic. Please, Mark, don't ask me to accompany any more fizz kids. I used to play this concerto with Casadesus and Rudi Serkin, and if you want me to have a younger artist, there is Brendel or the one who sounds like a killer fish.'

'Perahia?'

'*Ja*, that's a wonderful young man; but no more fizz kids!'

Heidi laughed. 'Tino, don't blame Mark. He didn't choose the pianist. You have to talk to Grubermann about that. Anyway, you were cross because he needed a haircut.'

'He needed a haircut, a shave, a bath, several years of playing chamber music with good musicians who know about such things as phrasing and articulation, and some very blunt instructions in good manners. I am told he is a great success because he scowls at audiences whenever he plays. It would not surprise me to learn that he also makes rude gestures with his "good" fingers. From now on, he can do them without me! So, we have replaced him with a badly under-rehearsed Serenade, and I will undertake the scowls and, maybe, the rude gestures.'

'I'll enjoy them all the more, but I will make a note that the young man in question is not on your list of preferred soloists! How is the soprano?'

Steigel raised his eyes to the ceiling, letting his arms fall loosely to his sides.

'She sang the Mahler as though it was Brünnhilde's Immolation. I explained to her that "Das himmlische Leben" is a child's view of heaven, full of good things to eat, and with a beauty and innocence that makes everything awaken with joy.' He began to sing: '"*Dass Alles für Freuden, für Freuden erwacht*", *nicht wahr?*' He paused dramatically. 'So now she sings it like the "Liebestod"!'

'You surprise me. She has a very good voice...'

'And a nice *tucchus* but, as Toscanini once demonstrated so physically...' He cupped both hands. '...if only her brains were as big as her mammary glands...' He chuckled with the memory.

Heidi, who was sitting in a corner, watching the display, smiled indulgently.

'You see, Mark, he doesn't change; just a little crankier every year. At the piano rehearsal, he gave her bottom a nice pat and told her she was a very talented young lady!'

'At my age, a pat on the bottom is all she can expect of me!'

'You're not so old, Maestro.'

'On the contrary, my dear Mark, I am becoming very old indeed and preparing to come into my own. I have already three score years and fourteen, and looking forward to the golden era of my career. You see, my dear, I fully expect to become a Grand Old Man of the music world, which gives me certain definite benefits. I will have outlived most of my contemporaries, and everyone will assume that the passage of time has bestowed upon me a certain God-like omniscience. This means that my programmes will become more and more eccentric and the critics will become more and more respectful and enthusiastic. It also means that I can make up more and more apocryphal stories about musicians that nobody will dare to contradict. When, at last, I go absolutely ga-ga and make no sense whatever, they will nominate me as one of the greatest conductors of my era!'

Mark smiled, and winked at Heidi.

'You sound as though you're in the best of form, Maestro. Did you enjoy the recording sessions in London?'

Steigel shrugged. 'Mark, recordings are neither good nor bad. Sometimes they please me when I hear them a year later. But they are a very useful means of making money and insuring that I have a little something for my retirement.'

Mark shook his head in mock despair. 'As bad as that!'

'Not bad, not good. Recording has very little to do with making music, my dear. There is no spontaneity, no inspiration, no imagination – just that stupid little red light and some idiot of an engineer telling you he heard the oboe playing a wrong note. It is a little like – forgive me, Heidi – self-abuse: the end result is a small pleasure, but the achievement is a solitary and altogether unsatisfactory occupation. You know, the young man at the studio told me I played it differently

16

every time he called a number at me. Of course I played it differently. I am not a machine!'

'Now you're getting carried away.'

Steigel relaxed. 'Well, perhaps a little, but these bright young record men irritate me. They always like to tell you how much they know about the music they can't play themselves. Did I ever tell you about the time Pierre Monteux was conducting the Debussy Nocturnes?'

'Probably.'

'Well, halfway through the rehearsal, the first violin asks him: "Maestro, why do you conduct this section this way?"' He waved his arms vaguely. 'And Pierre raised those magnificent shaggy eyebrows of his and said: "Because Claude told me to." Hah, what an answer!'

Steigel had been pacing the room, but he now stopped, dropping into a chair next to Mark's. His long, bony fingers tapped Mark's knee.

'Tell me, Mark, do I really want to go on this Japanese tour?'

'It's all arranged, as far as I know. You're supposed to leave ...'

'*Ja, ja*, I know all those things, but do these Japanese really want to hear Bruckner? Do they understand what Brahms is trying to get at? They keep sending me cables about television shows and millions of yen. I don't know what it's all about.'

'Why don't you give me all the papers, and I'll go through them for you.'

'Thank you, Mark, I was hoping you could do that. I don't know what they want.' He sat back heavily in the chair, closing his eyes. When Heidi spoke, her voice was apologetic.

'You see, my dear, it's a long way to go. Tino is not as young as he used to be. The journey could be very tiring, and we would be a long way from home if anything – if he were not feeling well. The family, the doctor – everyone – they are all here ...' Her voice trailed into silence. For a moment, her cheerful smile had faded. Her eyes were frightened. Mark hesitated before speaking.

'Why don't I have a look at the itinerary? There should be plenty of rest periods between appearances, and you could always make a little holiday of it; stop off and see one or two places *en route*.'

Steigel sat up again, frowning. 'I'm a conductor, not a tourist. I just didn't want to waste my time conducting for audiences who don't understand the music!'

'Yes, of course. Let me look at the papers, anyway.'

Steigel nodded, and settled back into the armchair, closing his eyes, as though the conversation had exhausted him. Almost immediately, Heidi, her smile restored, produced Mark's briefcase and coat.

'I think Tino should rest before the concert.'

'Yes, he should. Just send me all the Japanese papers and I'll sort them out. You have until the middle of next year to think about it.'

Steigel had not moved. He opened his eyes briefly, nodded to Mark, then closed them again. He suddenly looked, Mark thought, like a very old man. He walked to the door with Heidi, who kissed him on each cheek.

'Make sure he rests.'

She nodded. 'Don't worry, my dear, I always do. We'll leave about half an hour before the concert. Tino prefers to change here and walk across the road.'

'I'll see you then.'

He knew that, by the time the concert began, Steigel would be as refreshed and alert as ever, commanding his orchestral forces with the athletic skill of a gymnast. He remembered how, even in his nineties, Leopold Stokowski, barely able to walk and apparently clinging to life by a thread, could step on to a podium, his eyes blazing, his hair in magnificent, straggling disarray, and direct an orchestra with the concentration and intensity of a man half his age. Perhaps it was the constant calisthenics of conducting that kept them all going. He liked to think it was the music itself.

He never ceased to be impressed by the spectacular décor of the Musikverein. The warm opulence of that golden auditorium, with its baroque decorations, was a visual shock after the grey Viennese streets and the drab entrance passages of the building which housed it. There was a lush richness which, he felt sure, seemed to enhance the sound, adding a golden bloom. The dusty comfort of Geneva's Victoria Hall, despite its own acoustic excellence, could not compare with this magnificent setting. Vienna, once the focal point of a great empire, had never accepted that it was now the last stop on the line to Eastern Europe, but here, in the glow of the Musikverein's splendour, one could still believe, like the Viennese, that this was the centre of the music world.

From his box, on the right side of the hall, Mark scanned the audience for Willis, but there was no sign of him. By the time Heidi had guided him to his seat, the house was filled except for a few late arrivals, and the lights were lowered. There was friendly applause as Konstantin Steigel strode on to the stage, walking briskly. He paused to bow stiffly, then turned to the orchestra, his head down, awaiting silence.

He had been right about the lack of rehearsal for the Mozart. The strings were warm and delicate, their phrasing graceful, but the woodwinds were not together, and sounded poorly balanced. The horns were late in the opening chords, and their intonation occasionally slipped. By most standards, it was still very good, but Mark had heard Steigel conduct this Mozart many times before and could recognise what was missing. 'At least,' he thought, 'the solo violin is good.' And the music, well played or not, was still Mozart.

One of the eccentricities of the Musikverein is that, although the boxes flank each side of the hall, their seats are fixed so that they face directly forward. The listener must therefore either crane his neck to watch the stage, or face forward watching the audience. For a while, Mark turned towards the stage but, as the Serenade progressed from movement to movement, his neck stiffened. To relax for a while, he faced to the front, ignoring the musicians. Looking across the rows of seats, he was aware of a slight movement. A pale face, illuminated by the stage lights, was quite plainly turned in his direction. It was clearly Willis, the light catching his glasses, the shadows behind him outlining his puffy cheeks. Mark clenched his fists involuntarily. For a moment, their eyes met, and Willis inclined his head slightly before returning his attention to the stage. Mark did not move. He continued to watch Willis with intense concentration, willing him to look up again, but the man remained in profile only. In the pause between the third and fourth movements, Willis leaned over to whisper something in his companion's ear, but his gaze remained firmly fixed on the stage. Mark felt a slight tug on his sleeve. Heidi looked anxious.

'Is it so awful?'

'No, of course not.'

'You look unhappy.'

He forced a smile. 'I'm sorry, I wasn't concentrating. The performance is beautiful.'

Heidi shrugged. 'He has done it better.'

When the work ended, the audience applauded enthusiastically. Steigel bowed slowly, shook the first violinist by the hand and waved an arm (Mark wondered whether it might not be a fist) at the other players, who stood dutifully. He did not return for a second bow, and the house lights came up. Watching the audience disperse along the aisles, Mark caught Willis's eye again. He inclined his head towards the bar at the far end of the hall, and Mark nodded.

In his dressing room, Steigel was struggling with his bow tie, swearing. His face was covered with sweat, and his dress shirt clung to his body in damp, sticky folds. Mark entered the room with Heidi, but Steigel waved him away.

'Don't talk to me now, my dear. I'm too hot and sweaty, and I'm too angry to make small talk. Did you hear that idiot oboist?'

'It wasn't that bad.'

'It was bad enough. Go and have a drink for me. At least you can drown my sorrows. You can tell Grubermann that I have had enough. This is absolutely the last time. I'd sooner spend the rest of my time conducting for Japanese or pygmies! Heidi, did you bring another shirt?'

'Of course, Tino, I always do.' She had already unfolded a clean dress shirt, and set about helping him to dislodge a cuff-link.

Making his way downstairs, Mark spotted Willis standing in a corner of the bar, away from the crowd. He was deep in conversation with a slim, dark-haired young man. As Mark approached, he realised that the light in the auditorium had been deceptive. Willis had aged considerably in the seven years since they had last met. His cheeks had an unhealthy grey pallor and seemed artificially puffed out. What little hair was left on his head had thinned to pale streaks across the top of his scalp, and there were deep lines creasing his eyes and mouth in a permanent grimace. He had been a dapper little man, slightly portly, but always impeccably dressed. Now, his body seemed to have sagged, with shrunken chest and shoulders hanging limply beneath an oversized head. His suit was crumpled and ill-fitting, showing obvious signs of age. As Mark drew near, Willis peered at him across the top of his thick lenses.

'Mark, my dear boy, what an unexpected pleasure!' He raised a wine glass in salute. 'Not such a surprise, really; we're on your sort of territory. Terribly grand, isn't it?' He touched the young man on the shoulder. 'This is Quentin Sharpe, my assistant. He's my absolute shadow, and I can't imagine going anywhere without him.' The young man smiled and nodded, fingering a maroon bow tie. His charcoal-grey suit was cut to emphasise the slimness of his waist.

Mark kept his hands firmly to his sides, like a man standing to attention, acknowledging their greetings with a curt inclination of his head. His face was expressionless. Willis waved a wine glass towards him.

'What about a quick one? We'll never get through the crowd at the bar, but if you like, Quentin and I will share his glass, and you can have mine.' He giggled. 'Don't worry, I haven't got anything catching!'

Mark had not yet spoken, and shook his head. Willis looked around, beaming happily.

'Marvellous place, isn't it? I haven't been here for years. I'd forgotten how delightfully decadent it is.' Willis gave a theatrical sigh. 'This is nice, Mark ... so lovely to see you again. I must say, the years have been kind to you.'

Trying to control his voice, Mark said: 'I believe we have some business to discuss.'

'Of course we have, but we can hardly do it here, in the middle of a concert. Are you staying for the rest?'

'I expect to.'

'I see. Quentin and I thought we'd sneak out before the Mahler Fourth. It's a bit too heavy for our taste – all that maudlin self-pity. I can't see why he doesn't stick to something nice and jolly, like Haydn. Now, the Mozart was very pretty indeed, didn't you think? I'm sorry the pianist didn't show up. Quentin tells me he's quite dazzling.'

'Oh yes, he's really fabulous.' Quentin's voice was low and breathy. 'And terribly exciting to watch.'

Willis looked at his watch. 'I think if we're going to escape before the onslaught, we'd better make our exit now. If you're going to stay for the dreary part, Mark, why don't we meet as soon as we can get away?'

'Where?'

'There's a delightful little café called Hawelka, or something like that, on the Dorotheergasse. That's one of those little streets leading off the Graben.'

'I know where it is.'

'It's really rather fun. You always find a lot of artists and writers, and it's what I like to call "cheap and cheerful". I wish we had more places like that in London. Anyway, Quentin and I will head over there and keep a table warm while you do your bit for Mahler. I must say your life seems very enviable, Mark, and you're certainly looking very prosperous on it, so I suppose you have to put up with the boring parts too. Very noble!'

'As a matter of fact, I happen to enjoy it.'

'Really? Well, I suppose it's just as well. We'll pop off now, and you can come and find us as soon as you can get away. Then we can have a nice long chat – catch up on old times, eh? Cheers!'

He drained his glass and, with a knowing wink, linked arms with Quentin and headed for the exit. Mark watched their departing figures with a sense of relief. Seeing Willis again, but a diminished Willis who was a shadow of his former self, was reassuring. He made his way quickly back to the dressing room, where Steigel, looking calm and refreshed, greeted him with a charming smile.

'Ah, Mark, I hope the drink washed away the bad taste. Heidi, would you like to introduce our guest?' He waved in the direction of a tall, smiling man, dressed in a dinner jacket, who clicked his heels and bowed, announcing: 'Jürgen Krebs.' He offered a vice-like handshake and bowed again. Mark noted a strong aroma of after-shave.

Heidi took his arm. 'Herr Krebs is the Director of ADT, Mark. He wants to make a television programme about Tino.'

'Yes, I believe we have had some correspondence on the subject.'

Herr Krebs's smile broadened. 'Ah, you are Mr Holland from Geneva. I should have recognised you. I was planning to visit you last week, but they needed a new print of my Beethoven film in New York. You are joining us for dinner?'

'Unfortunately, I can't, but perhaps we can talk tomorrow morning? In fact, Maestro, I wondered if you would forgive me if I left a little before the end of the concert. I have to catch some other people while I'm here in Vienna, and they are leaving on the first plane in the morning.'

Steigel chuckled. 'I hope she's beautiful.'

'As a matter of fact, it's a he, and he's far from beautiful, Maestro. I hate to miss the end of the Mahler. It's one of my favourites.'

'Not tonight, it won't be, but I warned you about that already. Anyway, tomorrow is a better time. These days, by the time I finish a concert, my chief preoccupation is a good dinner and a long sleep. Now, go away, please, all of you. I want to think about music for a few minutes before those wretches out there destroy it.'

There were the usual formalities of rearranging the seating in the box when they returned. Mark offered the best chair to Herr Krebs, who insisted on seating himself in the row behind.

'This way, I can take a little snooze, if necessary. I am still jet-lagged from New York. Please!' He seated himself in Mark's chair, smiling benevolently, exuding goodwill and after-shave in equal proportions.

As the house lights dimmed again, Mark's eyes were drawn to the empty space vacated by Willis and Quentin. 'Why the hell would they want to talk to me about Glantz?' He had only a vague memory of a dark young man with sunken eyes, swathed in a cheap raincoat, with whom he had spent a few hours. He

23

had been one of a dozen such men, dirty and terrified, whom he had helped out of East Berlin during those years. He doubted that he would even know him again. Fifteen years was a long time to remember a face.

The orchestra ceased its tuning and, timing his entrance perfectly, Steigel again appeared on the stage, this time preceded by a beautiful young black soprano, dressed in a radiant wine-coloured gown. The audience applauded appreciatively.

From the first bars of the music, and the delicacy with which the violins played their opening phrase, building not to a *crescendo* but a *subito pianissimo*, Mark sensed that this was to be a great performance. The *sotto voce* reply of the cellos was superbly balanced, the solo horn was, at last, perfectly tuned, and the music ebbed and flowed, subtly changing, under Steigel's baton. This was to be one of those occasions when Viennese musicians lived up to their reputation. The first movement approached the final Coda, and Steigel led the strings back to their opening theme with an anticipation that brought Mark to the edge of his seat. He glanced across at Heidi and smiled. She nodded happily, and it occurred to him that she knew a great deal more about music than she pretended. Herr Krebs nodded vaguely towards him and whispered, '*Gut, gut!*' There was a hushed silence between the movements and Mark reflected that, for all their arrogance, at least the Viennese knew when they were hearing the real thing. New Yorkers rattled their programmes and looked at their watches, Londoners coughed and sneezed their way through everything, and the good burghers of Geneva and Zurich yawned openly, daydreaming of rich dinners and fat profits.

The great third movement, its pulse-beat emphasised by the double basses, began to unfold, and Mark leaned forward, closing his eyes. It was superb, the music sweeping over him majestically. For a moment, his attention was distracted by a sudden rush of cool air, as though someone had opened the rear door of the box. He wondered whether Herr Krebs, overwhelmed by jet-lag, had slipped out for a breath of fresh air, but from the corner of his eye he could still see the Director's well-tailored trousers and highly polished shoes. Once again, his attention was riveted by the great apogee of the movement:

a momentary silence, followed by a blaze of sound, the tim-panist striking his drums with two sticks in each hand and the orchestra rising to an apocalyptic climax. The effect was shattering, obliterating all distractions, and he found that he had been holding his breath.

As the strings returned with their serene harmonies, Mark glanced at Heidi, who sat, her eyes closed, absorbing the music. Herr Krebs had apparently fallen asleep, despite the power and volume of the sound. His arms had fallen to his sides, dangling loosely, and his head was bowed on his chest. Mark leaned towards Herr Krebs and, for a moment, stopped breathing. The Director was too still. There was something unnatural in his posture, and an angle to his body that only death could create. He recalled the sudden draft of cool air from a few minutes before. It could have been caused by some-one entering the box. At the same moment, Mark realised that Herr Krebs was sitting in the chair he himself had occupied during the first half of the concert.

For a moment, he felt a blind panic. His hands gripped the sides of his chair, and he prepared to lunge quickly towards the door at the rear of the box, but a long-submerged discipline overtook him, and he remained motionless, fighting against any sudden movement that might draw attention. Heidi had not yet opened her eyes but, as the music slowly faded, she leaned forward, her back to Mark, to watch the soprano on the stage, who had risen from her chair and moved to stand next to Konstantin.

Moving quietly, Mark stepped behind Krebs's chair, opened the door, and went quickly into the corridor outside. It was empty. The soprano had begun to sing, and he walked as rapidly as he could without arousing the attention of the sleepy attendant at the door of the hall.

The street outside was quiet, and he walked swiftly. A pulse was beating in his temple, but his face remained impassive. His senses, lulled by the music, were now fully alert to the slightest noise or movement. Glancing behind him, Mark made certain that he was not being followed, and doubled back on his route to make sure. Now, he was walking too quickly, and beginning to breathe heavily. Forcing himself to a slower pace, he tried to assemble the events, starting with the explosion in Geneva and the phone call from Willis. He paused for a moment, choosing a shadowy doorway, to light a cigarette. As he cupped his hands over the flame of his cigarette-lighter, he checked again for followers, but the street revealed no tell-tale movements. His cigarette glowed as he drew on it. For some insane reason, someone had just tried to kill him. There seemed little doubt that Krebs had been mistaken for him. But why? The cold sweat of fear dried on his forehead as a light breeze of night air brushed his face. Standing against the wall, in the open, he felt less vulnerable. Anger began to grow. 'That bastard Willis! He's got to be behind this!' He threw the cigarette into the gutter, where it sparked for a moment.

He moved forward again, close behind an elderly couple walking their dog. The animal stopped to lift its leg against a lamp-post, and he moved on, increasing his pace until he found himself amid other pedestrians. If he was being followed, he would be partially protected by the presence of other people around him. When he reached the corner of the Kärntnerstrasse, he found an empty phone booth and slipped inside. He dialled the police and spoke briefly, hanging up before the surprised officer could question him further. He was sorry to leave the discovery of Herr Krebs to Heidi, but she might still believe he had left before the man died. At that moment, his only instinct had been survival.

The Kärntnerstrasse, that great pedestrian precinct in the centre of the town, was still crowded with window-shoppers enjoying the first mild evening of spring. The old training had returned almost instinctively, and Mark relaxed his pace, joining the strollers and mingling with the crowd. Occasionally, he paused before a brightly decorated shop window, watching for any reflection in the glass that might betray a follower. In the distance, he could hear police sirens. Imperceptibly, he quickened his pace again, forcing himself to pause from time to time. 'My God,' he thought. 'All hell will be breaking loose inside the hall in about five minutes.' At the end of the street, he turned left, into the Graben. It was still too early in the season for the cafés to put out chairs and tables, and his footsteps echoed as he crossed the wide square towards Dorotheergasse.

He felt calmer as he entered the narrow, ill-lit little side street. When he found Willis, he would let him do the talking. Maybe the pieces would fit together.

The café was smaller than he remembered: noisy, smoky and, like so many of its kind, overheated. In one corner, a large table of Americans were shouting cheerfully at one another, announcing political solutions to the world's problems. At another, a group of students, heavily bearded and buried in ski sweaters, argued with exaggerated gestures. An elderly man, clutching a cup of coffee, was reading one of the house newspapers. Some Japanese tourists, laden with cameras, hissed and smiled appreciatively. Set slightly apart from the crowd, four men in shirt-sleeves, beer glases set in front of them, were talking quietly together in low voices, their faces glum. They, Mark thought, were probably the artists and writers that Willis found such 'fun'. Between the tables, bulky waiters in dinner jackets with shiny elbows negotiated trays of glasses and bottles. For a moment, Mark could not find Willis, but, entering farther into the heat and smoke, discovered the two men at the rear of the room, squashed together at a small table. Willis had placed a white hand over the younger man's, ostensibly to make a point in the conversation. He saw Mark, and waved.

'There you are! Had your ration of gasping emotion? I can't imagine how you survive it, night after night. What is the matter? You look quite put out.'

'Nothing. I stayed as long as I could, which meant having to hurry here.'

'You must be out of shape. You should join a health club, like young Quentin here.' He surveyed Quentin proudly. 'His body is quite perfect. Now, what are you going to drink?'

'Cognac.'

'You have developed fancy habits.' He waved to the waiter. 'And two more glasses of white wine, *bitte.*'

'Don't complain, Willis. It's all on expenses.'

'I know, but it's much harder to fiddle expenses if one has to pay out real money.' He settled back, watching Mark with pink lips pursed. 'Well, here we are, after all these years.'

Mark lit a cigarette. 'I think you'd better get right to the point, Willis. Something's happened, and I want to know if it's related to your bringing me here.'

'What's happened?'

'I'll tell you about it later, after you've told me what this is all about.'

'I see. You'll show me yours if I'll show you mine.' Mark did not return his smile.

'What have I got to do with Eberhard Glantz?'

'I'm glad you remember the name. The last time we spoke, you gave the impression that you'd forgotten him.'

'Believe it or not, I actually had, until you reminded me.'

'Well, let's see if we can bring you up to date. Quentin, why don't you give Mark some of the background.'

Quentin began to recite, almost in a monotone. 'The man we know as Eberhard Glantz was born in Köthen, now East Germany, on April 17th, 1944 . . .'

Willis raised a hand. 'I don't think his birthday's particularly relevant, but let it pass.'

'He was educated at local schools, but by the time he was sixteen showed a remarkable ability in physics and chemistry. At that time, he was more interested in becoming a concert pianist, but the powers-that-be obviously thought he would be of greater value to the State as a scientist. He was sent to the University of Leipzig at seventeen . . .'

'From which he graduated "summa cum laude", as our American friends like to say. He was the most brilliant student of his year; one of the best they ever turned out.'

Mark swallowed the rest of his brandy. 'None of this means anything to me. Good God, we only spent a few hours together in that bloody awful storm drain in Berlin.'

'Patience, my dear, it will all come out in a minute. When Eberhard graduated, they put him to work in one of their research units. He was an extraordinarily talented young man, and was playing around with all sorts of experiments in genetics.'

'What happened?'

'You'd never believe it, Mark, but that's because you're not a romantic, like me. Young Eberhard fell in love.'

'So?'

28

Willis sighed. 'She was some sort of lab technician and, well, you know the sort of thing: holding hands while they cut up the guinea-pigs and dissected the frogs.'

'I assume the authorities didn't care?'

'Not at all. The problem was that Helga – I think that was her name – yearned for a better way of life and, with a bright young man like Eberhard to support her, realised that fame and fortune, not to mention creature comforts, lay on the other side of the Curtain. That's where we came into the picture. You see, we weren't averse to lending a helping hand to anyone coming out, but we really didn't have the time or money to run a regular passenger service, except in special circumstances . . .'

'Like brilliant young scientists who might be useful?'

'Exactly.'

'And especially when Intelligence tell you that a very talented young scientist is working on the other side, and you just happen to know a "sympathetic" young woman who finds herself working alongside him?' Mark smiled bitterly. 'I used to work for you, Willis. Why don't you spare me all the euphemisms?'

Willis examined his fingernails rather carefully for a moment before replying. When he looked up, he smiled cheerfully.

'My dear Mark, you do have an unkind imagination. But to get on with the story, Eberhard joined you in that East Berlin storm drain for a few rainy hours one July evening, when you helped him hop over the Wall.'

'What happened to Helga?'

'She didn't get through. You really don't remember very much about that time, do you?'

'I was too busy trying to stay alive. You may also remember that I collected a bullet in the shoulder later that night.'

Willis nodded. 'Of course! I had forgotten. No wonder Eberhard felt so grateful.'

'And Helga?'

'Well, that was the evening we tried a multiple breakout. It involved a whole lot of diversionary tactics. Unfortunately, Helga's group never made it. They switched the searchlights on at the wrong moment, she got caught in the crossfire, and that was the end of that. For a long time he blamed us, but it really wasn't our fault, Mark – I assure you. The only benefit from the whole sorry business was that it convinced him there was no reason to go back.'

'None of which tells me how I come into the picture.'

'As I said, Eberhard wasn't very pleased with us, no matter how much we told him it had been an accident. And, very unfortunately, somebody let slip the fact that Helga had been, shall we say, associated with us for some time. When he learned that, he wouldn't come to work for us in Britain, so we had to make a sort of deal.'

'What sort of deal?'

'Really, Mark, there's no need to look so suspicious! We made a few arrangements with some friends of ours, and managed to get him a Swiss passport. He settled down very nicely in Geneva and has been working there ever since. Tell me, have you ever heard of a company called Suchim?'

'Not really, but I've seen the name. Aren't they something to do with pharmaceutical products? I seem to have seen a logo on aspirin bottles.'

'Exactly; it's one of those funny names made up from combining something like Suisse Chimie AG, whatever that means. It's a very big company, owning chemical plants and mines all over the world. They call them multinationals these days. The Swiss are very big on medicines, you know. It's one of their major industries.'

'All right, Willis, but I don't imagine you went to all this trouble to get your brilliant young scientist out of the East just to hand him over to some Swiss drug company.'

'No, not exactly.' He waved to the waiter. 'What about another cognac? All this talking is making me thirsty.' He ordered another round of drinks.

'What is your connection with Suchim?'

'I don't think I should go into all the details. I know you signed the Official Secrets Act, but it was a long time ago. Goodness knows, I'm not sure that I should be telling you half of this.'

'Then perhaps I can piece together a few ideas of my own.

30

Suchim is an officially registered Swiss company, dealing with pharmaceutical products, among other things. But, like so many multinationals, it is partly owned by a number of foreign stockholders, one of which is closely connected with some "colleagues" of yours.'

'You are a clever boy, Mark. I never did understand why you were so anxious to leave us. You could have gone far.'

'Not far enough, and I wanted to leave for the very reasons we are discussing. I hated the whole dirty business.'

'Oh come, come! Somebody has to undertake the job of protecting people.'

'It wasn't going to be me, and I had the strongest feeling that people were going to need protecting from their protectors. So, Eberhard Glantz went to work in a research laboratory which he believed to be Swiss, and you and Suchim were able to keep an eye on what he was doing. Is that about it?'

'That's exactly it. Like most scientists, he was much too busy working out equations and brushing up on Einstein to worry about who owned the company. He had a lovely, clean laboratory to work in, and a well-trained staff of his own, not to mention all the other little tax-free benefits of life in Switzerland.'

'What went wrong?'

'Well, actually, nothing. He did happen to stumble on an interesting theory. You know how it is: you pour the wrong chemical into the wrong test-tube, and discover Coca Cola . . . Well, it seems he was trying to isolate a number of rather unpleasant germs and came across a very nasty little virus of his own.'

Willis stared at his hands. He looked like a naughty schoolboy who had been caught red-handed.

'Oh Jesus Christ!'

'No, Mark, it really did happen that way. I am assured it is possible. If it's any consolation to you, he didn't manufacture anything.'

'But it could be manufactured?'

'Yes.'

'Just how nasty a bug is it?'

Willis kept his voice low. 'Very nasty indeed, I'm afraid. Of course, some of this has to be speculation, but it apparently takes the form of a colourless, odourless liquid that evaporates very rapidly, so that you can limit it to carefully selected areas.'

'And?'

'It would appear to reverse the process of what they have been doing in Israel, Jordan and various Middle Eastern countries all these years, turning a garden back into a desert, so to speak. It could have disastrous economic results in a heavy agricultural area.' He hesitated. 'There are also some side effects.' He nodded towards Quentin, whose voice remained a monotone.

'It induces an illness very similar to radiation poison: vomiting, loss of hair, followed by rapid weakening and death.'

Mark stared at them. 'Those are the side effects?'

Willis did not return his gaze. 'Basically, yes. They are the immediate effects, and they would be very difficult to trace. Among the survivors, if there are any, I understand that it also induces sterility.'

'God help us all!'

'Quite. I'm sure you can understand our concern that such a discovery doesn't fall into the wrong hands, Mark. Recent events in the Iraqi war have shown that not everyone is quite so concerned with the terms of the Geneva Convention. The real difficulty is that, once you've discovered something like this, you can't really un-discover it.'

'And they're sure it exists?'

'No question about it. These days, they can work these things out with computers to do the calculating.'

For a moment, they sat in silence. Mark glanced at his watch, estimating the amount of time before the news of Krebs would begin to circulate. Vienna preferred word-of-mouth to newspapers.

'You still haven't explained my part in this.'

Willis sighed and sipped some wine. 'Bad news always travels fast in these matters. It seems a number of people have learned about Eberhard's discovery, and are very anxious to talk to him about it. Of course, his secret belongs to us: we paid for it. The problem is that we believe some other people are trying to take it away. Eberhard is, quite frankly, a very frightened man.'

32

'Where is he now?'

'We don't exactly know. We talked to him a few days ago but as I told you, he has never trusted us. Even less than before, now that he's learned that he's been working for us all these years without realising it. As you may imagine, he's very unhappy about his discovery, and wants it put in a safe place. We managed to persuade him that we would look after it, and he was just about ready to hand it over when that damned bomb went off in Geneva.'

'And you called me. So it was a bomb. The evening radio reported a gas leak.'

'There was no point in frightening people unnecessarily.'

'And the apartment? It was supposed to be empty.'

'The apartment was Eberhard's. Fortunately, he wasn't there, or he would have been blown to smithereens. As soon as it happened, he took to his heels and ran, before anyone expected it. He called me from the French border – crossed over just beyond Lausanne – and said he was heading north.'

'Why did he call you?'

'I was his only contact. Someone from the other side just blew his apartment sky high.'

'Where do I come into all this, Willis?'

'I told you. Eberhard doesn't like us, and he certainly doesn't trust us. Someone is after him, and it's almost certainly our friends with the bullet-heads and the funny accents. So he doesn't know which way to turn or who to talk to.'

'I still don't see . . .'

'Except, of course, the man who saved his life, even stopped a bullet, all those years ago in Berlin. It's funny about coincidences. A couple of weeks ago, he saw you in Geneva, walking past his house. At first, he couldn't believe his eyes, so he kept a watch out for you. He even followed you home a couple of times. He said you spent most of your time with a very attractive blonde.'

'My God! Does he realise I wouldn't have known him if he'd come right up to me?'

'Certainly. He stood next to you one day, and you looked through him.'

'What am I supposed to do?'

'It's quite simple, really. You're the only man he feels he can trust. All we want you to do is bring him in. After that, we can look after him.'

'Despite the way he feels about you?'

'He'll have no further reason to mistrust us. Sooner or later, he has to throw in his hand with someone. I'd hardly be asking you to do this if there were any alternatives. After all, you're not one of us any more.'

'Thank God!'

'He's prepared to make his own way through France and, so far, he's been left alone. It's the only risk we're taking.'

'And after that?'

'He'll travel like any other tourist on the channel ferry, take a train to London and meet you at Victoria Station. It's not very difficult.'

'Then why all the cloak-and-dagger business in Vienna? Why didn't you tell him to come to my apartment in Geneva?'

Willis spoke with exaggerated patience. 'Because somebody, or maybe a whole lot of people, is looking for him in Geneva. He only just missed being blown to pieces. Even now, we're gambling on the fact that he got away unnoticed. You can fly to London first thing in the morning, pick him up at Victoria, bundle him in one of our cars, visit your friend in the music world, go to a concert or fly home to Blondie in Geneva, all expenses paid.'

Mark stubbed out a cigarette and swallowed cognac. Willis remained silent, watching him. Quentin occupied himself with the posters decorating the walls of the café.

'I think your story's a load of bullshit, Willis. I don't believe you accidentally discover viruses, either, unless you're looking for them.'

Willis sighed. 'All right. He was doing research in that field, but he still didn't expect to stumble on something as ghastly as that.'

'So he knew what he was doing?'

'Yes and no. He was working on an antidote to something else.'

'At least we're getting a little closer to the truth.'

34

Willis spread his palms flat on the table. 'It's the whole truth, Mark. Believe me.'

'There was still no reason to bring me to Vienna. I look after artists all over the place.'

'Quite wrong. We didn't want you to arouse any suspicion, and there was nothing more logical than for you to go to Herr Steigel's concert tonight. He was the only artist on your list appearing this particular Thursday evening at a place that would give you enough time to fly to London by midday tomorrow.'

'Why not have me fly directly to London? I go there quite often.'

'We considered it, but we had to play safe. After all, if we keep tabs on you, Mark, all these years later, why shouldn't our colleagues on the other side? For all they know, you're still working for us. It might have been just a little too coincidental for a bomb to go off round the corner from your apartment in Geneva, and for you to be winging your way into dear old Blighty on the next flight. You've got to credit them with a little intelligence.'

Mark leaned forward, keeping his voice low. 'I credit them with a great deal more intelligence than you appear to. This evening at the concert, one of your "colleagues", presumably from the other side, tried to kill me!'

For the first time since their conversation began, Willis's bland composure collapsed. He blinked several times, then slumped back in his chair. The lines cutting deeply into the sides of his mouth trembled slightly. He stared at the table-top, drumming his fingers in a meaningless tattoo. Quentin said: 'Oh God!' and, as if disturbed from a reverie, Willis glared angrily at him and muttered 'Be quiet!' When he looked up at Mark, his face was chalky.

'What happened?'

Speaking slowly and choosing each word carefully to avoid overlooking the smallest detail, Mark described the sequence of events following his return to the concert. His narrative was curt and direct, and neither man interrupted him. When he had finished, they remained silent. The noise of the café seemed to surround them like an invisible wall. He lit a cigarette, watching their faces. Willis was the first to recover. Producing a soiled handkerchief, he removed his spectacles and wiped his forehead. His face looked defenceless without the protection of the heavy lenses. Taking his time, he concentrated on polishing the glass and, with a final fastidious flick, returned them to his nose. He attempted a smile.

'This need not change our plans intrinsically. You're quite sure he's dead?'

'Certain.'

'How? Were there any external signs?'

'No; but I explained. The music was very loud, and it was a moment when everyone was looking at the stage. I felt a draft of cold air for a moment, which was almost certainly someone opening the door of the box, but I was too preoccupied with the music.'

'I understand. How was it done?'

'Any number of ways. The man was sleepy. He'd been complaining of jet-lag and he'd just flown in from New York. If he flew overnight, he could have been up for more than twenty-four hours. The concert hall was warm, and it would have made him drowsy. I don't have to tell you how these things are done, Willis. A quick jab with a hypodermic, a sniff of something lethal, or God knows what sophisticated new devices you've worked out in the past few years.'

Willis nodded silently. 'What makes you so sure it was intended for you?'

'He was sitting in my chair, so whoever planned the job probably checked me out in the first half of the concert. When I think about it, Krebs and I are both about the same height and build. He was sitting towards the back of the box, where there was less light to identify him.' Mark looked at his watch. 'We're going to have to move soon. They'll have found the body by now.'

Willis nodded again. 'You're sure you weren't followed?'

'As sure as I can be. You forget I was a professional. I doubled back and I double-checked half a dozen times in the ten minutes it took to get there. My guess, and I'm counting on it, is that they assumed they hit the right man and got out of the hall as quickly as possible.'

36

'You're probably right.'

'Which means I have a little time before they realise their mistake. I can't hang around here much longer.'

'One more question. What did you tell the police, and what made you call them at all?'

'As little as possible; simply that someone had died during the concert. I hung up before they could ask more.'

Quentin said: 'You should have called the hospital.'

Mark felt his anger growing. 'You're right, but I panicked. Next time somebody tries to kill me, I'll be sure to remember. I called them because I didn't want to leave Heidi Steigel alone. She's not a young woman, and God knows how it affected her. I did warn her that I'd be leaving early, and she didn't see me go. I hope she'll think I left before anything happened, and if your charming "colleagues" know their stuff, they may have made it look natural.'

Willis sighed. 'Then we could be in the clear.'

A white-hot anger filled Mark. 'You shithead!'

He blinked. 'I really don't see . . .'

'I just got away with my life, some poor bastard who knows nothing about your filthy business has just bought it, and your only bloody concern is that you're in the bloody clear! How about me, Willis? Am I in the bloody clear too?'

Willis looked round furtively. 'Please, Mark, keep your voice down.' He waved to the waiter. 'I think we'd better remove ourselves from here.'

'Not yet. Just stay where you are. What the hell happens now?'

Willis was flustered. 'For goodness' sake let me think. Do you want another drink?'

'No. I'm going to need all the concentration I've got for the next few hours.'

'Very well. Quentin, pay the man anyway. I don't want to hang around waiting for the bill when we leave.'

Mark leaned forward so vehemently that Willis shrank back, half raising his hands over his chest. 'I'm waiting for an answer, Willis, and it had better be constructive.'

Willis stared at his hands, his eyes almost closed, at a loss for words. He looked as though he might fall asleep. To Mark's surprise, Quentin took control, his voice hard and his manner calm.

'At this point, it looks as though you have no alternative but to see the job through.'

'Why?'

'Because, sooner or later, they are going to realise it was the wrong man at the concert and come looking for you. They may be after Glantz, but they've made the connection with you. I think they believe you're still working for us, keeping an eye on him in Geneva.'

'Then why kill me? That makes it a dead end.'

'Not necessarily. We must consider the possibility that they've found him already, but it's unlikely. If they have, there's no reason to come after you at all. If you are his contact, the best plan would be to remove you, leaving Glantz out in the cold, waiting to be picked up.'

'Which makes me the best target.'

'No, not if you bring Glantz in quickly.'

'Why?'

'The moment you bring him in, we'll make sure they know about it, and there's no further need to go after you.'

'If.'

'If you don't, they'll stay after you.' His eyes narrowed. 'Of course, you can stay out of the way until someone finds Glantz – either them or us – but that could take a long time. You might have to drop out of sight for months.'

'And destroy everything I've built over the past seven years. Shit!'

Willis had recovered. 'On the other hand, Mark, you could fly to London tomorrow, meet Glantz, and forget the whole thing.'

'Don't make it sound so bloody easy, Willis. If you hadn't called me in Geneva, I'd never have got involved.'

Quentin said: 'That's unlikely. The moment they went after Glantz, you were involved. You would probably have ended up under the sluice gates to the River Rhône, wondering what it was all about.'

Mark thought about it. 'You could be right. Why the hell didn't you bring him in as soon as he made his "accidental" discovery?'

38

Willis fiddled with his wine glass. 'We spoke to him briefly. He hadn't completed his work. Before we could call again, he'd done a bunk.'

Mark leaned back. 'In other words, horrifying as his discovery was, you weren't about to collar him before he'd completed work on it!'

Willis did not reply. Quentin looked at Mark steadily. 'What are you going to do?'

Mark stood up. 'We'd better get the hell out of here.'

Willis and Quentin stood also. Quentin said: 'You'll bring him in?'

'I haven't much choice, and you know it. I can sit and wait for them to take another shot at me, or disappear for God knows how long . . .'

'Or fly to London tomorrow morning. The early plane will get you in before noon.' They were standing in the doorway of the café.

'I can't risk flying from here. I'm supposed to be lying in the local morgue. Have you got a car, Willis?'

'Yes.'

'Good. I'll take it and drive to Salzburg tonight. I can pick up a London flight from there in the morning.'

'But it's registered in my name!' Mark was already walking towards the Graben.

'No problem. I take it you used a credit card?' Willis nodded. 'Give me the papers, and I'll hand it in at Salzburg Airport. I'm sure the Department can manage the extra mileage! You'll also owe me for all the airline tickets.'

'Mark, I think you're being unnecessarily . . .'

Mark rounded on Willis, towering over the smaller man. 'Willis, just get me the car! Whom do I contact in London?'

Quentin replied. 'We'll contact you. If you can get to Victoria by one o'clock, we'll have a man standing by the newsagent in front of the departures board.' He reached into his breast pocket and took out a small photograph. 'This is a recent picture of Glantz. He knows what you look like.'

Mark pocketed the picture without bothering to look at it. Turning to Quentin he said: 'I have to pick up my overnight bag from the hotel. I haven't had time to check in, so I left it with the concierge. I'm round the corner, at the Ambassador.'

'Good. While you walk round there and collect it, I'll bring the car to the front door. We're parked nearby. Is there anything else you need?'

For the first time, Mark smiled. 'The list is too long! Do you still use the old number in London?'

'No. Here's my card.' He handed over an elegantly engraved business card, inscribed 'Quentin Sharpe, Arts Consultant', with a Central London telephone number. 'You're going to arrive very early in Salzburg.'

'Not if I drive slowly. There should be an all-night café somewhere along the road.'

Mark left them, retracing his steps to the Kärntnerstrasse and the rear entrance to the hotel. Vienna's small, poorly lit side streets suddenly appeared ominous. At the hotel, the concierge expressed concern.

'Herr Holland, a young lady from your office has been calling all evening. She said it was urgent you call her back.'

He took his bag. He had forgotten to call Anne-Marie earlier, but there was no time now. 'Thank you. If she calls back again, will you tell her I'll be calling her a little later?'

'Of course. You are leaving so soon?'

'Unfortunately, yes. A slight change of plans.'

Willis and Quentin were already waiting in the square outside the hotel. The car was a small Opel, and they had left the engine running. Quentin nodded towards it and said: 'I'm glad you're not in a hurry. It's an Avis, by the way, and the papers are in the glove compartment.'

He was surprised when Quentin shook his hand. He had not anticipated the gesture, and the younger man's grip was unexpectedly firm. Hovering behind him, Willis waved limply without speaking. With his shoulders hunched against the cooling air, he seemed to have shrivelled. As Mark drove away, they remained standing by the door of the hotel.

He drove slowly, making his way through a dozen side roads and one-way streets until he found the Autobahn-West, heading toward Linz. Even then, as the lights of Vienna began to recede, he did not accelerate. Every minute or so, he checked the rear-view mirror for headlights that remained constantly in view, but there were none. By the time he reached the open countryside, the traffic diminished to an occasional car, travelling faster than his on the outside lane. He switched on the radio, and found a late-night station. The car was warm, so he lowered the window, resting his elbow on the door, and settled his shoulders more comfortably against the back of the seat. 'My God,' he thought, 'it's almost as though I'm enjoying myself!'

Salzburg and Zurich

Half an hour down the road, he found an all-night garage with a telephone booth, and called Anne-Marie. It was already late, but she picked up the receiver almost as soon as it rang.

'Anne-Marie? It's Mark.'

He heard her gasp. 'Mark, where are you? I have been trying to find you all day, but the hotel said you never checked in. Are you all right?'

He kept his voice casual. 'I'm fine. There wasn't time to check in. When I left Konstantin and Heidi, I spent the rest of the day with Grubermann at the orchestra office and went straight from there to the concert.'

'Where are you now?'

'Believe it or not, I'm halfway down the road to Linz.'

'Where?'

'Linz. I'm driving to Salzburg.'

'Salzburg! Mark, what is happening?'

'Darling, I can't talk for very long. I've got some people with me: a German television director and his wife. He's got a huge opera project for Bianca Morini, and he needs to discuss it in detail. But he must be in Salzburg for an early morning meeting with his partner and the festival committee, so I agreed to drive over to Salzburg with him and talk on the way.'

He was slightly ashamed by the ease with which he told his story, even though he had rehearsed it carefully in the car. The fabrication of an imaginary television director seemed like a cynical afterthought and, for a moment, his mind's eye visualised Jürgen Krebs sprawled in his chair in the Musikverein. To add credibility, he held the phone away from his face and called out: 'Just a minute, Werner. I must speak a little longer.' Returning to the phone, he said: 'I'm sorry, darling. You sound upset.' It was like the old days: anything but the truth would do, as long as he made it plausible.

Anne-Marie was unusually distraught. 'Of course I am upset, Mark. You're behaving in such an odd way. I have been trying to find you all day, and you just . . . disappeared! You could have been in an accident.'

'But there's nothing wrong.'

'You usually call. I didn't hear from you.'

'I know. I'm sorry, but I couldn't get to a phone. If there had been time to check into the hotel, I would have called you from there, but you know how Grubermann is.'

'You're sure there is nothing wrong?'

'Absolutely. Why do you ask?'

'I don't know. I've been worried ever since that phone call from London.' Mark said nothing. 'You told me they said there was a bomb, but on the evening news they reported it as a gas explosion. Why would anyone think there was a bomb? You behaved so strangely all day yesterday.'

'I know. He must have got it wrong. These stories are always exaggerated.'

'And then you acted so strangely, going to Vienna without any notice. Did you see the man?'

Again, Mark remained casual. 'The one who called from London? Yes, I saw him for half an hour. It turned out he wanted us to represent some artists his organisation has been sponsoring. I told him the usual things and said we were over-loaded already, but they're going to send all the material anyway, so we should expect it in a couple of days. You know how it is with Arts Council representatives. They have no idea of the commercial music world. In the meantime, this tele-vision project for Bianca looks very good. It's a huge budget.' He hoped his voice was suitably enthusiastic.

'Mark, please tell me you are not in any trouble.'

'Trouble? Darling, I'm in the best of spirits. What is it?'

'I don't know. I have a feeling. Did you meet Mr Glantz?'

'Who? Oh, no. He was one of the artists they want us to look after. He's a violinist of sorts. I can't say I've ever heard of him.'

'But you said you met him in Germany a long time ago.'

'Yes, I did, but I couldn't place him. I meant I hadn't heard of him since.'

She was silent. 'Hello. Darling, are you still there?'

'Yes.'

'Is everything under control at the office?'

'Yes.'

'How did the meeting with the Suisse Romande go?'

'They had to cancel after all.' Her voice was expressionless.

'What is it?'

She paused for a long time. 'I feel foolish. I've been going out of my mind all evening, imagining things.'

'What things?'

'I don't know.'

'Oh darling, I'm sorry. I should have called you earlier.'

'No, it's not that. I think what I'm trying to say is that I didn't realise I was so dependent on you.'

'Is that so bad?'

'I'm not sure. I don't know what I think any more.'

'You don't sound very happy about it.'

'No, I don't think I am.'

'We'll talk about it when I get back. Can you do something special for me?'

'Yes.'

He chuckled. 'I haven't told you what it is, yet! I'm going to leave Werner and his wife in Salzburg. They're staying at the Goldener Hirsch, of course. Where else would a successful television director stay?'

'And you'll come home?'

'No, I can't. It's all a matter of timing. The producer of this television project is in London at the moment, meeting Bianca's husband, and he wants me to fly straight there to settle the negotiations. He's only going to be in London for another day and a half, after which he disappears back to Iran or Saudi Arabia or somewhere like that. I've agreed to meet him for lunch at the Connaught.'

'Oh Mark!'

'It shouldn't take more than a day or so to sort it out. It's a very big project, darling. They're talking about filming a package of three operas and a biographical film. It could be terribly important for Bianca.'

'So you'll fly directly there from Salzburg?'

'I could, but I don't want to. You see, I need various documents and a change of clothes. I only took the barest essentials in my overnight case, and I must look more than respectable if I'm going to meet an oil sheikh in London. He's probably Eton and Oxford, if I know the type. And there are Bianca's files and her five-year diary from the office. I had no idea this was going to happen.'

'I can meet you in London.'

'No.' He replied a little too fast.

'You don't want me?'

'Don't be silly. I want you more than you'll ever know, but there's no point in dragging all the way there.'

'Then come to Geneva. I can meet you at the airport.'

'That's the problem. All the morning flights out of Salzburg go via Zurich, which means changing planes before flying to Geneva. I don't think I can make it on time. Have you got an *ABC* at home?'

'Yes, I have a copy next door. Wait.' In the silence that followed, Mark spoke softly to himself. 'This isn't your world, darling. It's never going to be.' He rested his head against the glass of the window. It felt refreshingly cool. A moment later, she returned, and he could hear her leafing through the directory.

'Mark, the Zurich plane comes into Geneva at eleven-fifteen, but the next flight doesn't land in London until one o'clock. You'll be too late.'

'That's what I thought. Look, darling, could you meet me in Zurich?'

'Zurich? I suppose so. Wait a moment, while I check the flights. Your first flight is five past nine from Salzburg, arriving at five to ten, so I could take an early flight from Geneva to meet you there. Then, there is an eleven-thirty flight from Zurich to London – Swissair 804 – arriving at quarter past midday. Does that give you enough time?'

'Just about. Darling, you're wonderful. I hate to get you up so early. It means going to the office for Bianca's papers.'

'I don't mind. Mark, I don't sleep very well when you're not here.'

'My offer still stands.'

'I know.' Her voice had relaxed. 'I'm still "thinking about it".'

'So am I!'

'What clothes do you want?'

'There's a grey pin-stripe, and could you choose a couple of shirts and ties? You know what I like. You choose them for me anyway.'

'Yes.'

He kept his voice casual. 'There's one other thing. Could you bring my movie camera?'

'Your camera? Why?'

'There's something wrong with it that needs adjusting.'

'But Mark, Geneva is full of camera shops!'

'I know, but I've always taken it to a place in Bond Street. I've been dealing with the same little man for years. He knows all its quirks. You'll find it in the top drawer of my dressing-table.'

At last she laughed. 'Mark, you are the one with the funny quirks!'

'I know. Look at the way I love you.'

Her voice was soft. 'And I love you, too, Mark. I'm beginning to realise that more. Where shall we meet?'

'Anywhere easy.' He looked outside, to the Opel. 'What about the Avis counter on the arrivals floor?'

'Yes. And Mark . . .'

'I have to run, darling. Werner's getting anxious.'

'Please be careful.'

'I will. Goodnight, my love. I'll see you in a few hours.'

Walking slowly back to the car, Mark paused. He felt grubby. It had been so easy to persuade her, adding one lie to another without faltering. Rain was beginning to fall, cold heavy drops spattering the ground. They seemed to slap his face. Werner, the film director! With sudden anger, he slammed the car door behind him and pressed his foot hard on the accelerator. The rear wheels kicked stones across the gravel forecourt of the filling station.

He arrived in the outskirts of Salzburg a little after four. It had been a painfully slow journey through heavy rain. His eyes stung, and his head throbbed from the constant, hypnotic vibration of the windscreen wipers. Knowing that everything would be closed for at least two more hours, he drove down a quiet suburban street, turned off the engine and allowed the car to coast to a stop. The night air was crisp and icy, and the windscreen misted in a few minutes. Pushing the driver's seat back as far as possible, he tilted the seat back so that he was almost reclining. There was still enough heat inside the car, but he covered himself with his raincoat.

He was very tired, but too uncomfortable to fall asleep and, as he shifted fitfully, he tried to remember fifteen years back to the night in Berlin with Eberhard Glantz. Had they talked about anything? He searched his memory, recalling only that the haunted young man, dirty and frightened, had curled himself into a corner of the storm drain, oblivious of the flow of muddy water in which they were crouching. They had shared cigarettes and a bar of chocolate, and he remembered telling Glantz to save his energy. In those days, his German had been less fluent.

Memories became clearer. Glantz had whistled a Schubert melody under his breath and they had exchanged lines from German lieder whenever they could think of something appropriate. It had kept them occupied for an hour or more, until the cold and the water had driven each man into a solitary agony, waiting for the signal to move. It came just before dawn – a whistle, repeated twice. They had crawled out of the drain and made for a point on the wall where workmen had left some sacks of cement. They gave just enough extra height to scramble up to the surface and over the top. The signal had been to tell them that the East German guard was changing, allowing a few seconds of distraction. In the darkness and the rain, Glantz had slipped, and Mark had practically lifted him to the top of the wall before clambering up the slippery surface. As they half jumped, half fell to the other side, there had been distant gun shots, and then the machine-gun had opened fire on them. He remembered shouting 'Zig-zag!' hoping the German would understand, as they ran for cover. Then, the shocking pain and the blow that had thrown him to the ground. He had managed to pull himself up, staggering blindly towards the sheltering buildings. His final memory was of lying flat on his back, looking up towards a grey sky, streaked with pale light. Willis loomed above him, his legs made unnaturally long by the perspective, his face a distant white globe in which two lenses glinted. He had been trying to say something. What was it? Something like: 'The stupid bastard slipped!' Then he had blacked out. He had never seen Glantz again. After his wounds healed, they had moved him back to London.

At seven-thirty he awoke when a heavy lorry rumbled past. He had been sleeping for nearly an hour. Straightening the car seat, he opened the door and stepped out. The mountain air was cold, and a thin drizzle of sleet was falling. His legs and arms were painfully stiff and numbed, and he walked up and down, swinging his arms to restore circulation. An old man, dressed in a padded coat, walked past, eyeing him curiously. He attempted a smile, and nodded in the man's direction, but the other clicked his tongue disapprovingly, shaking his head, and hurried past. 'He probably thinks I've been out drinking all night.'

Starting the car, he drove into the lower part of the town, by the river, in search of a café. Out of season, Salzburg was grey and deserted, the leaden sky reflecting the dark hillside and the stones of the buildings. The elegant baroque architecture appeared and disappeared in clouds of sleety rain, and the little riverside souvenir shops looked wan and desolate. He found a workmen's bar in a side street, and ordered a pot of coffee. The proprietor, a dour man in shirt-sleeves and apron, glanced at his dishevelled, unshaven face, and left the coffee on the counter, to return to the back of the house through a door behind the bar. From a room upstairs, pop music was blaring from a radio, and a woman shouted angrily until the volume was reduced. There was a basket of rolls on the counter. They were stale, but he ate one hungrily, drinking the bitter black coffee until he felt revived. Sitting next to a steamy radiator in the corner, he stared out of the window, watching occasional passers-by, coat collars turned up, lean into the rain. No-one entered the café. On the wall by his table, a fly-spattered poster advertised last summer's festival. He bought a packet of cheap cigarettes from a machine, paid the proprietor when he looked back in, and returned to the car.

By eight-thirty, he had checked the car back with Avis and bought a ticket to London. Taking his overnight case to the men's room, he shaved and washed in one of the hand-basins. His eyes still felt gritty but the shave refreshed him. The tiny airport was almost deserted and, after passing through the immigration counter, he found the duty-free shops had not yet opened. There were only a dozen passengers on the flight and, waving aside the air hostess with the coffee wagon, he settled back and slept for another twenty minutes.

Anne-Marie was waiting at the Avis counter. She was dressed in a long grey woollen overcoat, high at the neck, and leather boots. In Zurich too, the bright sunshine of a few days earlier had given way to rain and sleet, but she still wore her oversize sunglasses. Her face looked very small behind them. He put his arms around her, and she clung to him, her head pressed against his shoulder, saying nothing. He was about to speak, but she pressed closer, reaching up her fingers to close his lips. At length, she relaxed her grip and stood back.

'You look terrible.'

'I didn't get much sleep. We arrived later than we expected.'

'I didn't sleep either.'

'But you still look beautiful. I'm sorry to make you get up so early.'

'It didn't matter. I couldn't sleep. I've been so worried. I know it's foolish, but I have.'

'But why?' He took her hands. 'There's nothing the matter.'

'I've had . . . bad dreams.'

'I'll be home by tomorrow evening – tonight, if I can make it. Then we can both sleep.' He smiled. 'Afterwards!'

She tried to smile, but her face was drawn. He could see muscles rippling the surface of her jaw. 'Mark, don't go away again; not for a while.'

Placing his arms around her again, he held her gently. 'I won't. I promise.'

'I feel so childish. I know you have to go away. There's always someone you have to see. But not for a while?'

'No, not for a long while. Once this trip's over, there's no reason. I've been travelling too much this year. I meant it about the mountains this weekend. Do you think we could stay away longer? What does next week look like?'

'Not much. Frau Emmi will be in every day to look after things. She could take messages.'

'Then we'll plan it for certain.' He looked up. The girls at the Avis counter had been watching them, giggling. He winked at one of them.

'Darling, I think we're making a spectacle of ourselves. The Avis girls think we're trying harder than they are.'

She gave a pale smile, but let go. 'Don't be so English! Do you want to check your baggage in?'

'I may as well. We have plenty of time. Let me transfer a few things from one case to the other.'

They found an empty counter, where he made the changes to his bags, handing Anne-Marie the overnight case.

'I still don't know why you bother to take that old camera all the way to London. You never use it.'

'I know, but it's a perfectly good camera. I'll stay at the Westbury, and my camera shop is a few steps up Bond Street. With any luck, my man will fix it while I wait. If he does, we can take it with us at the weekend. Maybe I'll make a movie about you. It will give me the excuse to watch you all the time.'

She laughed. 'You don't need an excuse!'

'The sort of look I had in mind is best hidden behind a camera! Let's get a coffee and work out where to go when I get back.'

When she linked her arm through his, her stride was jaunty. As they passed the Avis counter, she stuck out her tongue at one of the girls, who looked shocked until she laughed.

When they called Mark's flight, she clung to him again.

'I hate to let you go.'

'It's not for long.' She nodded sadly.

'Mark, please take care of yourself.'

'I will. Don't worry, darling. I'll be home tomorrow.'

'You'll call me?'

'As soon as I can. I won't be at the hotel until the meeting finishes. I've no doubt that the oil sheikh has a dozen other meetings scheduled after mine. Either that, or a dozen wives to go and look after. Speaking of which . . .'

She kissed him on the lips. 'I told you I was thinking about it.'

'What is there to think about?'

'But you will call?'

'As soon as I can. And you will think?'

'Yes.'

As he waited in the exit lounge for the narrow bus that would take him across the tarmac to the plane, it occurred to Mark that she had never once mentioned Vienna. He hoped it was a good omen. He was also glad that it meant he did not have to concoct any more stories for her. He was not sure how successful he would be when she was looking at him.

London

The sky cleared over the coast and, uncharacteristically, London was bathed in bright spring sunshine. The pilot flew the 'scenic' route, following the River Thames on a due west course. From his window, Mark could see the skyscrapers of the City and St Paul's Cathedral, dramatically lit by the slanting beams of light, and other landmarks came slowly into view. Approaching Westminster and the centre of the town, he had forgotten what a green city it was; not only the great parks in the centre, but the tree-lined streets and the countless squares. Watching for familiar buildings, he realised how much he missed London. For all its daily irritations: the constant lack of money, spartan comforts, the drab, limited ambitions, the eternally petty political bickering, it was a stately, civilised city, constantly changing visually – he noted yet another 'high-rise' under construction – but somehow remaining secure and unchanging. It would always be 'home'.

Fortunately, the flight was early, despite the heavy weather they had left behind, and the Swiss pilot announced the local time with a certain smug satisfaction. Mark set aside copies of the *Züricher Nachrichten* and *Tages Anzeiger* that he had been reading, and watched the houses draw closer as the plane turned south of the town and banked sharply, making its final approach over the lush open spaces of Kew Gardens and Sion Park. He had checked both Swiss newspapers and a copy of the *Herald Tribune* for any mention of Krebs in the news items, and cursed himself for not buying an Austrian paper in Salzburg. A Viennese newspaper would have been better still. No other town in the world devoted the centre spreads of its newspapers to three or four pages about music or musical events. 'I'm getting too old for this kind of job. Missing a night's sleep wouldn't have made me so careless in the past.' He also made a mental note to telephone Konstantin and Heidi as soon as possible. He would need to elaborate some different stories for them when he called.

As he came out of the customs hall in Terminal Two at Heathrow, he was greeted by the usual busy crowd behind the barrier, awaiting the incoming flow of passengers: rows of vacant faces, bored by the long pause between touch-down and final clearance through immigration and customs, intermingled with uniformed chauffeurs and drivers from the car-hire companies, holding up their boards printed with the names of people or organisations. It seemed to grow busier every time he came to London: more faces, more colours, more varieties. Walking swiftly, he ignored the crowds and headed for the exit, when a voice, quite close to his ear, said: 'Mr Holland?'

A man wearing a chauffeur's peaked hat was holding a board on which was printed 'London Arts'. He wore a dark suit with a tightly knotted navy-blue tie. It was the old identification the Department had always used. He hesitated for a moment, looking at the man. He was of medium height, heavily built and with the scarred face of an ex-boxer. His sandy hair was long at the sides and back, reaching out beyond the chauffeur's headgear.

'It is Mr Holland, isn't it?' His voice had a London accent, despite a façade of 'posh' aspirates.

'Yes.'

The man picked up the overnight bag and, from the bulky shape where his sleeve met his armpit, Mark could see that he wore a shoulder holster.

'I thought it was you. The car's just outside in the park.'

Mark hesitated. 'I wasn't expecting to be met.'

The man moved forward with a rolling gait. 'I know, sir. They phoned ahead and thought you might like a lift into town, seeing as it's getting late. They thought you'd be in a hurry.'

'That's very thoughtful.' They pushed their way through the crowded terminal. 'I don't think I remember you.'

'No, you wouldn't, sir. I've only been on the job a couple of years. They gave me a picture so's I'd know you.' He headed

53

for the exit. 'I'm parked upstairs.'

He led the way up the passenger ramp to the bridge connecting the terminal to its car park. Mark followed. There was something wrong. Perhaps the man had identified him too quickly, but he should not have been there, waiting for him. Quentin had said they would find him, but their first contact was to be at Victoria Station. Something did not fit. Walking slowly, he followed the chauffeur over the pedestrian bridge above the road, side-stepping a large Indian family with a trolley piled high with suitcases. The chauffeur left his bag at the corner of the parking floor.

'I'm parked a bit further round, sir, if you'd like to wait here?'

Mark nodded. As the chauffeur disappeared round a row of cars, he considered taking the bag and walking back into the terminal. By the time the other man returned, he could be in a cab, heading for the town. On the other hand, the man could be genuine, and it was getting late if he was to be in Victoria by one o'clock. He was still uneasy when the car arrived. The chauffeur placed his bag in the boot and opened the rear door. Mark moved to the front.

'I'll sit up front, if I may. I prefer the view.' The man said nothing. Mark's experience had been that most drivers preferred this small, democratic gesture, but this chauffeur obviously disapproved. Was it that he preferred to keep him at the back of the car, away from the controls? It might just be reverse snobbery. As Mark entered, the chauffeur said: 'Don't forget the seat-belt. It's the law now, you know.'

They drove in silence for several minutes as the man made his way out of the airport to the M4 motorway. His Mercedes moved rapidly into the outside driving lane, hissing past traffic at a speed well above the limit.

Mark smiled. 'Lovely day. It's been filthy in Austria. Usually, it's the other way round.'

The man relaxed. 'Oh yes? Been like this all week here. We're not used to it. Probably means we're going to have a wet summer!'

'How's the football this season? Liverpool still on top?'

'Don't know. I don't really follow it.'

'I didn't think there was any way of avoiding it.'

'Oh, I don't bother with the telly. The hours I keep, there's no use planning to watch anything. Most of it's rubbish anyway!'

'I suppose so.' Mark found that he was suddenly very alert, brushing aside the torpidity of a night without sleep and the gentle cradling of the planes. Could he detect a trace of an accent in the man's voice? And, even so, it need not mean anything. He could be London Italian, London Greek, London Maltese, London anything. These days, there were so many variations in the local dialect.

They drove on in silence, leaving the fast part of the motorway to enter the raised section before Chiswick. Bright sunlight fell on his face, so that he half closed his eyes.

'What an amazing day! I always associate London with fog and damp, except for my childhood years. Have you ever noticed how you only seem to remember the sunny days from when you were young?'

'It's not such a bad old climate, sir, and we need our share of the rain. Otherwise we wouldn't have anything to complain about, would we? I went down to Spain for one of them package tours one year, but I didn't think much of it. It was too hot, you couldn't find a decent glass of beer, and the food was rubbish!'

'I suppose so.' As Mark's anxiety increased, he cultivated a relaxed attitude, stretching back comfortably. 'We had a beautiful view on the way in. The plane came right up the Thames, all the way from Gravesend to Hammersmith. You could pick out every building on the way. Are you a Londoner?'

'Born and bred, as they say. I can't claim to be a real cockney, though. I grew up in Twickenham, which is a bit too far out for a sound of Bow Bells. But my Dad and Granddad were, round Southwark. I live just off Edgware Road myself.'

It was only a small error, but to Mark it seemed conclusive. Just as a New Yorker, despite the nomenclature, always calls the Avenue of the Americas 'Sixth Avenue', a Londoner 'born and bred' would never refer to 'Edgware Road', even though street signs are printed that way. For some historical quirk, it is always 'the Edgware Road'. The man was no Londoner. He could still be mistaken, but it was not worth taking the chance, especially with a man carrying a gun.

They were approaching Hammersmith when the chauffeur veered to the left, to leave the main stream of traffic. 'I'll try Hammersmith. It gets blocked further in with road works on the Cromwell Road. After that, we can cut through the back of Shepherd's Bush to the Westway and across Maida Vale.' It was clear that he was not heading towards Victoria, to the south.

'Good idea.' Mark kept his voice impersonal, while his mind raced. Within a few minutes, they would be in Central London and, if he did not make a move soon, they would reach their destination and whatever reception had been planned for him. As the car slowed in the heavy filtering traffic, he considered jumping out. The man would not be able to follow him, and it was unlikely that he would risk a shot with cars and lorries surrounding him to prevent his escape. From the corner of his eye, Mark noted that the doors were locked through the car's central locking system, which would further reduce his chances of leaping out unexpectedly. It would also mean leaving his travelling bag behind. He leaned back in his seat, yawning ostentatiously, and considered further possibilities. There was little time left. The driver manoeuvred the Mercedes expertly between buses and taxis until they entered the express road climbing to the high-speed Westway leading to Paddington and Maida Vale. As they passed on to the overhead roadway, Mark tapped his pockets and swore softly. The driver glanced in his direction.

Mark smiled. 'I don't suppose you would have a cigarette on you?'

'No. I don't smoke, sir.'

He fidgeted again. 'I've just run out. I wonder if you wouldn't mind stopping when we go past a tobacconist?'

The driver looked sullen. 'We're almost there.'

'I know, but there's nothing worse than not having a cigarette when you want one.' He laughed lightly. 'If I actually had one left, I probably wouldn't bother to smoke it!'

The man did not reply, steering the car smoothly to the Paddington exit. In a minute or so, they would be in Maida Vale. Still casual, Mark crossed his legs, stretched his arms and sighed. 'Anyway, there has to be a place just around here. It won't take a minute.'

'I can't stop here, can I?' The man's voice was almost plaintive.

'That's all right; just as soon as you can.' Mark left no doubt in the request.

They were now entering that area known as Little Venice, crossing the Grand Union Canal by the boat basin and still heading north. Without speaking further, the driver turned right on Blomfield Road, running along the side of the canal.

Mark kept talking. 'This was always one of the nicest parts of the town. I used to think I'd love a little house overlooking the water.' He laughed dryly. 'Not that they're so little, and not much chance on my salary!'

The driver said nothing, his chin set in a stubborn line. He filed into the Edgware Road, heading north again for a few yards, then suddenly turned left, into a small street. He stopped the car with a slight jolt, and nodded in the direction of a tobacconist-newsagent.

'There's your shop.'

'Thanks very much.' Mark made as if to open the door, then stopped, slapping his trouser pocket.

'Oh good Lord, I haven't got any English money! I was on my way to the bank when you found me, and I clean forgot about it.'

The driver started to put the car in gear, when Mark spoke again, placing a hand on his sleeve.

'Look, I wonder if you could do me a tremendous favour. If I give you some foreign money, would you lay out the cash for a packet of cigarettes?' He reached into his trousers and took out a note. 'I've got a Swiss ten-franc note here. You can have it. Any bank will give you about three quid for it. What about it?'

For a moment, the man hesitated, torn between greed and his previous irritation. At length, he turned and took the money with a sly grin.

'Fair exchange?'

'Of course.'

'I won't be a jiffy.'

He stepped out of the door and, to Mark's relief, left the engine running. As soon as his broad back had disappeared behind the door of the shop, Mark moved swiftly. Drawing up his knees and pressing firmly against the gear lever to prevent it from changing, he threw himself across the front of the car, wriggling into the driver's seat. Keeping one eye on the door of the shop, he slipped the automatic drive and started to edge the car forward. There was still no sign of the chauffeur. He accelerated rapidly, and the powerful car leapt forward with a squeal. Facing forward, he saw a brick wall racing up to meet him. He was in a dead-end street.

Jamming a foot on the brakes, he threw the wheel sideways, so that the car slewed round, lurching violently. There was a grinding, metallic crash as the tail of the Mercedes struck the wall, but he spun the wheel and accelerated again as the machine bounced forward and started for the exit at the end of the road.

The chauffeur had run into the street and was standing in the centre. Mark braked for a moment and, as if frozen, the two men stared into each other's eyes. The chauffeur reached into his coat, and Mark accelerated again. The man brought out a Smith and Wesson Special and, grasping it in both hands, his feet astride, police-style, he aimed down the sight. The gun roared.

Inside the car, there was an explosion as glass shattered, and Mark felt a thick shard graze his temple and cheek. He threw himself sideways and, even as his head hit the seat, felt a white-hot slash of pain in his upper arm. A moment later, there was an ugly thud as the car hit the man, followed immediately by a jolting crash as it hurtled into a tree on the left side. Mark was thrown to the floor by the force of the impact. His hand grabbed the gear lever, putting it into the 'Park' position and, as his head cleared, he could still feel the engine running. There was a high, squealing sound coming from the power steering. He scrambled back into the driving seat, forcing his legs to swivel in the narrow space and gritting his teeth against the throbbing pain in his right arm. Straightening his body, he threw his left hand forward, to push out some of the shattered windscreen.

The laminated glass had not become opaque, but there was a jagged hole, from which slivers still fell. To his right, he could see the chauffeur lying on the edge of the road, face down, a trickle of blood oozing from the corner of his mouth. His eyes were open and sightless, his body twisted and broken. To his left, Mark could see an elderly man, dressed in a grey overall, in the doorway of the shop. He was stumbling forward, calling, but Mark could not distinguish the words. He threw the car into reverse, and pressed the accelerator viciously. The car wrenched itself free with a further grinding and, as it gathered speech, he changed gear and forced the machine forward again.

The steering wheel was sluggish, and he could hear a wheel rubbing against twisted metal, but the Mercedes skidded towards the corner. The old man backed into the doorway, frightened, as Mark reached the main road, glancing quickly to see if there was any oncoming traffic. From the corner of his eye, he was aware of several pedestrians standing on the pavement, but their faces were a white blur. He moved forward again, dragging the steering wheel into a hard left turn and braking fast. The car slid round the corner, to a chorus of motor horns and howling brakes, then straightened. He pressed the accelerator to the floor and raced towards traffic lights, the wheels of the Mercedes spinning wildly before they gripped the surface of the road. Glancing for a second in the rear-view mirror, he could see a number of people running in the road behind him, pointing in his direction. The traffic lights were changing as he sped through at sixty miles an hour.

His right arm was throbbing painfully. From the feel of it, the bullet must have passed through the outer flesh, so that he was not totally disabled. He could feel blood running down the side of his cheek, where the glass had cut him. The rush of air through the broken screen cooled his face and, as his nerves relaxed, he realised that he was panting like a sprinter. With great effort, he slowed the vibrating car, which was fighting his control, to a more reasonable speed. Ahead of him, approaching rapidly, there was another set of traffic lights, still green, and as he reached them he braked and accelerated, skidding the car through oncoming vehicles in a hard right turn which carried him up a gentle slope towards Hamilton Terrace.

Checking in the rear-view mirror to make sure he was not being followed, he allowed the car to slow down again, and drove almost sedately up the hill. At a slower speed, the car was sluggish and noisy, but responsive enough to keep moving. He guided it gently through several more traffic lights and turns, until he found a quiet, tree-lined street. Still moving slowly, he edged the car into an empty parking space and stopped, leaving the engine running. He checked again in the rear-view mirror, but he had not been followed. The battered Mercedes made no further complaints. Its engine purred quietly.

He closed his eyes and sat for a moment, waiting for his hand to stop trembling. His right arm still throbbed, and he reached across gingerly with his left hand. The fabric of his jacket was torn and, as his fingers probed, there was a flash of pain where they found the wounded flesh. Although it hurt, it seemed to be only a surface graze. The chauffeur must have fired off two shots before he had run him down. Twisting the rear-view mirror round, he examined his face. There was a shallow cut on his left temple and another on his cheek. Blood had run down his face in a long, red-brown stripe. With a handkerchief, he dabbed the smarting skin gently, to remove the worst of it. There was glass on the dashboard and seat, and he lifted the larger pieces clear and threw them on the floor. Then he leaned back in the seat and closed his eyes.

He had to get rid of the car, as quickly as possible, before the police found it. There had been enough witnesses to take the number and, in any case, it would look like a wreck. Unless he ran into a police patrol, he still had a few minutes, perhaps half an hour. But where could he go? In his present state, spattered with blood, his clothes torn, he was more than conspicuous. It occurred to him also that, for the moment, he had no English money. When he had persuaded the chauffeur out of the car, he had been telling the truth. Reaching into his left pocket, he found Quentin's card and memorised the number. It was time to move again. The clock on the dashboard registered five to one. There was no hope of reaching Victoria.

60

The car moved off unsteadily. It responded slowly, and turning was noisy and difficult. Letting his right hand rest on his lap, he steered with his left, moving slowly in search of a telephone box. He stayed in side streets, where there was little traffic. A woman in a small car drove past him in the opposite direction. She looked at him curiously. At length, he found a telephone. Overhanging trees half obscured it from view. He parked the car a few yards away and, risking that it would start again, turned off the engine.

The damage to the car was more extensive than he had anticipated, likely to draw attention. The broken windscreen was jagged and cracked, there was a bad dent on the front right wing, and the front left headlight was folded in on itself, the bodywork crumpled where he had hit the tree. At the rear, there was more damage: a long scrape on the right wing and a missing tail light. He walked round to the front and, with his left hand, tried to pull the twisted metal away from the wheel, allowing it more room for turning. It bent back a little, but the effort sent slivers of pain through his right arm.

In the telephone box, he dialled the operator and asked to make a reverse-charge call. Taking a chance, he gave his name as Quentin Sharpe. She put him through almost immediately. The girl at the other end had a perky, cheerful voice.

'London Arts. Hello, Quentin.'

Mark took a deep breath. 'Can I speak to Quentin, please.'

'I thought it was Quentin calling.' She sounded suspicious.

'No, I'm trying to reach him. Is he there?'

There was a slight pause before the girl spoke again. 'Sorry, there must have been some sort of mix-up. Who's calling?'

'A friend of Quentin's. I need to speak to him urgently. Is he there?'

'I'm afraid not. Quentin – Mr Sharpe – is out of the country at the moment.'

'Do you expect to hear from him?'

The girl's voice was cautious again. 'He does call in sometimes. Would you like to leave a name?'

'Mark Holland.'

'All right, Mr Holland. Does he know where to reach you?'

'No. I'll have to call you back later.'

'I can't guarantee that he will call.'

She was about to ring off, when another thought struck him, or perhaps he had been avoiding it.

'Just a moment. Do you have a Sally Faulkner working there?'

The girl sounded puzzled. 'Miss Faulkner?'

'Yes.'

'Miss Faulkner does work here, but I'm afraid she's not in either. I think she said she would be in later. Would you like to leave a message for her?'

'No, don't bother. I'll call back later.'

He hung up, and remained standing before the telephone. He had not expected to learn that Sally was still there. When he had left, he had always assumed that she would leave too. But he was not sure whether he could face her again. When he had left the Department, she had been one of the 'casualties' in his life.

His arm was beginning to throb again, and there was a small patch of blood spreading on his jacket. Returning to the car, he found his raincoat lying on the back seat. He tried to put it on, but moving his right arm was too painful, so he compromised by hanging the coat around his shoulders to cover the jacket.

It was only a gamble that Sally still lived in the same flat after seven years, but at least it was within a few minutes' driving distance: a converted house off Primrose Hill. He could not, for the moment, remember the name of the street, but he would know it when he saw it. They used to walk on Primrose Hill on Sundays, to watch the people flying kites.

The car started easily, and he edged forward experimentally. The front wheel no longer caught against the crumpled metal so frequently, making it easier to negotiate the corners. Keeping to the smaller streets, he made his way through the back of St John's Wood, avoiding the busy High Street. He stopped at a light on Ordnance Hill, and looked up to see a cyclist peering down through the window at him.

'Gawd, you look as though you just went through a wall!'

He smiled ruefully. 'Just about. I'm trying to get it to the garage.'

The young man gave the car a critical examination. 'Hardly

worth it, mate. You'd be better off collecting the insurance.'

The light changed, and he moved off. He followed the quieter roads to the north of Primrose Hill until he found the street he wanted. Chalcot Crescent. How could he have forgotten the name! There was a parking place nearby and, taking his bag from the back of the car, he draped his raincoat over his shoulders. He was moving painfully. When he reached the door, he rested a moment before looking at the several nameplates and their accompanying bell pushes. The card still read 'Ground Floor A – S Faulkner', and he recalled that she always used her first initial only, both on the door and in the telephone directory, to avoid unwanted callers. He pressed the button, and could hear a bell ringing. Nothing happened. He tried again and, this time, thought he heard a sudden swell of distant music, cut off within seconds, as though somebody had opened and closed a door. There were footsteps in the hall, and the front door opened.

'You!' Her voice was shocked, and she drew in her breath sharply.

'Hello, Sally.' She was wearing an old green sweater and jeans that were frayed at the ankles. She was barefoot. It made her smaller than he remembered. Her black hair had been cut short, and there were unexpected traces of grey in it. When she spoke again, her voice was low and angry.

'What are you doing here?'

'I'm sorry. I couldn't think of anywhere else to go. Believe me, if I could have, I would never have bothered you.' He lowered his head wearily.

She stepped closer, looking at his face. 'What on earth's happened? Have you been in an accident?'

'Sort of.' He tried to stand straight, and the raincoat slipped from his shoulders. He saw her eyes travel to his jacket, and heard the intake of her breath, but her voice was calm.

'You'd better come in.'

He hesitated. 'I hate to do this to you.'

'Oh, don't be so bloody silly! If you really meant that, you wouldn't be here. How bad is it?' She helped him across the hall. He turned to pick up his bag, but she said: 'Leave it there. I'll get it in a minute,' and led him into the living room. There

63

was a record playing, and she crossed to the hi-fi and lifted the playing-arm clumsily, so that it scraped the surface. He sat down slowly while she went to the kitchen, to return with a bottle of brandy. She poured some into a glass, handing it to him silently. He drank it quickly, feeling the liquid burning his system, but it helped.

'Thanks. I needed that.'

'You look as though you need a good deal more than that. Wait while I get your bag and shut the front door. Can you get your coat off?'

'If you give me a hand.' She had already returned, leaving the bag in a corner.

'We'd better do something about your arm first. I'll have a look at it, but you'd be better off in a hospital. I'll get some scissors. We'll probably need to cut the sleeve loose.'

'I don't think it's as bad as it looks.' He stood again, and she helped him out of his jacket, slipping it downwards off his shoulders, to avoid moving his arm. It was painful, but quick. A moment later, she had taken a pair of sharp nail scissors and cut away the top of his shirt-sleeve. The blood was still quite wet and slippery, allowing her to ease the material over the wound and off his wrist. The skin stung, but he clenched his left hand tightly, remaining silent. She examined his arm carefully.

'That must have hurt.'

'It did.' He tried to smile.

'You should let a doctor look after it. There's a kind of ridge, but it doesn't look very deep. I've got some first-aid things next door. We can at least clean it.'

'Thanks.' She went into the kitchen again, and he looked around the room. It had not changed very much. The bookcase had been extended, and the curtains were different, but he did not notice any other immediate changes. When she returned, she carried a tray covered with various items: a bowl of hot water, some gauze and cotton wool, bandage, a tube of ointment and a spray can. She lifted this first.

'This is some kind of anaesthetic, but I think it's only intended for mosquito bites or minor burns. I don't know how effective it will be.'

64

She sprayed a fine mist on his arm, and he flinched more from the coldness than from pain. It made his skin feel slightly numb.

He said: 'It seems to work.'

Working slowly, she washed the wound, dabbing at it gently. Sharp needles of pain accompanied each movement, but the anaesthetic continued to work. While she cleaned the wound, her attention fully concentrated, he watched her face. After seven years, he had not expected her to look the same, but an ageing process was cruelly apparent at close quarters. The fine, high cheek-bones were there, but the skin covering them was coarser, the lines at the corners of her eyes and mouth more permanently fixed. There were shadowy patches below her eyes, with tiny blue veins. She wore no make-up, but he had the impression that she had not bothered with her appearance for a long time. For a moment she glanced up, and their eyes met, but her face remained impassive, and she returned to her work with greater concentration.

When the cleaning was finished, she made a small pad of gauze, covered it with antiseptic ointment, and laid it gently over the raw skin. Holding it tightly enough to keep it in position, she wound a bandage round his arm. Her closeness suggested an intimacy between them, but she worked coolly and efficiently, as impersonal as a nurse.

When the bandage was in place, she poured more brandy into his glass, and filled a glass of her own. Mark drank quickly. His arm still felt numb, but the pain had faded. The alcohol made him light-headed. At last, Sally sat on the sofa, watching him. When she spoke, her voice was calm.

'Why, Mark? Why me?'

'I had nowhere else to go, I swear it.'

'What happened?'

'It's a hell of a long story, and I don't know where to start. For what it's worth, I seem to be working for the Department.'

'You left years ago.' Her voice was bitter. 'Eight years ago, next September. What do you mean, you're working? Have you rejoined?'

'No, I've been seconded, if that's the right Civil Service

term, by Willis and Quentin.'

'Quentin?' She looked thoughtful. 'He's long since your time. You must be telling the truth.'

'Why should I lie?'

She stood, angrily. 'Lie? Oh, for Christ's sake! How can you, of all people, ask a question like that!'

'I'm sorry. I meant I had no reason to lie about Willis. They dragged me back in, if you want the truth, fighting all the way. I never wanted to see or hear of the bloody Department again, but they forced me in.'

'Thanks very much!'

'I didn't mean that. Look, I can't excuse what I did to you. I thought about it for weeks . . .'

'How very conscientious of you!'

'All right. I behaved like a bastard when I walked out. I admit it. The only reason I came here is that I had nowhere else to go.'

In the silence, Sally walked over to the window, staring across the street. When she spoke again, her voice was bleak.

'I suppose I've rehearsed what I would say to you, if we ever met again, a thousand times over. Now it doesn't seem to matter. Anyway, I've done it all in the wrong order.' She turned back to him. 'You'd better tell me as much as you want me to know, sort yourself out, and leave. You could at least have warned me you were going to show up like this. It doesn't do much for my self-confidence.' Unconsciously, she smoothed her sweater over her waist.

'I would have phoned. Believe it or not, I didn't have the price of a call.'

'What's going on?'

'Have you ever heard of a man called Glantz – Eberhard Glantz? He's an East German; at least, he used to be.'

'No.'

'And do you know anything about a Swiss pharmaceutical company called Suchim?'

'No. Should I?'

'I would have thought so, considering where you work.'

'Not necessarily. I don't work for the Slug.'

'The Slug?'

66

'H W Willis. One of the girls in the office gave him that nickname years ago. We work in the same building again – part of the last set of budget cuts – but I see little of him. I'm involved with another department.'

'And you wouldn't know what Willis and his boys are up to?'

'It's more than likely. Listen, Mark, when you left, I asked for a transfer. Nobody was particularly surprised. They probably checked me out pretty thoroughly for the next few weeks, to make sure I wouldn't follow suit. Anyway, I switched jobs and moved to the house in Highgate. It was more convenient from the flat.'

'Who were you working for?'

'None of your business. Sorry, but I've only got your word for it that you're back. Mentioning Willis or Quentin Sharpe doesn't give you the right to pry. Anyway, the usual budget cuts came round. They sold the house in Highgate for a nice profit, and I went back to the old place.'

'I'm sorry.'

'Oh, forget it! You were supposed to be telling me.' She sat down moodily, stretching her legs in front of her. Mark waited a moment or two, wondering how much he should tell her. There seemed little point in keeping secrets.

'Look Sally, everything I tell you is restricted, but that doesn't mean a thing to me. I don't work for bloody Willis or anyone else unless I'm forced to, so I have no qualms about discussing it. But I would suggest you forget anything you hear.'

'I understand.'

He told the story, piecing it together in small sections, starting with Willis's phone call. He never mentioned Anne-Marie by name, but when he spoke of Zurich, Sally interrupted.

'Why did you fly to Zurich to meet your assistant? Why not straight to London?'

'I wanted one or two extra things if I was going to maintain my cover. I could hardly explain that I was on some wild goose chase after a mad bloody scientist.'

Her voice was soft. 'I don't see why you needed to explain anything. You come to London quite frequently.'

'You knew that?'

'Yes, I knew. People talk from time to time, and I checked your files through a friend after your "disappearance". It's one thing I find hard to forgive you for, you know. I never go to concerts any more.'

'But why?'

She stood again. 'For a silly, feminine reason. I suppose that's what makes me angry. I knew the chances were minimal, but I didn't want to risk running into you by accident.'

'I see.'

'No, I doubt whether you do. Anyway, you left Zurich this morning. What happened next?'

Mark continued to talk, leaving no details out. She listened gravely, scarcely moving until he had finished. As he let his head fall back, she walked behind his chair, running a cool finger across his forehead. Her voice was soft.

'That's quite a story. What are you going to do next?'

'Rest a little, I hope, but there are one or two things that need to be looked after first. There's the car.'

'What about it?'

'I need to move it away from here. It's parked a few doors away. If they know as much about me as they appear to, the chances are that they'll put one and one together when they see it parked outside your house.'

'All right, we'll move it in a few minutes. What next?'

Mark stood. His legs felt shaky for a moment, but he fought the nausea by pacing steadily. 'If I'm going to keep my sanity, I've got to know if that chauffeur really was after me. I have no proof, but I'll swear he wasn't from the Department. Sally, you know who looks after transportation these days. Can you find out for me?'

She did not speak, but walked out of the room, closing the door. He remembered that she kept the telephone next to her bed. While he was waiting for her, he walked to the bookcase. Her collection had grown over the years, paperbacks mostly, with an occasional hard-cover of a novel. The book of Auden that he had given her was still there. Opening a recent Graham Greene, he noticed a short, handwritten inscription inside the front. 'All my love, darling – T.' She entered the room quietly and, seeing the book in his hand, said: 'It's rude to read other people's dedications.' She had changed into a blue dress, high at the neck, with flat walking shoes. Mark returned the book to the shelf, feeling guilty.

'Did you learn anything?'

'Yes. We didn't send anyone to the airport today. All the drivers are accounted for. Your conscience needn't bother you, unless Willis and Sharpe are using a new private service . . .'

'Whose drivers carry guns?'

'I suppose not.'

'Does anyone know where Willis is?'

'Not really. They think he's on his way to London, but nobody's sure. You seem to forget it's Friday, and people are more concerned with going home. We're really only civil servants at heart.' Her manner was more friendly. 'Friday or not, I've got to go to the office this afternoon, and I'll see what I can find out for you. You're not in much shape to move around.' She paused, as though making a decision. 'You can stay here for the moment, if you like. It's safer than going to a hotel.'

'Thanks. I still haven't got any money.'

'If you give me some of yours, I'll change it for you.' He reached painfully into his right-hand pocket, and took out a small wad of Swiss notes, which he handed to her. 'I may as well look after the car, too.'

'No! Look Sally, I've already imposed on you too much. The police will be looking for that car. I can't get you involved any further!'

'Oh, stop being so bloody noble, Mark! It really doesn't suit you. There's a repair place just on the other side of Camden Town, with a sign on the wall offering estimates. I'll take it in there and leave it for an estimate. The police won't have notified anyone yet. The garage men have never seen me before, and they're never likely to see me again. Besides, if you're playing for time, it's better to have me deliver the car. By now, half a dozen eye-witnesses have already described you.'

'I still don't like the idea.'

'It makes more sense than anything you can suggest.' She looked at her watch. 'I'd better get going. Make yourself at home.' There was a slight edge to her voice. 'You should be able to remember where everything is!'

'Do you mind if I make a phone call? It's to Switzerland.'
She shook her head. 'Sally, I don't know what to say to you. I
really was desperate, otherwise I wouldn't have walked back
into your life...'

She laughed. 'Walked back into my life? Oh, come on,
Mark, you're talking like a character in a Barbara Cartland
novel! You haven't walked back into my life. I never wanted to
see you again – no, that's not true. Of course I was curious.
Anyway, now that you've reappeared, it's not as bad as I expected. You're looking well, apart from a few cuts and
bruises...'

'So are you.'

'No, I'm not. I'm overweight, my hair needs washing and
I'm no longer in the first bloom of youth. I'm a survivor.' She
took a deep breath. 'Did you leave the keys in the car?'

'I must have.'

'I thought so. Which way is it?'

He pointed. 'I don't think you can miss it. It's a dark-
coloured Mercedes; at least, it used to be.'

She looked at her watch again. 'I'm late. If you do want to go
out, the spare keys are hanging in the kitchen, next to the
coffee machine, but I wouldn't, if I were you. Get some rest
instead. You may need it.' The door closed behind her and, a
moment later, he heard the front door close.

The room seemed very silent, except for the ticking of the
carriage clock on the mantelpiece. Seeing it there reminded
him that she always checked her watch a dozen times when she
was feeling nervous. He stared at the various pieces of furni-
ture: the sofa with a frayed arm, the small gate-leg table that
had to be opened for meals, the expensive hi-fi set next to the
bookcase. He remembered the weeks he had spent here. How
long had it been? Less than two months, if he discounted the
time spent in Germany and Austria. They should have been
happy, if only the other events had not occurred. He shifted in
his chair. It was all long ago, in the past. He had changed lives
since then.

The carriage clock chimed, and he checked his watch against
it. It was quarter to three. 'That stupid clock never did keep

accurate time. No wonder she used her watch.' He walked to the bedroom, looking for the telephone. The room was exactly as he remembered it: small and cramped, with a heavy wardrobe that occupied too much space. He had once promised to replace it with one of those prefabricated do-it-yourself closets with sliding doors. Sitting on the bed, he dialled his Geneva office. After a while, Anne-Marie answered.

'Hello, darling. How was the flight back to Geneva?'

'Mark!' Her voice sounded pleased. 'I had not expected to hear from you for hours. Have you finished already?'

He laughed. 'No, we've hardly started, but I took five minutes out to call you.'

'I'm glad. Mark, I feel ashamed for being so upset last night.'

'Don't apologise. I know it sounds selfish, but I'm glad you were. I think it brought our lives into better focus.'

'Perhaps. Are you going to the Westbury later?'

'No.'

'Oh?'

'I ran into Charles Holmes, and he offered to put me up.'

'Do I know him?'

'I doubt it. Charles looks after Bianca's London engagements, if she ever agrees to do any. She doesn't like the taxes here, or the fees, but he still lives in hope!'

She laughed. 'Can you give me his number?'

'Yes.' He gave her the number of the flat, reading it from the dial. 'Don't call me here if you can avoid it. The telephone is in his bedroom, and I don't want to disturb him.'

'I understand. Will you be home tomorrow evening?'

'I hope so, but I can't promise. Everything is fine, but it does take a while to organise. I'll call you again tomorrow morning if I don't call tonight.'

'Make it tomorrow, Mark. I have to go to the opera tonight. I promised to hear that new tenor – you remember? – and Madame Renaud and her husband have invited me to supper afterwards. I won't be home until very late, so you would have to disturb your friend.'

'Madame Renaud? Sooner you than I, darling. What are they doing?'

'*Tosca*. They're letting him try out in Spoletta, with a promise that he can have a bigger role next time. Why didn't you stay at the Westbury?'

'No reason, except that Charles offered the bed. I thought I might as well save the money.'

She laughed again. 'You're getting more Swiss all the time!'

'All the better; then you won't have to marry a foreigner. I love you, Anne-Marie.'

'I love you too.'

'Enjoy *Tosca*, despite Madame Renaud.'

'I will, but I would rather see it with you.'

'Next time, you will. Take care.'

'You too, Mark. Take special care of yourself – for me.'

He hung up, and the room was suddenly silent again.

There was nothing to do now, except wait. He knew that Sally could give him the latest information about Willis and Quentin, and there was no point, even if he could manage it, in going to Victoria. If Glantz arrived, they would have to rely on the look-out by the news-stand. He was surprised that Willis had not made some arrangement with the Immigration Department to grab him when he landed off the ferry. They would not have needed him at all. Instead, he was sitting in Sally's apartment, waiting for instructions, just like the old days! And, Barbara Cartland notwithstanding, he had not wanted to drag her into it. When he had severed all ties with the Department, she had been so integrally a part of it that he knew she would never understand his actions. She had never really known what his job had involved. It had been mysterious and exciting, but he had never told her the details. Perhaps it was the difference in their ages. And perhaps, if he had cared for her more deeply at the time and had not been so preoccupied with his own conscience, he might have told her more. Instead, he had taken the coward's way out and 'disappeared' from the Department, from London and from her life. Willis would have understood that. He was in the betrayal business.

He walked to the living room and looked through her record collection. It had changed subtly. All the old records were still there, but there were a lot of new albums that he would not have associated with her taste in the past: Original Cast albums of more than a dozen musical shows, a Frank Sinatra set and even a number of pop idols like Billy Joel and The Police. In the past, Sally had never listened to anything but classical records and the occasional spoken word. He had given her the Emlyn Williams readings of Dylan Thomas, and they had once had a flaming row when he had accused her of being an intellectual snob. 'I wonder if the new records are the influence of the elusive "T"?' He felt slightly ashamed. 'I'm spying on her, too. Anyway, if I'm going to see this thing through, I may as well be ready.'

He chose one of the older records which had always been a favourite of theirs: Elisabeth Schwarzkopf singing the Strauss Four Last Songs. Walking over to his overnight bag, he unzipped the cover and took out his camera. It was a medium-sized 8 millimetre Eumig, with a plastic pistol-grip, which he had 'modified' many years earlier. Sliding two small catches under the main case of the camera, he lifted it clear of the moulded plastic pistol-grip. There was no camera mechanism inside. He turned the metal camera casing over, removing a number of items that were clipped to its inner sides: a short, metal barrel, a silencer, and a chamber and firing mechanism. Running along the top of the plastic pistol-grip was a ridged steel strip. The gun barrel clicked into position at the front of the metal ridge, and the chamber and firing mechanism slid along the ridge from the other end until the two met with a low, metallic snap. The silencer screwed to the end of the barrel. Inside the camera case there was also a small pouch, which he unrolled. In it were a trigger, which he screwed into the chamber containing the firing mechanism, and a clip containing six cartridges, which locked to the bottom of the camera base. He removed the cartridges from the clip. The rear of the firing mechanism pulled back slightly, and he pressed the trigger. The firing-pin snapped forward. He eased it back, and pressed again. The gun was in good working order. He returned the cartridges to the clip and inserted it, cocking the trigger and setting a small safety catch.

It was an ugly-looking weapon, a cross between a New York street 'zip-gun' and a small Sten. With .30 bullets, it was not very accurate, and it was inclined to kick wildly. At close quarters it was deadly. It took only seconds to assemble, and he had carried it on and off planes many times. Security officers at airports never gave a standard make of camera a second glance.

The record side ended, and he walked over to the machine, switching off the power. His arm was no longer throbbing, although he was aware of a constant soreness, but his eyes seemed to be full of sand and his head ached. Going to the bathroom, he washed his face carefully. The cuts had dried, and he found a piece of adhesive plaster for the larger of the two, on his temple. He thought of taking a bath, but waves of tiredness flooded over him. Taking the gun, he walked to the bedroom, and placed it under one of the pillows. He kicked off his shoes and lay back. The room felt pleasantly warm, and he closed his eyes. Somewhere in the garden beyond the window, a bird seemed to be singing its heart out.

When he opened his eyes again, it was dark. For a moment, he was completely disorientated but, as he reached out his right arm, a sudden twinge of pain reminded him. He lay back, staring upwards at the darkness and, as his eyes became accustomed, he was aware of a faint light from beneath the door, which provided enough illumination to make out shapes in the room: the oval mirror on the dressing-table by the window, the straight-backed chair next to the wardrobe. From next door, he could hear faint music. It sounded like one of the songs from *Cats*. His head felt light, but with a dull ache and, moving slowly, he sat up. He tried his right arm cautiously. It was sore and slightly stiff, but the pain was negligible. He turned on the bedside light, closing his eyes for a moment, and sat on the edge of the bed. Then he stood and, feeling his senses return, made his way out of the room.

Sally was in the kitchen, standing by the stove. She was humming to the music from the radio. When he entered, she looked up with a light smile.

'I didn't expect you to wake up for another hour or two. How are you feeling?'

'I'll let you know in a minute or two. I must have passed out like a light.'

74

She nodded. 'I thought you might. I looked in a couple of times to wipe your brow. You were having bad dreams. How's your arm?'

'Much better. It doesn't really hurt any more – just slightly stiff. Thanks.'

'You should still see a doctor, when you have a chance.' She busied herself with the cooking pots, examining the contents.

'What time is it?'

She looked at her watch. 'About nine.'

'I must have slept for about six hours.'

'It's the best way to recover. I hope the radio didn't wake you.'

'No. How long have you been back?'

'A few hours. I didn't see any point in waking you.'

'I see.' He sat down at the kitchen table. She had laid two places, and there was a bottle of wine. 'Did you learn anything at the office?'

'Quite a lot.' She turned to him, and her face was sombre. 'If you're worried about the chauffeur, he was definitely not one of ours. In fact, our people seem to have been quick off the mark. They took him over as soon as the reports started to come in.'

'What did the police say?'

'We asked them to keep it quiet. There was something on the six o'clock news. They described him as a runner for the local bad boys in the gambling world. It's been reported as a vendetta of some sort. The newspapers will be full of it by tomorrow morning.'

'Oh.'

'There were several descriptions of you, each one contradicting the other. I think you're supposed to be a "hit man" for one of the East End mobs. The story is that you were imported from Birmingham, and the police are looking for you in the Midlands.'

'What about the car?'

'Some of our people picked it up from the place in Camden Town. They're going over it, but they don't expect to find anything. After that, it will probably go to the knacker's yard.'

He sighed. 'So it's as simple as that?'

'That part of the story is, yes.' She continued to work at the stove. 'I didn't know what time you would wake, so I made a stew. Are you hungry?'

'Yes, I think I am. Perhaps it's the smell of the cooking, but I haven't eaten since yesterday. Can I do anything?'

'You could open the wine. It's only plonk.'

'From the northern slope of the supermarket?' It was an old joke they used to share, and she smiled.

She was silent for a while. 'I'm sorry. I behaved badly earlier.'

'No you didn't, and I'm grateful you were here.'

'You would have managed somehow. It was a shock to see you again, without warning.'

'I'm sorry.'

She laughed self-consciously. 'There's no point in both of us spending the evening apologising to each other. I'm glad you're feeling better. You must have had a rough twenty-four hours.'

'I did. It's hard to believe there was a time when I did that sort of thing for a living.'

Sally transferred food to the table, and they sat facing each other. The stew was delicious. He remembered that she liked to cook and, glancing up, he raised his eyebrows and nodded appreciatively. She had put on a little make-up to cover the shadows beneath her eyes, and he caught a faint wisp of her perfume. Mark ate hungrily, enjoying the food and the wine, which helped to shake off the aching lethargy of a few minutes earlier. When they had finished, she made coffee in a small espresso machine. He took out a cigarette.

'Do you mind if I smoke?'

'Of course not. There should be an ashtray somewhere.'

'Is there any news of Willis?' His question changed the mood of the meal, and he sensed her withdrawal, but her voice was calm.

'He's expected back this evening. He knows where you are, and I left a message for him to call if it was necessary. Otherwise, he could let you sleep it off and call in the morning.' When she turned to face him, she looked serious. 'I did a little reading this afternoon.'

76

'Files?'

'No, a couple of print-outs. I'm not really supposed to see a lot of that information, but I've been there a long time, and I know a lot of people. They won't mind, especially as you're staying here.'

'I wanted to talk to you about that. I'm well enough to leave any time, if you would prefer me to.'

'It's probably better to stay.' Her voice was impersonal, but he was pleased by her reply.

'I don't want to get in the way.'

'I'll tell you if you do. We have company, by the way.'

'Company?'

'They'll keep a watch on the house for the next twenty-four hours, in case anyone saw you drive here. In a way, it's easier if you stay put. Let's take the coffee next door. I don't like the smell of food when I've finished.'

'It was delicious.'

'You were hungry.' She smiled.

When she handed him his coffee cup, their fingers touched for a moment. He wanted to thank her, even to take her hands in his, but she moved away to sit by the fire. Instead, he asked: 'What did you read at the office?'

She shrugged. 'Basically, confirmation of your story.'

'Glantz and his little "discovery"? It's filthy!'

'Yes.'

'I suppose you don't know whether he showed up today?'

'No, but I don't think he did.'

'What happened to him?'

'Nobody knows.' Sally looked at him. 'Mark, you need to take care of yourself in this business.'

'What does that mean?'

'Simply what I say. They've dragged you into a very slimy operation.'

'It always is, Sally. That's what I couldn't explain to you.'

Her voice was soft. 'You never tried.'

'I shouldn't have had to.' She stood up, hurt and angry. For a moment, he thought she was going to cry, and moved towards her, but she shook her head angrily, biting her lip.

'That was a lousy thing to say!'

'I didn't mean it the way you think. Look, you're right, I behaved very badly when I left London. I should have talked it over with you, tried to explain what was happening, but I was mixed up and confused and, if you like, sick of the whole damned way of life. I just wanted to drop out.'

'No matter who you ditched on the way? Why did you do it? I hadn't done anything to you.'

He paced the room. 'There was a sequence of events; all the circumstances seemed to come together at the same time, and I exploded. The whole thing had stopped making any sense.' She did not interrupt him, even when he paused to find the right words. 'At the beginning, it was all so easy and clearly defined. We were the goodies, they were the baddies, and it was our job to get them, whatever the cost. But, as time went by, it stopped being so simple. It was no longer a case of good triumphing over evil – us against them – whatever the cost. It had turned into a kind of insane game, where winning was all that counted, whether we were right or wrong, no matter what it cost.'

'It was always that, Mark. You're being childish to imagine it could be otherwise. You weren't playing cricket!'

'I'm not suggesting that we were. I'm simply saying that, somewhere along the way, our motives had so blinded us that we were prepared to do anything, just as long as we came out on top. And we didn't care who or what we destroyed on the way. We were no better than they were. Do you remember Perry Smith?'

'Of course.'

Mark stared angrily at the electric fire in the fireplace. 'Dear old lovable Perry Smith – Peregrine Arthur de Vere Smith. There's a good name for a cricket team! He was a good-natured, charming, inconsequential, upper-class idiot. He never even worked for us on a full-time basis. He never had more than two consecutive thoughts in his head, and he was the perfect cover, as a fun-loving playboy who jet-setted around the world, having a good time.'

'All right. Perhaps he was all those things. He knew what he was doing for us.'

'But he didn't! He was a well-intentioned fool whom we

78

used and abused because he could afford to slope around without arousing suspicion. He thought he was Lord Peter Wimsey, or something like that, and we played on his fantasies. You know what happened to him?'

'Not all of it. I know he was arrested in Prague and died trying to escape. He was a brave man.'

'Bullshit! He was a fool, Sally. I haven't got all the details, because I never had all of them myself. But I can tell you this: Perry was sent to Prague with a load of false information. We knew it was false, even if he didn't, because we wanted him to be arrested. We deliberately set the Czechs on him. It wasn't an accident. He didn't have a hope the moment he stepped off that bloody plane.'

'That's happened before. You have to believe in a cause.'

'Without knowing what you're doing? Without knowing you're being sacrificed for the cause? We engineered Perry's escape, Sally. We arranged it because we had to convince the Czechs that he was carrying the genuine stuff. And that meant that we had to make sure that he got caught a second time. My God, I stood in a clump of trees on the Czech side of the Austrian border one lousy freezing day in 1976, and watched "dear old Perry" through a telescope. He was cold and tired and frightened out of his wits and, when he passed me, he thought he'd made it across. And that silly horse face of his was lighting up with a big stupid smile. He started galloping across the open ground when the border guards opened fire. He was still grinning when he hit the ground!'

'Oh God.' She was very still.

'But that wasn't the entire story, because I was holding a Czech rifle at the time, the same model as theirs, and it was my job to get him if they missed him. I was watching him through the telescope on my rifle, and it was only because they did a good job that I didn't have to finish it for them. It was a cold-blooded murder either way, and for what? So that they would drag him back to Prague, find the second set of dummy information that we'd planted on him, and lose one point in the game. He was carrying a set of false codes that H W Willis had dreamed up to mislead them. It fooled them for about eight days, after which they guessed what we had done, and the whole operation was written off as a flop. And when he learned about it, Willis shrugged his fat little shoulders, muttered something like "Back to the drawing-board", and planned something else.'

Sally closed her eyes. 'Good God!'

'God had nothing to do with it, Sally. H W Willis, assisted by me, was deciding who should live and who should die, whether they wanted to or not, whether there was any point to it. I remember the night I came back from Austria, Sally. You were irritated because I didn't want to make love. You thought I'd been with another woman!'

She did not reply, sitting motionless in her chair, her eyes closed. Mark watched her, but she would not look at him.

'There were others, too; not as cold-blooded, perhaps, but equally despicable. I'd become nothing more than a hired assassin, killing on either side; it no longer mattered which. We weren't trying to catch spies any more, or help fugitives into the land of the free. We had progressed far beyond that, and it was a matter of our side scoring points off theirs.'

'Why didn't you tell me you felt like this?'

'You'd never have understood. You were young and enthusiastic, filled with the same sort of good intentions that Perry had. For your own safety, it was better that you didn't know. Do you remember the night we had that argument about the extremes of left and right, when I said they weren't opposite poles, but side by side? Did you believe me then? And do you think the Americans would have landed on Grenada in the name of democracy if the coup had been a right-wing, fascist takeover? Would a peasant, working in the fields, be any better off under a fascist, totalitarian state than a Marxist one?'

'Why don't you ask the peasants working in the fields in Afghanistan?'

'I'm not defending the Russians, for God's sake! I'm saying that we've reached the point where we're no better than they are.'

Sally looked up angrily. 'Are you telling me that you really believe there's no difference between what we stand for and what they want?'

'Of course there's a difference, but the difference between the way we go about it and they go about it is increasingly less and less. Look at Latin America. For years it's been feudal, people living like animals, because it happens to suit a limited few.'

Her face was contemptuous. 'In a minute you're going to start throwing in good old catch-phrases like "vested interests".'

'What the hell do you think they are? You won't face the reality of the situation. We're not talking about some union leader, in the comfort of Liverpool, lecturing the workers. Why is everybody so uptight about Latin America swinging further and further to the left, as though it was some special intrigue developed by the wicked Russkies? It was inevitable. I don't support it and I'm not pleased that it's happening. I'm simply not surprised.'

Her anger subsided momentarily. 'All right, so you can sit back comfortably in Switzerland and say "I told you so" . . .'

'Not all right. I'm trying to tell you why I wanted out. There were no moral arguments left to justify what I was doing. It had become our system versus their system, and we were supposed to break any rules, do anything – however immoral – so that our system came out on top.'

'You can't reduce it all to some simplistic moralising because you were involved in a few ugly undercover incidents.'

'I'm not trying to, but I knew that I couldn't go on being a part of it. I had to get out of the whole filthy business, so I went, without ever looking back. And I managed pretty well until I was dragged back in because I can be useful to another of Willis's little operations.' He dropped into a chair. 'You've managed to cover a hell of a lot of ground with "ugly undercover incidents": murder, deceit, betrayal for starters. We're not talking about clicking our tongues because the West German government buys the odd busload of East German technicians for hard cash. You don't know what goes on . . .'

She rose to her feet, furious. 'Don't tell me I don't know what I'm talking about! I'm not concerned with one man who suddenly got pangs of conscience and walked out on everything and everyone he knew without even . . . I'm talking about brave, dedicated men, who believed in what they were doing and didn't whimper about it. They knew there were no Marquess of Queensberry rules, and some of them were prepared to die, if necessary...' Her voice broke, and she stopped in mid-sentence, swallowing hard to hold back tears. But her eyes misted, and a single tear coursed down the side of her nose, leaving a shiny trail. She sniffed at it angrily and sat down, burying her face in her hands.

For a long time, neither spoke. At length, Mark asked softly: 'Is this the "T" whose inscription I poked my nose into?'

She shook her head, still masking her face with her hands. 'None of your bloody business!'

'I didn't mean to criticise you, or anyone special to you.'

She looked up, staring into the fireplace. Her voice was still angry, but under control. 'I didn't become a nun after you disappeared, you know. God! How arrogant can you get?'

'I didn't think you would. I hoped you wouldn't.'

She was calmer. 'I know. I'm sorry. I shouldn't have attacked you like that. Anyway, I asked for it. I wanted an explanation, and you tried to give me one. I'm sorry about Perry, too. I didn't know what had happened to him.'

'It was all a long time ago. Put it down to battle fatigue. Who is "T"?'

'Someone I used to know.' She shook her head and blew her nose noisily.

'I don't want to pry.'

'Then don't ask questions!' She was silent for a while, repairing her face with a crumpled Kleenex. She sighed. 'Oh, what the hell! His name was Tony. Silly, isn't it? He always signed everything with a "T", even though his name really began with an "A". It always struck me as inconsistent.'

'Did I know him?'

'No. I only met him a few years ago. It's funny; I didn't really like him very much at first; he wasn't my type. And I certainly didn't want to get involved with him.' She looked at Mark. 'Once was enough!'

'What was he like?'

She thought about it. 'Nice. I know it's a useless sort of

word, but if you ask me to describe him quickly, he was a nice man. He was very different from you: very relaxed and easy-going. He was always cheerful and friendly. You would never have guessed he was working for us. He wasn't the intellectual type. He never seemed to read anything except the Sunday supplements. I think he preferred a night out with the boys more than anything else. When we went out together, it was usually to meet all his drinking friends at the local. He had a marvellous capacity for making friends. Oh, sometimes we went to a show. He loved musicals, especially if they had senti-mental endings.' She smiled. 'He couldn't stand my classical records. They depressed him. But he made me laugh, which I hadn't done for a long time, and he looked after me. He made me think I was the greatest thing since sliced bread. I can't im-agine how he managed, half the time. Whenever he was alone with me, he was shy and clumsy, especially when he was trying to look sophisticated.' She laughed. 'The first time he took me out, he managed to knock a bottle of wine over; then he jumped up to fix it, and poured soup all over my lap.' She smiled at the memory, but there was sadness in her voice. 'I suppose he was a comfortable man, easy to be with, once he stopped knocking things over. He wasn't very handsome, and his clothes looked as though he had slept in them, but he was good to me and good for me. God, I must have given him an awful song and dance when he first started seeing me. I was so bad-tempered and neurotic, but he wouldn't take no for an answer. He said he'd assigned himself to me as a special pro-ject: to turn me back into a human being.'

'He sounds like a good man.'

'I never realised how good. He lived here for a year or so. Just showed up one day with all his stuff in a couple of suit-cases, and said he'd given up his flat, so I couldn't turn him out in the rain. It happened to be a lovely, sunny day, and he looked so silly, standing there, that I just laughed, and he moved in. He wanted to marry me – "make the old girl honest" – but I wouldn't.'

'Why not?'

She looked at Mark. 'Because I'd been hurt, and determined never to be hurt again if I could help it; something melodramatic like that. I know it's childish and self-pitying to talk like that, but my life was pretty messed up after you left. It took a long time to get over.'

'I'm sorry, Sally.'

'Oh, it's too late for apologies. Maybe I should have noticed more, and talked to you about it at the time. You were obviously going through all sorts of private horrors, but you never let me know. Do you realise that I had no idea that anything was seriously wrong? I just thought you were more than usually moody. I suppose I was pretty innocent. I wasn't that young, but I was very naïve. Anyway, I told him I didn't want to get married and to stop pestering me. We were perfectly well organised as we were.' Mark nodded thoughtfully. 'It wouldn't have surprised me, though, if he had shown up one day and whipped me down to the Registry Office without warning. I'd probably have said yes out of embarrassment for him.'

'Then what happened?'

She walked over to the sideboard, to pour the last of the wine into her glass. Her voice was colourless when she spoke.

'He went away on a job, and never came back. I don't know exactly what happened or why he was there, but there was nothing very dramatic about it – no border guards on the Czechoslovakian frontier. He was in a fight, the silly fool, in a Belfast pub.' She shook her head helplessly. 'I still don't know what the hell he was doing there. Anyway, a man pulled a knife on him, and the next minute he was on the floor of the bar.' She emptied the wine glass in a single gulp. 'I suppose that, if he had to go, at least it was the sort of place he would have chosen!' When she looked at Mark, she was close to tears. 'So it seems I have a deadly effect on people. One look at me, and they don't come home!'

Mark stood, to go to her, but she waved him aside.

'I don't want your bloody pity, for God's sake! You asked me who "T" was, and I've told you!'

'When did it happen?'

'Six months ago. I'm over the worst part, but I do miss him. I miss his cheeriness, even when it was irritating, and his good nature. They were good for me. I'm not even sure that I loved him, but he was nice to have around the place. Perhaps that's what real love is like.' She turned to Mark, and her eyes were angry. 'So don't tell me we're all rats in a sinking ship, or that we're all slimy, dishonest killers with no moral sense. Some of us did care, and still do.'

'Of course.'

'And if there are horrible parts, or things we should be ashamed of, it's because they go with the things we have to do, and we have to accept them. It may not be very pretty. I'm not trying to whitewash anyone, least of all that little slug Willis, but what happened to you was on the outer limits of our lives. Most of the people are just nice, simple and uncomplicated, doing a day's work. I was going to say "honest" day's work, but they don't make up the rules.'

'All right. I accept that.'

'No you don't, but I'm jumpy enough to make you agree, if only to keep the peace. I won't cry again, so you don't need to feel nervous. How are you feeling, by the way?'

'I'm better. The sleep did me good.'

'You still don't look so hot. What are you going to do?'

'There's not much I can do. Wait for Willis to call in the morning, finish the job, and go home. There's not much else I can do, is there?'

'Well, try and see a doctor as soon as you can. That's only a temporary job on your arm. Do you want me to have another look at it?'

'No, thanks. It's not giving me any trouble. I'd sooner leave it alone.'

She spoke softly. 'You're lucky, Mark. In a day or so, you can go back to your musical world and forget all this. Not many people get a second chance.'

'I know.' He took her hand. For a moment, she pulled back, but he held it firmly. 'Sally, I'm sorry. I wish I could make it up to you.' He pulled gently at her hand, so that their bodies touched. Sally allowed the movement, but remained immobile. At length, she said: 'I know what you're trying to say, Mark. It all happened a long time ago.' He released her hand, and she stepped back. Their eyes did not meet.

She yawned. 'I don't know about you, but I'm suddenly very tired. It's been a hectic day, one way and another, so I'm going to kick you out of here and make up the bed.'

'I'll sleep in here.'

'Don't be silly. You're much too tall for the sofa, and I fit comfortably. I've often slept here before, when friends stay over. It's very comfortable. So we both might as well rest properly.' She paused, diffidently. 'And thank you for listening. It sometimes helps to talk about it.'

'Sally, I wish there was something I could do. I didn't mean to hurt you . . .'

She smiled sadly. 'I know you didn't. But you needed to hurt someone at the time, and I was the handiest candidate.'

'You deserved an explanation. I should have told you what was happening to me.'

'Yes, you should have. You should have understood that I wanted to know, instead of being so noble about it.' She smiled. 'Now, if you wouldn't mind getting out of here, I'm going to bed.'

She came to him in the night. He had been sleeping lightly, and awoke to find her nestled against him, her face very close to his. In the pale light from the doorway, he could see that her eyes were open, watching him. There was a light scent of jasmine, mingled with the warm, earthy perfume of her body. As he placed his arm against her back, drawing her closer, her hands held his face, her mouth gently welcoming.

In the morning he was awoken by the telephone, which rang twice and was silent again before he could lift the receiver. Sally was no longer there but, pinned to the pillow by his head, there was an envelope. He recognised the large, tidy handwriting.

Mark –
The telephone ringing was me! I thought I had better wake you before it got too late, so, if I have, it means that it is 8.30. Sorry to play games, but the truth is that I didn't want to face you. If we have to hate ourselves in the morning, I'd rather do it alone.

I have a few more confessions, since I'm telling the truth

and nothing but. I know about your 'constant companion' in Switzerland. She's listed along with a few other personal details in those print-outs I read. I'm not apologising for what I've done, although I'm not exactly sure why I did it. It wasn't revenge or jealousy – at least, I don't think it was, even if you were mine first. Call it a momentary fling, or a nostalgic gesture, or just the need to feel close to someone again. If it hurts you to know this, I'm sorry.

You'll find your money in the envelope. I forgot to give it to you last night. Talk about reversal of roles! Sorry it isn't a lot, but you didn't give me very much. At least the exchange rate is good. Tell Willis to give you something out of his 'slush fund'. He's probably sticking it in his own mattress, if I know him!

In case you need to get in and out of the flat this morning, there's a spare set of keys in the envelope. The bigger one is for the front door. You may as well hang on to them for the moment. You can always stick them on a piece of card and post them to me when you have finished with them. One day, you might even like to deliver them in person. I promise I'll behave a bit better if you decide you'd like to.

Please be careful. Willis is a devious man. I know it's not very likely that we'll see each other again, but, for what it's worth, I'm glad there was this one time.

Love, S

The phone rang again as he was finishing a second cup of coffee. This time it was Willis.

'Mark, my dear, I believe it's the English woman who's supposed to say: "Feeling better?"'

'Spare me your schoolboy humour, Willis. What's going on?'

'Quite a lot, quite a lot. You seem to have got yourself in a nasty spot of trouble yesterday.'

'I didn't get myself into a damned thing. You put me square in the middle of it, and it's about time you took me out again.'

'We will, Mark. Don't be such a fuss-pot!'

'For God's sake, you cold-blooded bastard! I don't live in

your world any more. I missed being killed by the grace of God, spent the night driving through the Austrian mountains, got shot up by some trigger-happy maniac, and you call me a fuss-pot!'

'Very well. I'm sorry. It was a little joke in my usual poor taste. How is the wound? I heard it grazed your arm. I can send a doctor round to have a look at it.'

'My arm isn't giving me any trouble for the moment, and it's not what concerns me. I've had enough. Just get me out of this whole bloody mess and I'll worry about my arm. Where's Glantz?'

Willis hesitated. 'I'm afraid there's a slight hitch.'

'What sort of hitch? Is he here or isn't he?'

'He isn't, Mark.'

'Then where the hell is he?'

'It appears he's in New York.'

'Where?'

'New York, NY, USA. He never took the ferry. After promising to come in yesterday, he had a change of heart. He never even went to Calais.' Willis sounded hurt. 'Instead, he took a train from Lyon to Paris, lay low for a day or so, and flew to New York.'

'In God's name, why?'

'Well.' He hesitated again. 'I think I told you already that Eberhard doesn't really like or trust us.'

'Neither do I.'

'He decided at the last minute that he wouldn't be safe here, despite all our guarantees, and he was scared of being recognised anywhere else in Europe, so he hopped on a transatlantic jet. The man's paranoid, but I must admit he knows what he's doing. If you're going to disappear for a few days or weeks, the best place to hide would be a nice big city, where you can be anonymous.'

'I can't see you taking it quite so philosophically, Willis. What sort of pressure are you putting on him now?'

'I?' His voice expressed surprise. 'There's very little I can do, under the circumstances. Of course, I did happen to mention that I would be in touch with some of my colleagues in the American constabulary. After all, he's not a very suitable candidate for American residence, is he? Our friends over there get so nervous if you so much as mention East European affiliations.'

'You really are a nasty bit of work! The poor devil's scared out of his wits. You're after him in England, God knows who's after him in Switzerland, and now you're threatening him with the FBI, the CIA and, knowing you, the New York City police as well. Why the hell don't you let him go?'

'We will, just as soon as he hands over one or two little pieces of information. You seem to forget, Mark, that it's rightfully our property. We're only trying to get it back. After that, he's free to do what he wants.'

'Where? He daren't go back to Suchim.'

'We can make arrangements to accommodate him. The world's a big place, you know.'

'Not big enough, from my experience. What do you have in mind?'

'Well, Mark, I know you're not as fit as you should be, but do you think you could keep going just a little bit longer? You see, he is still prepared to talk to you. I never would have guessed you had such a fatal attraction for him . . .'

'Oh, stop it, Willis! My only attraction is that I'm one of the few people lately who hasn't either blackmailed him or bullied him or tried to kill him. All right, I'll talk to him. Give me his number.'

Willis hesitated again. 'I'm afraid it's not quite as simple as that. You see, I told Eberhard you would meet him in New York.'

'You told him . . .'

Willis continued quickly. 'I know it's imposing on you, Mark, but we must resolve this matter before anyone else finds him. He's agreed to a meeting tomorrow evening, and you should be able to come to any arrangement necessary and fly back to Geneva on Monday.'

'I was supposed to fly back to Geneva last night.'

'So if you leave on Monday, it's only two days longer than anticipated. That's not so very long.'

'How the hell am I supposed to get there?'

'We've booked you on the three o'clock flight today. It gets you in at five-thirty, New York time. I made it later than absolutely necessary.'

'Why?'

'In case you need a visa. I've got this absolutely charming friend at the American Embassy standing by in case there's a problem.'

Mark laughed, feeling close to hysteria. 'Willis, if I didn't despise you so completely, I'd laugh this whole thing off! You're unbelievable! Suppose I told you my arm was killing me, and that I was in no shape to go anywhere, including Switzerland?'

'But you didn't. That's why I asked you.' His voice was smug. 'Mark, let me offer you one small inducement. If you'll complete this assignment, apart from having served your country . . .'

'Bullshit! My country has no idea what is going on.'

'That's something you'll never know for certain. Anyway, as I was saying, if you complete this final mission, I promise you that we will never contact you again.'

'I don't believe you. Why should I?'

'Don't believe me if you don't want to, but the offer is there. I think I can give you proof. Do you trust Miss Faulkner?'

'Sally? I suppose so.'

'Very well. When this little job is finished, all reference to you will be erased from our files. Computers can be deprogrammed, you know. Sally Faulkner uses our machines, and she knows how they work. When you return to Geneva next week, you can call her for confirmation that you have been removed from the memory banks. 'How's that?'

Mark hesitated. 'I suppose so. I don't trust anything you offer, Willis. You can probably pull the wool over Sally's eyes too.'

'But I won't. If you think about it carefully, you're never going to be very valuable to us again. Your presence has been noted by some of our friends on the other side of the fence.'

'That argument makes a little more sense to me, Willis. I can't imagine any altruistic gesture on your part. All right. I'll go. I still don't believe half you've told me, but it's worth the gamble.'

'I am glad. I'm sorry you feel so strongly about us. It's so much nicer to be friends.'

'That's not going to happen. My visa is still valid, by the way, so your co-operative American friend can go home.'

'Very good. Are you sure you wouldn't like a doctor?'

'Quite sure. What do you want to do?'

'Quentin will come round for you in a car at one o'clock, to give you plenty of time for the airport.'

'Tell him to bring some dollars. I'm damned if I'm laying out any more money for you.'

'Of course. You're going to be there for two days. Would five hundred be sufficient?'

'Yes, but I'm still going to send you a bill for the rest.'

'Very well, dear boy, as long as you fill in the correct form.'

'Not a bit of it! I'm not an employee. Take it out of the Special Fund. Am I going first class?'

'Oh, dear me, no. I'm afraid the budget doesn't run to that kind of thing for any of us these days. The best we can manage is Club.'

'Some things never change, Willis! You'd better give me a London number where I can reach you at all times.'

'Quentin will bring everything you need. Don't worry.'

'Willis, I'll keep worrying until this whole sordid little operation is finished.' He thought for a moment. 'I'll be staying at the Mayflower Hotel on Central Park West and Sixty-second Street. I always do.'

'Good. When Glantz calls us today, I will tell him to call you there any time after seven o'clock tomorrow evening. All you have to do is talk to him. Agree to anything he demands, within reason, provided he gives us what we want.'

'That's a pretty wide-ranging authority.'

'Not really. We're prepared to barter, if it becomes necessary.'

'I see.'

'Good. Be ready for Quentin, please.' The line went dead.

Mark sat on the bed, staring at the phone. His eye noticed Sally's note, and he re-read it, wondering whether he should leave a note for her. 'Not yet,' he thought. 'I don't know what to say. Just about anything will be wrong!' Picking up the phone again, he dialled Anne-Marie's apartment.

To his surprise, she accepted his story quite calmly. It was essential to fly to New York immediately, to see Bianca, because, without her agreement, the project would fall through.

'I thought you might have to go and see her. You'll find her at the Mayflower.'

'Yes, I know. I'm sorry, darling. I was looking forward to our weekend together.'

'It's all right, Mark. I understand.' Her voice was very controlled.

'We can still go away when I return. If I'm quick, I can be home by Tuesday.'

'Don't make promises – and don't worry. There will be other weekends. Shall I call ahead and book your room?'

'Thank you, darling, it would be a help. I love you, by the way.'

'And I love you. Please take care of yourself.'

'I will. Goodbye.' She seemed very far away.

He went into the bathroom and, working slowly with his left hand, unwound the bandage over his arm. The flesh was raw and angry, but there did not seem to be any serious inflammation. He found a wide piece of adhesive plaster and, adding a little of the antiseptic ointment, stuck it over the damaged skin. It took up less space, and was moderately comfortable.

In the bedroom, Mark reached under the pillow and removed the gun. Sally must have known it was there, but she had made no comment. He dismantled it quickly, recreating his camera, and packed it on top of his clothes. Walking through to the living room, he chose a record of Fauré Nocturnes and put it on the player. The languorous, nostalgic melodies and subtle harmonies filled the room, and he stood by the window, looking into the street outside. A man was sitting in a small red car, parked a few doors away, reading a newspaper. He appeared to be reading with great concentration, but, after ten minutes, Mark noted that he had not turned the page. Presumably the man was part of the 'company' that Sally had mentioned the night before. He looked at his watch. There was nothing left to do but wait for Quentin to arrive. In the air, there was still a faint scent of jasmine.

New York

The yellow taxicab, which seemed to operate with neither springs nor shock absorbers, rattled up the hill that marked the start of the Triboro Bridge, and Manhattan's famous skyline came into view. It gave Mark little pleasure, despite the brilliant, ice-blue skies and dazzling sunlight. He remembered how, twenty years earlier, he had always felt a sudden surge of excitement, deep inside, as the multi-shaped skyscrapers loomed majestically. But that had been twenty years earlier, when the world had been a younger, more innocent place. In the intervening years, as the whole world had deteriorated, New York – the most concentrated city of the Western hemisphere – had deteriorated with it, emphasising the downward slope on which civilisation was travelling. When he had first visited the Big Apple, it had been a dynamic, optimistic merry-go-round, vibrating with enthusiasm and ambition, where even the ever-friendly waiter in the overpriced restaurant explained that he was really a brain surgeon between jobs, and where 'mugging' was something that Jack Benny and Milton Berle did to entertain hysterical audiences. That was before hard drugs had destroyed the human spirit, and the Arabs had destroyed the old economy. Even the New York cabbies, some of the cheeriest, most garrulous experts on any subject in the world, had been replaced by sullen, hirsute young men, silent behind the armour-plating of the protective plastic screens that separated passenger from driver. And the old optimism had gone, replaced by neurotic anxiety, from the corporate executives who snarled their way through a day fraught with fears of redundancy or replacement, to the ever-present little old ladies, their faces etched with disappointment, who clutched handbags tightly for fear that the street gangsters would pry them away. The cab lurched over a particularly spine-

93

shattering pot-hole and Mark thought to himself: 'They still haven't fixed the road!'

It was one of those deceptive New York March days. The blue of the sky and the brilliance of the sun in the crystal air suggested a Mediterranean balminess, but the temperature was well below freezing. In the short distance between the terminal building and the cab, a vicious wind had cut through Mark's thin raincoat. A droning newscaster on the rado interrupted his endless sales pitches to advise New Yorkers that light snow was on the way. The cab bumped and ground its way along the fast-moving East Side Highway, and Mark noted the innumerable new buildings that seemed to have sprung up in the year since he had last visited the city. Like the favourite restaurant in the mid-town area that had disappeared to provide space for a car park that would, in turn, become a multi-story tower, the new apartment buildings appeared as if from nowhere, to cast their giant shadows on the nestling brownstones. As one observer had commented: 'It will be a great city when they finish it!'

The Saturday traffic was light as they made their way across town from the Drive, and cruel gusts of wind sent eiderdown-coated women scurrying between the smart shops on Madison Avenue. In Central Park, the trees were still blackened skeletons. They had shed all trace of leaves, standing naked and apparently dead during the onslaught of the winter months. Their outpouring of foliage, when the first, sudden heat of April replaced the winter ice, always amazed him. There was a hard whiteness to the ground that witnessed the last of a previous snowfall, or perhaps a heavy frost. Mark looked out of the steamy taxi window and shivered.

He entered the hotel lobby to a blast of hot air, and was signing in when a familiar voice, accustomed to being projected across the great opera stages of the world, hailed him.

'Marco, darling! It is you?'

Bianca Morini, her arms superbly upraised in the gesture that had made her the finest Adriana Lecouvreur of the day, was standing in the centre of the lobby. Several guests turned to stare, and two bellboys broke off their conversation to gaze admiringly. She was sheathed in a full-length sable coat, cinched tightly at the waist to emphasise her hourglass figure, and she held the dramatic pose with the confidence of a star until Mark had walked the twenty feet that separated them. He planted a kiss on each proffered cheek, murmuring 'Hello Bianca', and her arms enfolded him in richly perfumed fur. The theatricality of the gesture was slightly marred when she moved her right leg forward so that her thigh was placed squarely between Mark's legs, oscillating gently but firmly. One of the elderly bellboys blushed.

Mark unwrapped himself with difficulty. 'I hoped I would find you.'

'Darling, I am always here for you.' She moved in again, thigh at the ready.

'How's Ettore?' He hoped the inquiry might deter her, but Bianca's long-suffering financier husband was aware that her emotional promiscuity was endemic. On the other hand, so was her passion for luxury, and she always returned to him, giving herself with exhausting generosity.

'Ettore is wonderful!' Her smile broadened wickedly. 'And in Los Angeles for a week.' The thigh started to move in again. 'You were looking for me, and you have found me!' Her voice rang with triumph.

Bianca's rise to fame as an opera singer was based on, in addition to stunning beauty, great musical talent and a dramatic skill that many of her colleagues sorely lacked, a number of well-publicised events in her career. At a nubile twenty-five, she had been the companion of an Italian cabinet minister, until her marriage the following year to a Greek shipping magnate. When he, in turn, died two years later of a heart attack, it was strongly rumoured that this was brought about by Bianca's amorous excesses, and she rapidly became the toast of Rome and the darling of the *paparazzi*. She did not marry again for several years, whetting journalistic appetites, but her name was constantly linked with successful figures in the public eye: leading film actors, a racing driver, the host of a television series (whose wife once poured a bowl of pasta over her at Alfredo's), and one of Italy's best-known directors. She had been a vocal student, and had always considered herself a singer, but it was only when she began appearing regularly on the arm of a popular young Swedish tenor that Bianca's formidable operatic talents became apparent. It was possibly because she had not overtaxed her voice in her earlier years that it blossomed so superbly when she was already in her thirties. Within two years, she was singing major roles, and her first film, in which she appeared monumentally topless for one brief scene, became a collector's item in later years when she persuaded Ettore to buy up all the existing prints. She finally married Ettore when the tenor, whose top C was beginning to crack, sought solace in the arms of a Rumanian baritone and, although her name still appeared occasionally in the gossip columns, her marriage to the patient Ettore was a success. He was an understanding man, who adored Bianca with the dedication of a lifelong opera-goer, and delighted in using his financial skills to convert her considerable fees into a series of highly profitable tax-free corporations in various corners of the globe. At thirty-eight, admitting to thirty-five, she was in her vocal prime, and her voluptuous body was guaranteed to keep the sleepiest of opera patrons wide awake. But Mark recognised that, despite the delightful scandals that surrounded her, together with traditional Italian displays of operatic temperament (she once refused to appear in the third act of *La Fanciulla del West* because the conductor had dared to interrupt the applause to continue the opera), Bianca had a redeeming quality which earned instant forgiveness: she was a great artist. And, when she was not performing to the gallery or whoever happened to be watching, she was also a warm and charming friend: kind, and with a genuine sense of humour.

As Mark turned to the waiting bellboy, Bianca linked her arm through his, bestowing on him a heavy sampling of the famous Morini bosom as she pressed closer. 'What can I do for you, my darling?'

Mark walked with her towards the elevators. 'I was hoping we could make some plans for the season after next. I've brought your five-year diary, so we can look through the empty spaces. By the way, Charles in London sends you his love. He still thinks you should accept Covent Garden's offer.'

She pouted. 'Only if they meet my conditions, darling. My

fee is to be the same as Placido's – but after taxes!'

'I don't think they'll buy that, Bianca.'

'Then I don't sing there.' Covent Garden was dismissed with a wave. 'But I have other things to talk to you about, *caro*. Come to my suite. Are you hungry? I will have something sent up.' She sighed sensuously, more out of habit than intention. 'I will make you very comfortable.'

'I'd love to, Bianca, but I'm expecting a call. I've only just arrived from London. Aren't you on your way out of here at the moment?'

She waved aside the question. 'If you are tired, you must rest, dear Marco. I want you warm and refreshed. Listen, you must talk to Abe for me.' Abe was her American agent. 'It's about a contract he showed me.'

'Which contract? You have so many . . .'

'Some record company. I don't remember which one it is. A man came to see me last week. Marco . . .' Her voice was petulant. '. . . they tell me they want to record all their operas for the next three years, but only if I pay for them myself. What sort of a contract is that? Ettore is expected to provide the money!'

'Really?'

'The insolence! In New York, they call that the chootz-bar!' She made it sound like an Italian word. I told Abe: if they provide the money, I sing the operas. If Ettore pays the money, who needs them? *Ecco*! Then they tell me they want me to record all kinds of songs – pop songs, Broadway songs, folk songs – any kind of songs except the songs I sing! I think they confuse me with Liza Minelli. It's another good Italian name! Tell me, who is Johnny Roberts? Should I know him?'

'He's a country and western singer.'

'A cowboy? Why would I make records with a cowboy? Ah, wait a minute! They have seen my Minnie, and maybe they think I am a cowgirl! What is this Johnny Roberts: a tenor? a baritone?'

'Well, I suppose you'd call him a baritone. They don't really identify them that carefully. He sings popular country and western songs. He's very successful.'

Her hands waved in Italian, fingers carving and weaving. 'A

cowboy singer! Do they know who they are talking to? I am not a horse! Please, Marco, talk to Abe for me. Tell him to explain to them: Morini doesn't sing cowboy songs!' Her eyes narrowed to a speculative gleam. 'Do you think they know Clint Eastwood? For him, I would sing cowboy songs!'

Mark laughed. 'I'll bet you would, Bianca.'

'And you'll call Abe for me?'

'I will. I was planning to call him this afternoon.'

'Wonderful! Dear Marco, you are my true friend.' She moved closer. 'Listen, *caro*, call me as soon as you are rested. You can call me any time you like – any time.'

'I will. I'll call you in the morning.'

She shrugged. 'You must be very tired, darling! Tomorrow morning? No, I have to make television interviews all day. The people are so boring, and they always ask me the same questions. Do you know what one fool asked me? Who was my favourite soprano. At first, I thought I would name at least three dead ones, but then, I thought again, and I told them that I love them all. If they have to appear on the same stage as I, they have real courage! But I will finish by the evening. Call me then, as late as you like.'

'I'll try, but it might be quite late.'

She smiled, giving his arm a final, pneumatic squeeze. 'That's my favourite time, *caro*. Come to me, and we will have a nice cosy chat. And then, when the business is finished, we will relax and enjoy ourselves. I do not sing again until Wednesday, so we will have plenty of time. *Ciao!*' She kissed him, lingering on each cheek, her knee caressing his leg. Then, with a further dramatic display of hands and arms, swept towards the front door of the hotel, where a nervous uniformed chauffeur awaited her.

The bellboys followed her exit, fascinated. For a moment, Mark thought they were going to applaud. She would have been delighted if they had.

When he had unpacked his few clothes, leaving the camera unchanged for the moment, he called Abe Sincoff. It was already too late to disturb Anne-Marie in Switzerland, six hours ahead. Abe was one of Mark's oldest friends in the music world, a genial manager whom he had befriended when he was still working for Willis. They had first met at a concert where Mark was supposedly sponsoring a young Australian cellist. When he had finally broken away from the Department, Mark had sought help and advice from Abe, who had provided both. Like most managers, he shared artists across the Atlantic with local representatives who understood the domestic situation, and Abe had helped establish Mark in Europe by passing several excellent young American artists to the care of his office in Geneva. As Mark's own roster had grown, Abe had offered American representation, making them partners in various ventures. Years later, and with some success to his credit, Mark still regarded Abe as his mentor. Few weeks passed without a telephone call to discuss mutual problems, and Mark knew that, however brief his visit, he would find time to see his friend. They shared the formidable task of representing Bianca, and his presence in New York gave him the excuse of working on some details of her career. Abe was surprised to hear his voice.

'Hey Mark! You sound like you're next door. Where are you calling from?'

'New York. I'm at the Mayflower.'

'You should have told me you were coming. What are you doing here?'

'Just a quick visit, to talk to Bianca; and you, of course.'

'Great! Listen, you want to come round? No, wait a minute. My sister-in-law is coming in from Queens. That I wouldn't do to you.'

'That bad?'

'I'd rather go to an all-Stockhausen concert on a Saturday night! And there's only one thing worse than an all-Stockhausen concert on a Saturday night...' He paused for Mark to add the punch-line.

'An all-Stockhausen concert on a Sunday afternoon!'

'In Baltimore!' Abe always had the last word. 'So, you're at the Mayflower? You know Bianca's there?'

'I just saw her in the lobby...'

'And lived to tell the story. Jesus, that lady is some broad.

She makes me worry for my virginity.' Mark smiled. The vision of Abe, sixty-two and balding, with a roly-poly face that was perennially wreathed in smiles, defending his honour from the endless charms of Bianca, was hard to imagine. He was the archetype of the contented family man, with a daughter in her final year at college, a son already established as a dentist, and a loving, sympathetic wife who worried and constantly fussed over all of them.

'Don't let Bianca scare you, Abe. She acts that way out of reflex action.'

'It's not *her* reflexes I'm worried about! How about tomorrow?'

'Free all day.'

'Great! I'll tell you what we'll do. Myra and I will pick you up around twelve and show you a good old New York tradition: brunch at the Tavern on the Green. We can walk there from the hotel.'

'Sounds good.'

'It's a great place, if you haven't been there already. In the old days, I would have taken you to the Lower East Side for some good whitefish, real pumpernickel and black bread in a genuine New York Jewish restaurant, but these days down there it's all Puerto Ricans and *schwartzers*.'

Mark laughed. Abe was the only man he knew who could make racial discrimination sound entertaining. 'Abe, you're a racist!'

'No I'm not. I miss the old days. It's just that you English fairies never got over losing the dear old Empire.' He essayed Noël Coward: 'Pity we lost Indiah!'

'Abe, your English accent sounds like something out of Paramus, New Jersey!'

'Well, you know what they say, kid: wake an Englishman up suddenly, without warning, in the middle of the night, and he talks just like the rest of us! Listen, you want to come over anyway? Myra can take her sister into the kitchen, as long as she promises not to contaminate the food.'

'No, but thank you. I'm still on European time.' He looked at his watch. 'It's past two in the morning in Geneva.'

'OK, pal, then I'll see you tomorrow. I didn't tell you about the catch.'

'I knew there had to be one!'

'You're coming to a recital at Alice Tully in the afternoon. I've got a young pianist making his début there. You're going to like him.'

'Sure, Abe. Why not?'

'So much so that I may just have you representing him in Europe for the next couple of years – before I hand him over to the big boys!'

'All right.'

Abe feigned exasperation. 'Hey, schmuck, you're never going to learn. Don't be such a pushover! At this point, you should be screaming at me that you can't handle the artists you've got, and why am I bugging you with some cock-a-mamie new pianist. Then, before I can say more, you lay two of your artists on me, and say there's no deal unless I handle them for the United States and Canada.'

Mark laughed again. 'Abe, I only said I'd come to the concert, but I'll keep your suggestion in mind for next time.'

'Oh boy! How's the beautiful Bianca?'

'More beautiful than ever. I was hoping we could discuss some film ideas I've been thinking about. She would be sensational on the screen.'

Abe chuckled. 'She already was. Didn't you ever see that movie?'

'No, Abe. It was before my time.'

'Well, keed, you miss something. If she's going to make a movie with a pair of jugs like that, it had better be in Cinemascope!' He turned away from the phone and shouted: 'So you open the door, Myra. It's your sister!' Returning, he said: 'Listen, I'd better run. It's the Creature from the Black Lagoon and her prey! You're going to like this kid I've got. He's a fine pianist.'

'I'll look forward to it.'

Abe again pretended anger. 'Don't give me all that cool! This is New York. You've got to think in superlatives! Believe me, with what you'll earn from him, you can give up that crummy hotel and move into the Carlyle.'

'I'm happy where I am, and it's convenient for Lincoln Center. The Carlyle's to hell and gone on Madison Avenue.'

'That's the trouble with you, Mark: no class!' There was a further interruption, as he made effusive welcoming sounds to the Creature from the Black Lagoon and her husband. Into the phone, he whispered: 'She's wearing a hat, for Christ's sake! Civilisation has come to Roosevelt Boulevard. Maybe it's just that she had her hair dyed punk-style. I'll wait and see if it comes off.'

'You'd better go, Abe.'

'We'll pick you up in the lobby. Did Bianca tell you about her record offer?'

'She mentioned it, a little unhappily.'

'I'll tell you more about it tomorrow. What I didn't tell her is that they asked if she'd agree to pose for the cover with no bra in a wet shirt. The sad part was that they meant it! All right, Myra! The whiskey's in the cabinet, where it always is. Your sister should know where to find it by now! I gotta run. Sleep well and rest. Bye!'

Mark hung up, smiling. New York might have deteriorated, but New Yorkers still liked to talk as though they were on the Johnny Carson Show. It was always showbiz! He walked over to the window, to look across the dark expanse of Central Park. There was a light snow falling, the flakes illuminated by the street lamps. Across the street, the pavement was already turning white in the freezing air.

The room had a walk-in closet, self-illuminating as the door opened. Entering, he examined the jacket he had been wearing in London when he arrived. The brown stain on the arm was not very noticeable, but the tear in the cloth made it unwearable, leaving him only with a pin-stripe suit. There was probably a twenty-four-hour tailor somewhere in the city, who could repair it overnight. One of the advantages of New York in the old days was that there was a service for every need round the clock. Today, he was not so sure.

He considered having a meal sent up by room service, but decided against it, having little appetite after the plastic trays of plastic food that had marked the passage of the hours during the flight from London. In-flight meals were never very good, but they helped to pass the time. He was tired, after two nights with little sleep. His memory lingered with Sally, wondering whether she had decided that it would be safe to return to the flat again. Perhaps Willis had already told her of his departure. It was hard to know how much they communicated with each other, but he had the feeling that she had not told him everything she had seen in the computer print-outs. After those first, nervous hours together in the flat, she had shared his bed with great tenderness, tempering her passion to his exhaustion. Rediscovering the hidden secrets and delights of her body, and remembering her urgent response, had given him greater pleasure than he cared to admit. He wondered whether Anne-Marie would understand such a momentary lapse into his past life. A shadow crossed his mind. Sooner or later, he wanted to tell Anne-Marie about the past and what it had involved. There should be no secrets. He had thought about telling her before, but it had all seemed remote in the clean, placid atmosphere of Geneva. How could you tell a quiet, well-educated, albeit beautiful, Swiss girl that you had spent fifteen years of your life scrabbling around in a dirty underworld where death had no dignity and was sometimes the most dignified alternative to what you were doing? He ran a hot bath, relaxing into it and feeling a sensuous tiredness flow through him. If Willis kept his promise, this would be the one last time. He could return to his new life in a few days, and bury it forever. In a month or two, it would be in the past, and he would find a way to tell Anne-Marie about it. But not yet.

He awoke at eleven, feeling rested and with that slight suggestion of a hangover from oversleeping. He was grateful that he had remembered the 'Do Not Disturb' sign on the door. There had been too many other rude awakenings in hotels around the world. When he flexed his arm, there was only a slight soreness. Brilliant sunshine, streaming through the curtains, gave the room a cheerful glow. Looking out, he could see that there was a sprinkling of snow on the ground. It was the only time of year when New York looked clean. Reaching for the telephone, he gave the operator Anne-Marie's number in Geneva. It rang steadily for several minutes, but there was no reply.

Abe and Myra were waiting in the lobby when he came out of the elevator. Abe's round face, supported by several creases of chins, lit up with a broad smile.

'There you go, sleeping beauty! How do you get to look so good if you're in the music business?'

'I lie about my age a lot.'

'You're learning, kid, but your timing is off.' He had half closed his eyes, turning down the corners of his mouth in a Semitic gesture learned through generations of Jewish humour. At his side, Myra, equally bulky around the hips but with the thin, angular Spanish face that must, somewhere in the past, have had Sephardic ancestry, nudged Abe out of the way.

'Take no notice of him, Mark. He's just jealous. And how is Anne-Marie?' They had spent a happy few days together in Switzerland the year before, when Abe was making his annual Grand Tour of European offices.

'She's very well, and sends you both her love.'

'And when's the wedding?' Myra did not openly disapprove of Mark's free-ranging association with Anne-Marie, but took the view of any good Jewish mother. Anne-Marie could – God forbid in such a set-up! – be her own daughter.

'Just as soon as she says yes.'

'So what are you waiting for, a nice good-looking young man like you? The girl has problems?' The majority of Myra's comments contained a question-mark, with an upward intonation at the end of the sentence.

'No problems, Myra. She just values her independence.'

'Independence, what's that? If you wait this long, how old are you going to be for your children and grandchildren?' Myra was already anticipating the increase of her own family to a second generation, although both her children had steadfastly ignored heavily underscored comments on the advantages of married bliss. It was a constant subject of conversation at the family dinner table.

'Oh, leave the kid alone, Myra. He only just got here.' To Mark, he added: 'You're going to freeze your ass off. It's cold out there. You want to take a cab?'

'No, of course not. The fresh air will do me good. I've been cooped up in planes and hotels for days. I like your coat, Myra. Is it mink?'

Abe beamed proudly. 'It's twenty-three concerts, two television appearances and a Japanese tour, but who's counting?'

The Tavern on the Green, situated in Central Park, in addition to being a tourist mecca, was also a favourite New Yorkers' restaurant for the traditional Sunday brunch, which consisted of anything from an extended breakfast to a full Sunday dinner, 'with all the trimmings'. Abe, who seemed to know every maître d'hôtel in the city, led them past busy queues of guests to the crowded central room of the Tavern, an art-deco palace from whose glass roof hung dozens of coloured crystal chandeliers of various shapes and sizes. Mark found that, as ever, the glittering room reflected New York very well, with its combination of gaudy ostentation and comfortable informality. Many of the diners were in shirt-sleeves and casual clothes, with a smattering of sports jackets and business suits. There were a number of family tables, with young boys dressed in formal suits that made them look like midgets. As in all New York restaurants, the noise was intense, and the decibel level of conversation immeasurably higher than anywhere in the world. He could never understand why New Yorkers felt such a driving desire to shout at one another when they met. Something to do with living in a highly competitive society. Fortunately, the head waiter, greeting Abe like a long-lost friend, shepherded them to a corner table by a window, where the sound was reduced to a comfortable level. After the ritual of ordering food and drinks, they settled back to enjoy the frosty view. The white ground was undisturbed and, every now and then, a gust of wind sent delicate sprays of frozen snow dancing in the crisp air.

Abe nodded. 'I tell you, kid, it's the greatest city in the world. Any time you want to come and work in my office, I'll make you a trade.'

'No thanks, Abe. I like Geneva.'

'That's why I offered the trade. I'm not so dumb! I could use a few years in that clean Swiss air, paying those teensy-weensy Swiss taxes and eating all that Swiss candy. You've got it made.'

Myra interrupted. 'Don't you believe him, Mark. He loves New York. Every time I talk him into a European trip, he spends one half of the time complaining about the food, and the other half talking to his office in New York. I'm lucky if I can get him to take more than two weeks' vacation. If he had his way, he'd spend it in Central Park.'

Abe sighed. 'I guess you're right. Did I ever tell you about a friend of mine – a publisher – who was sitting in Paris with some friends one January? He hated it. Couldn't stand the food, couldn't stand the waiters, couldn't stand the town. So he says: "That's it! I'm through with travelling. What am I doing in Paris, France? I can't even find a bagel to put my lox on. From now on, I'm going to be in New York. Period. New York is the only city in the world. There is no other place worth being in, and I'm spending the rest of my life in New York City. If anyone wants to see me, they're going to have to come to New York, because that's where I'm going to be. I'm staying in New York, and I'm not moving." So a friend of his says: "Sam, today is Tuesday, January 25th. If you were in New York today, where would you be?" And Sam thinks about it for a minute and says: "January 25th, where would I be? In Miami; where else?"' It was an old joke, but Abe laughed happily, retelling it. Mark laughed too, but Myra looked puzzled.

'I don't get it, Abe. If Sam wanted to live in New York, why would he be in Miami?'

Abe laughed more, holding his wife's hand affectionately. 'What New Yorker spends January in New York, Myra? Don't let it worry you. You have to be Jewish to understand it.'

Myra was offended. 'Abe, I am Jewish!'

'Not really, honey. You're from Orange, New Jersey. You have to be from New York City to be really Jewish!' Myra looked perplexed, and returned to her scrambled eggs and lox, while Abe winked at Mark.

'So how's the beautiful Bianca?'

'She's fine, Abe. She said I must talk to you about some record contract she was offered.'

Abe repeated the gesture that combined omniscience, philosophical acceptance and *weltschmerz*. 'Listen, what can I tell

106

you? The record companies here don't want to make classical records any more. They don't sell a hill of beans, and a *good* record is one that sells. Anything else is a no-no. This funny little guy came to see us. He had a nervous tic and made so many faces I thought Bianca was going to bop him one for making a pass. He's running scared, they're all running scared, peeing in their executive pants in case their records don't sell and they get kicked out on their executive asses!'

'It can't be as bad as that.'

'Sure it can. They're working for companies that think millions every time they sign a pop star. Who needs some classical broad that's going to sell a few thousand records?'

'Then why bother?'

Abe shrugged. 'Image. Institutional advertising. It looks good in the annual stockholders' report, and it gives the chairman of the corporation something classy to send his friends for Christmas.'

'It's not like that in Europe. Even in Switzerland which, God knows, is hardly the centre of the music world, there are little companies.'

'Sure there are, with little overheads, and they pay little fees in little amounts of francs and marks and drachmas, or some other funny money. Europe's different. Music's a traditional way of life. You see kids in all the opera houses and concert halls. Going to a concert in New York is a status symbol – something to tell Mrs Garfinkel you did last Thursday. The European companies are all that's left of the classical business, and they do it with a little bit here, a little bit there. In New York, everything's got to be bigger and better. This is Successville. We leave the art side to nice English fairies like you!'

Myra looked pained. 'Abe, that's rude!'

Mark smiled. 'Don't worry, Myra. He's just jealous because I still have my own teeth and hair!'

Abe laughed, slapping his leg. 'So who's got hair?'

'What about Bianca? She said they want her to sing with a country and western star.'

Abe dismissed the matter with a wave of his hand, the light glinting on his gold watch. It had been a present, surprisingly, from Fritz Reiner. 'They thought they were doing her a favour. They wouldn't know what to ask her to sing if they had the budget.'

'But why the cowboy songs?'

'Because the latest trick is called a crossover record, which means you get classical artists to make pop records, but you put them out on the classical label. If you hit lucky, you can sell a lot.'

'You think Bianca should do that sort of thing?'

Abe waved a hand. 'Nah, Bianca's different. She doesn't need the exposure and she sure as hell doesn't need the money. I told her not to bother about it and sign a European contract. You can handle that, kid. I like the movie idea, too. So anyway, I went back to the record company last Friday. The little man made faces at me and watched his telephone as though it was going to bite him. By the time I left, he was looking relieved.'

Mark was thoughtful. 'It's not a very hopeful situation.'

Abe smiled. 'There's still penty of action in Europe. You have to change with the times here, Mark. New York's a showcase city. We see all the best artists. They all play here, but it's still only a showcase, like the one in a hotel lobby. If you want to buy the goods you have to walk three blocks to find the store that sells them. And if the critics say an artist is good, he gets an ovation. If they don't like him, he plays to empty houses. New Yorkers don't have time to find out for themselves. Why do Broadway shows close on the strength of a few reviews? At the prices you pay for two on the aisle and with so much on your mind, who's got the time? People are too busy working at being a success. They need someone to tell them what's "in" and what's "out", from music to movies to theatres and restaurants.'

'I suppose so. The first time it struck me was when *Annie Hall* opened. I happened to be here about a month later, and every third girl that passed me was wearing a floppy white shirt and a big tie, to look like Diane Keaton. It was more like a uniform.'

Abe sighed. 'It happens all the time, even the way we talk. A few years back it was all computer language, with "input" and "demographics". Before that, it was do-it-yourself psychiatry, and we were all "relating to" and "identifying with" each

108

other. There's always some new buzz word. Can anyone tell me what "glitzy" means?' Myra looked vague. 'It doesn't matter. By next year, it will be something else. New Yorkers live for change and success. Why d'you think they give famous people such a hard time, crowding them wherever they go?' He rolled his eyes dramatically. 'Success, my boy! They hope some of it's going to rub off on them!'

'That happens everywhere.'

'No, it doesn't, Mark. Myra and I were in a little restaurant in the South of France a few years back, and David Niven was standing at the bar, talking to some friends. Everyone left him alone. They almost ignored him. If that had been New York, they would have been hanging over him, trying to start up a conversation. Jesus, half the pop stars have to hire armed guards to keep trespassers off their property!'

'We have the same thing, Abe. It happens to pop stars everywhere.'

'Not as much as here. Success is the name of the game, kiddo. If you can sell the public on an idea, this is the place to do it. Remember that violinist who came up a couple of years ago: the nutty one who glared at the audience and refused to take a bow? The word got out that this was the greatest player to hit the stage since Heifetz. Myra and I went to his début at Carnegie Hall, and I'll be goddamned if the audience didn't give him a standing ovation when he walked out!' He shook his head in amazement. 'Where else in the world would you get a standing ovation *before* you played a note?'

There was a pause. Myra said: 'Eat your food, Abe. It's getting cold.'

Mark looked at his friend. Between smiles, his face was deeply lined. 'You sound bitter, Abe.'

'No, kid, I'm not bitter; I'm a realist. If that's the way the public calls the shots, that's the way we have to play the game. My problem is that I remember Heifetz. Now it's the hype that counts, not the talent.' He looked up suddenly, his face breaking into a warm smile. 'Hey, why am I talking like this? You're about to hear the greatest young pianist this side of the Mississippi, and I'm warning you it's all a big hype!'

Mark put a hand on his arm. 'I know what you're telling me,

109

Abe, but I also know you wouldn't want me to hear him if he wasn't good. When you invited me to the concert, you were paying me a compliment.'

Abe blinked, as he always did when he was embarrassed. Myra looked on approvingly. Mark lit a cigarette. 'I'll steer Bianca away from the cowboys. The Old West would never be the same after she got through with them, and for all you say, you still love this business or you would have got out years ago.'

Abe smiled back. 'There was only one thing I forgot to add about New York. We love to complain and we exaggerate a lot!'

Myra watched them happily. Then she took command. 'Abe, you eat! For Pete's sake have your lunch while there's still some heat in it. You want your stomach to rumble all the way through the recital?'

Abe's young pianist was a twenty-six year old graduate from the Juilliard School of Music, who had been playing modest professional recitals on the 'college circuit', with an occasional concerto engagement with one of the lesser orchestras that could not afford a 'name' artist. The famous were often available, but at $10,000 and $15,000 an appearance, the funds were not. His New York début was an important moment in his career, and Mark was surprised to see the hall reasonably full. Abe had done his work.

The young man had chosen a pleasant, conservative programme, the first half consisting of a group of Scarlatti sonatas, followed by the Chopin B Minor Sonata. Mark tried to listen impersonally, although he did not enjoy Scarlatti on the piano. 'Pianistic' playing, with subtle use of pedals and *legato* finger work, seemed inappropriate. It took all the sting out of the music, smoothing the harsh, at times dissonant harmonies and making each piece a polite *salon* entertainment. The plucked strings of a harpsichord gave the music the earthy, Spanish sound it deserved. The young man had, like any pianist of his generation, strong sure fingers. He played smoothly and accurately, with dazzling runs and well-controlled dynamics, and the audience applauded sincerely. Abe nudged him and winked, but Mark reserved judgement. He could be yet another of those 'fizz kids' that Konstantin abhorred. The Chopin was different. He played it with flair and daring, managing to blend the lyrical with the dramatic and drawing long, fluid lines of melody that were never overstated. It was an outstanding performance, and the audience applauded wildly, calling him back to take several bows before the lights came up for the intermission.

Mark turned to Abe with a smile. 'You've picked yourself a winner. He's excellent.'

'I told you.'

'I liked the second movement of the Chopin. You don't often hear a pianist who can make both hands talk. All you usually get are the right-hand fireworks.'

Abe mopped his gleaming forehead in the well-heated auditorium. 'Jesus, Mark, you sound worse than a goddamned critic! What that kid has is charisma. You could see the audience responding to it. And it sounded the way I like to hear Chopin. Come on, we'll go see him backstage. I can't stomach all those arrogant young broads sounding off like experts in the foyer. There's always at least three, loud-mouthing their theories and scoring points off their friends. You see, kid, it's even competitive in this town when you're in the audience!'

Myra looked at Abe with triumph in her eyes. 'I told you to eat your lunch while it was still hot.' She turned to Mark. 'When his stomach's playing up, he hates the audience. If he's digested properly, he smiles like everybody's rich uncle and calls them "nice kids".' She shook her head in disgust. 'So go and talk to the boy. I'm going to the powder room.'

They found the young man sitting in the dressing room, staring at the wall in despair. His eyes were glazed and his face was disconsolate. Hovering in the corner was a worried-looking woman in her fifties, dressed in funereal black, searching through a carry-all for a clean shirt. Mark guessed that she was the artist's mother. Abe patted the pianist gently on the shoulder, waving to the woman.

'It's going really well, Alvin. The Chopin was great! How are you feeling?'

Alvin looked up, scarcely recognising Abe. Then, as if shaking himself out of a daydream, said: 'A bit better. I threw up twice before I went out. But I screwed up the Scarlatti.'

'Nonsense, it was beautiful. This is my friend and associate, Mark Holland. I hope he's going to look after you when you get to Europe.'

Mark shook hands. 'Congratulations. I'm enjoying it very much.'

Alvin still looked dazed, speaking mechanically. 'Well, thanks. I screwed up the Scarlatti, you know,' he added conversationally. An unhappy expression came over his face. 'And I think I'm going to throw up again.' He pulled a handkerchief over his mouth and made a dive for the toilet.

His mother hovered by the door, listening anxiously. Abe walked over and patted her on the shoulder. 'Don't worry, Mrs Hudacek. It's quite normal. Your first New York recital is a pretty frightening ordeal.'

She shook her head. 'I guess so. I've never known him act up like this before. He was fine in Ann Arbor.'

Abe guided her to a chair. 'But this is New York. Débuts are always the same. If he plays the second half anything like the first, he's going to get wonderful reviews. Mark my words: this could be the start of a very big career for him.'

'I guess so, if it's what he wants. I always hoped he would find a real job.'

The second half was equally good. Alvin played the Alban Berg Sonata with great command, making its complexities take shape, and ended with the dramatic Prokofiev Sixth Sonata. It was all virtuoso playing, but he managed to add touching gentleness where it was called for. The piano sound was big and robust, and as his hands drove down on the keyboard for the final chords, the audience erupted hysterically, calling him back to the stage several times before he sat again at the piano for the compulsory encore pieces. These were greeted equally enthusiastically, and the cheers were genuine and deserved. As the lights came up, Mark could sense the mood of the audience. He felt some of it himself. Abe was smiling happily, helping Myra into the new coat.

'There's nothing wrong with this New York audience, Abe.

They knew what they heard.'

He shrugged. 'Oh, Alvin does it the hard way – with real talent!'

'You should have told me before. He's special.'

'I didn't want to push him too quickly. He's young, with plenty of time. He needs to prepare repertoire. I'm interested in a long-term career. He can get rich when he's old enough to appreciate it.'

'Will you send him over to Europe?'

'Next year, if you want to find him some dates, but nothing too fancy. He's good, but he's got a lot to learn.'

'I'll see what I can do. Send me whatever you've got on him.'

Abe grinned. 'There's a package on my desk, waiting for you.'

'I should have guessed!'

Abe ushered Myra towards the dressing room, but Mark halted them for a moment, looking at his watch. 'If you don't mind, I think I'll leave you here.'

'You don't want to see him again?'

'I'd love to, but it's getting late and I promised to call Anne-Marie. It's already after eleven in Geneva.'

Myra nodded approvingly. 'More important that you should call her. Pianists you can hear any time. And tell her from me that she shouldn't play games with you. A nice girl like that should be married and raising a family.'

'I don't know about the second part, Myra, but I'm working on the first.'

'So work a little harder!'

'I will. Please give my apologies and tell him how much I enjoyed it. I look forward to seeing him in Geneva. And thanks for a lovely lunch.'

Abe took his hand. 'Sure. That dressing room's going to be a madhouse for another hour. The adrenalin will have hit his system by now, and they're going to have to hold him down with steel cables.' He chuckled. 'He'll probably want to go out and play the whole programme again – especially the Scarlatti! You sure you don't want to join us later at the Tea Room?'

Myra shook her head. 'He never changes. There's a recital at

Lincoln Center, but he still takes the boy to the Russian Tea Room!'

'Why not? It was good enough for the great ones. You go to one of those smart-ass new Lincoln Center places if you want. I like the Tea Room!'

'It's too far.'

'In New York, nowhere is more than five minutes. Call me tomorrow, Mark. Beautiful Bianca's looking for action.'

Mark left them, arguing comfortably as they pushed their way past the queue of well-wishers which had formed outside the door of the dressing room. For a début recital, the line was long.

Outside, it was snowing. Heavy flakes were falling, and they struck his face in wet patches. Traffic hissed over gleaming streets and, as he walked briskly back to the hotel, the doormen of several apartment buildings were already out on the sidewalk, spreading pebbles of chemical that would prevent the snow from settling. They crunched underfoot.

At the front desk, he found two message forms from the telephone operator. A 'Mr Gluns' had called at five-fifteen, and would call back later. There was no return number. Also, a Miss Monno from Geneva – please call a.s.a.p. Once in his room, he called Anne-Marie. She sounded relieved to hear his voice.

'I called earlier.'

'I was at the office. I wanted to catch up on a few things.'

'You sound worried.'

'I think I am. I'm not sure.'

'What is it?

'The office. I think someone has been in it.'

'How do you mean?'

'It's difficult to describe. Everything is in the right place.' She hesitated. 'But I have the feeling that someone has been looking through all our papers.'

'Is anything missing?'

'Not as far as I could see. I can't explain, Mark. Everything is where it should be, but it feels as though it has all been moved, and then returned to where it should be. I know it sounds foolish, but I have the feeling that someone has been looking through the office, reading all the files.'

'Did you talk to Frau Emmi? She might have been doing some tidying.'

'Perhaps, but Frau Emmi has not been here since Friday. We left together. I do not seem to be making very much sense, do I?'

'Do you want to call the police?'

'The police?' Her voice was alarmed. 'There would be nothing to tell them. Nothing is missing. In fact, everything is exactly where it should be. I just have the feeling that it has been – moved.'

'How about the cleaners? They come in late. Perhaps they've hired someone new, who's moved things out of place.'

'But nothing is out of place! Oh Mark, I wish you were here!'

'So do I, darling, but don't worry, I've nearly finished. It shouldn't take much longer.'

'How is it going?'

'Very well, but slowly. I'll get away as soon as I can.'

'I know you will. I'm sorry. I feel I'm being neurotic again.'

'No, but it could be something quite simple. If you are still worried, why don't you give the police a call? They can keep an eye on the place.'

'No, it isn't necessary. I feel foolish for telling you about it. When do you hope to finish?'

'Tonight, or tomorrow. I'm not sure. After that, I'm on my way, on the first available flight.'

'I hope it is soon.'

'So do I. I miss you.'

'And I miss you.'

'We have a lot to talk about when I come home. There are things we have never talked about before.'

Her voice was calmer. 'Your mysterious past?'

'Partly. If you're going to marry me, darling, and you are, aren't you?' She was silent. 'I don't want to have any secrets. Myra Sincoff says to tell you not to be so stubborn, and say yes.'

'You saw Abe and Myra? How are they?'

'Very well. The same as ever. They think you should marry me immediately. Myra wants children!'

She laughed lightly. 'Then perhaps I had better!'

'You mean that?'

'When we have talked. I wish you were here now.'

'I do, too, darling, but I won't be much longer.'

'Yes, and I am sorry I worried you with my feelings about the office. It was just a strange sensation.'

Mark frowned. Could someone be interested in his office in Geneva? He kept his voice light. 'There's sure to be a simple explanation. My guess is that it's a new cleaner, but if you're worried, please call the police. That's what they are there for.'

'I will, if I am still worried. Talking to you about it makes it less important. I must miss you.'

'Well, it won't be too long, and then I can escape this awful place.'

'Is it so terrible?'

'Not really. It's just me. I've changed, and it's snowing and bloody cold! I'd rather be home with you.'

'Yes.'

'I'll call you as soon as I'm clear. Sleep well, and don't worry.'

'All right.' Her voice was shy. 'I love you.' She had never said it before, unprompted.

'And I love you. You'll never know how much. Goodnight.'

'Goodnight.'

Sitting in the darkened room, Mark remained immobile. It was time to tell Anne-Marie. He wondered why he had waited so long. Shame, perhaps? There was so much to explain. He could not start to do it on the telephone. As soon as he returned, he would tell her the whole story: how he began, what he had done; every detail and every event, including all the lies and half-truths. It would be difficult, but there was nothing to hide any more. He would find a way to explain.

The plaster on his arm itched, and it occurred to him that he would have to find an explanation for that, too. He could hardly tell Anne-Marie that he had just happened to walk into a passing bullet. It was a relief to think that there would be no

116

further reason to cover the truth.

Looking at the telephone messages in his hand, he assumed that 'Mr Gluns', who had called earlier, was Glantz. A German accent would sound like that, and New York telephone operators rarely asked callers to spell their names. Why had he called so early, when Willis had told him it should be after seven? Perhaps the tension was taking its toll. It was only a little after six, and he lay back on the bed, trying to piece together the events of the past three days. Unanswered questions still nagged his brain, and he cursed himself for an inability to see the whole picture clearly. But then, that had always been part of Willis's technique, to manipulate people like players on a chessboard. Each one had a particular function, but only Willis knew the overall strategy. The bastard! There could even be someone else, a *doppelgänger*, lying on a bed in another hotel in the city, awaiting a similar call from Eberhard Glantz. It was not above Willis's mentality to play games like that. Perhaps that was why his contact was Quentin. Was Willis controlling someone else? He sat up for a moment, then shook his head in disgust. 'My God, he's making me paranoid now!' And yet there were still too many unexplained events. The answers they had offered him in Vienna had been too pat.

He was dozing, and the phone woke him with a start. It was too dark to see the time, but he switched on the bedside lamp before lifting the receiver. It was eight-ten. His heart seemed to be beating faster.

'Hello?'

'Herr Holland?' The voice had a pronounced accent. It was hesitant, cautious.

'Yes. Who is this?'

'You were expecting my call.' It was a statement.

'Yes.'

'Then you know who I am.'

'Yes, I do. We are supposed to meet.'

'You are alone?'

'Yes.'

'And you will come alone?'

'Yes.'

'Very good.' There was a long silence.

Mark spoke first. 'Do you mind if I identify you?'

'No, I do not think so. Why is it necessary?'

'I'd like to be careful.'

'Very well.'

Mark waited for a moment. Then, holding the phone a little away from his mouth, so that the sound would not be too piercing at the other end, he whistled a few bars from Schubert's 'Rastlose Liebe'. The words to the song were: '*Dem Schnee, dem Regen, dem Wind entgegen, im Dampf der Klüfte, durch Nebeldüfte*' ('Through snow, rain and wind, in damp ravine, through misty haze . . .'). He had whistled it that night, in Berlin fifteen years ago. It had been a sad joke, to describe the storm drain in which they were hiding. He listened, and, at the other end of the line, there was a slight chuckle, and the caller whistled the next phrase: '*immer zu, immer zu* . . .' It was Eberhard Glantz. When he spoke again, his voice was warmer.

'You remembered.'

'Yes. I'm sorry to be suspicious, but I thought it best.'

'You are right. When can you come to me?'

'As soon as you like. Where are you?'

'I am in an apartment building in the city, not very far from your hotel.'

'I'll take a cab.'

'Very good; the address is one-nine-five East Seventy-fifth Street. It is between Lexington Avenue and Third Avenue, on the south corner. I am in apartment eighteen-H. There is a doorman that you must pass, and the apartment is in the name of Dwyer.' He might have been lecturing a class of science students.

'Who is Dwyer?'

'The owner of the apartment, but I did not meet him. I rented from an agency. He is away.'

'Very good. I'll leave immediately.'

'It is still snowing. There are not so many cabs.'

'Then it will take me a little longer.' He hung up.

He wondered whether he should take his gun, and decided that it would not be necessary. Glantz wanted to meet him, and there had been no suggestion that he was being watched. He

118

left the camera on the bedside table but, before leaving the room, decided to take a few precautions. Tearing a small piece of paper from a message pad, he placed it in the door of the closet, close to the hinge by the floor. If the door was opened in his absence, the paper would fall to the floor. He put on his raincoat and, opening the front door of the room, placed another sliver of paper against its hinge. On the outside, he hung the 'Do Not Disturb' sign.

It was still snowing, and the streets were already lightly covered. Even the busy road outside the hotel had a wet brown-white surface where the traffic had passed over it, but there were now few cars moving in the street. The city was un-usually quiet in the heavy storm, and the constant hum that one felt rather than heard was reduced to a minimum. Mark approached the doorman hopefully, and the man shook his head doubtfully.

'You may not find a cab in this, mister. Nothing's moving. Best thing to do is wait for someone coming in.'

Ten minutes later, their patience was rewarded when a cab made its way to the hotel entrance with some new arrivals. Several other guests were waiting under the awning. The nearest turned to Mark.

'You want to share? Which way are you headed?'

'Across town.'

'So am I – the East Eighties.'

'Fine. I want Seventy-fifth.'

They each handed the doorman a generous tip, and gave the driver their instructions. He turned in his seat.

'I'll have to go round Central Park South. There's no Park traffic.'

'That's OK.'

'Sure, mister, just so you know how I'm taking you. Some weather, eh?'

Mark had found that snowstorms engendered a special camaraderie in New York. Competition ceased to be so fierce, and people cheerfully joined forces against the elements. The man sharing the back seat said: 'Goddam city shuts down whenever it snows. You'd think they'd be prepared.'

The driver snorted. 'Nah, they wait till the last minute.

Someone makes a bundle out of the snow clearing. It happens every year the same.'

Mark said: 'It's late in the year for a storm like this.'

'It was on the radio all day,' the driver said, by way of explanation. He inched past a car that was skidding uneasily on the slippery surface, its engine running too fast.

The other man grunted. 'They say we're causing too many disturbances in the atmosphere.'

'Yeah,' said the driver. 'Fuckin' Russians!'

The building was a typical New York apartment house, some twenty stories high, with a covered awning to the street. Because his fellow passenger was continuing uptown, Mark alighted at the corner of Seventy-fifth and Third Avenue to walk the last few yards to the front door. He left a ten-dollar bill with the driver, who thanked him happily. Someone was profiting from the weather, and it was Willis's money anyway. As he trudged away, the driver called out: 'Have a nice evening!' The doorman called the apartment on the house telephone before allowing Mark to pass through the lobby, and he was finally granted permission to take the elevator.

He pressed the front door bell and waited for what seemed to be an unusually long time. It was probable that Glantz was watching him through the glass peephole above the number plate, perhaps to satisfy himself that Mark was alone. At last, he opened the door narrowly, leaving just enough space for Mark to pass through. There was no light in the foyer, and Mark followed him to a living room, from which he could hear the sounds of voices. It startled him, but as he entered, he saw that it was a television set. On the screen, two young girls were speaking in Swedish.

'You have not changed greatly over the years, Herr Holland.' Glantz's voice was low and guttural.

In the subdued light of the room, Mark was able to see his face. The photograph that Quentin had given him had not been very accurate. Mark recognised the thin face with sunken eyes, closely set, but he had not expected his hair to be so prematurely grey-white. His teeth were long and uneven, and he was wearing rimless glasses, which had not been in the photograph. He was dressed in a dark brown suit, tight at the waist and rather crumpled, with an open-necked yellow shirt. He wore no shoes, and his general appearance was untidy. He had not shaved, and dark shadows ran either side of his chin. Glantz stood very still, watching Mark cautiously, like a trapped animal. His hands were trembling slightly.

'Would you like coffee? I do not drink much alcohol, but there may be some in one of the cabinets.'

'Coffee would be very good, thank you.'

Glantz walked to the kitchen and, while he waited, Mark's attention was drawn to the television screen. To his surprise, one of the girls was now naked, lying on her back. The other was removing her blouse slowly, smiling seductively. She leaned over the naked girl and began kissing her breasts, her head moving slowly downward over her body until it reached her thighs. The soundtrack consisted of nervous giggles, accompanied by sensuous sighs, which grew in intensity. From his memories of bland American television programming, it was shockingly unexpected. At his side, Glantz spoke, his eyes on the screen.

'You enjoy, perhaps, these movies? I find them very – relaxing.'

Looking past the television set, Mark saw the winking green lights of a videotape machine. There were several cassettes lying next to it, with lurid covers. Eberhard Glantz apparently had a predilection for pornography.

'I don't often see these films.'

Glantz continued to watch. 'They are excellent quality. The photography is very well made, I think.'

The moans of the girl on the screen had now increased in intensity, gathering as she reached her climax. The sound was artificial, and Mark assumed that it had been added at a later stage in the production. Glantz watched, fascinated, until the final orgasm had ended, then nodded his head, like a surgeon inspecting his work, and switched off the machine. When he spoke again, his back was turned towards Mark. He spoke calmly, but was clearly in a highly nervous state, stretched to the limit of his endurance.

'They have explained the situation to you?'

'Only the broadest details.'

'My life is in danger, Herr Holland.' His voice was almost a whisper, and his fists, hanging loosely at his sides, were tightly clenched, the knuckles white. 'If I had not left my apartment early that morning ... you see, there was an experiment in the laboratory that was critical in its timing...' His voice broke off, and he walked to the video machine, turning off its power switch. The green light ceased blinking.

'What did you do?'

'I drove away. For the first few minutes, I drove without thinking, anywhere to be away from the house. And then I made a quick plan. My passport was in my briefcase. I had expected to need it shortly. And I had money. I had been to the bank the day before.' His sentences were clipped, with pauses between them. He turned to face Mark, the light catching his glasses. For a moment, reflection from the lenses reminded Mark of Willis.

'We had been talking for several weeks.'

'Who?'

'Herr Willis, of course. He began to call me, very friendly, to ask me how I enjoyed my work at Suchim. He was very polite.'

'I didn't know he had been in so much contact with you.'

'Oh yes!' His voice was bitter. 'He had been very much in contact with me!'

'And had you reached any sort of – understanding?'

Glantz paced nervously, while Mark drank the coffee. It was bitter, and only vaguely warm.

'There was no understanding, Herr Holland; but there was much to be understood. Every day, he began to call me, and every day he began to tell me a little more. It was like a torture, but his voice was always very polite – very English!'

'I see.'

'No, Herr Holland, I do not think you see. He explained to me about my life in Switzerland, and my work at Suchim. He told me that I had been working for him – for that man! – since the day I arrived in Switzerland. He said that I was an employee of the British government.'

Mark said nothing. Anger had helped to conquer the other man's fear. He continued to pace angrily.

122

'I did not know. For fifteen years, I did not know! I am a respected man, Herr Holland. I am a Swiss citizen. And then, he began to increase the pressure on me. It was incredible! That man! I had almost forgotten him, but he kept telephoning me! He told me all the things I did not know. That I had worked, all those years, for him! That my records, my theories, my experiments were for him! He said that I belonged to him, Herr Holland! That I, and everything I had worked on, belonged to him. I told him that I would destroy the papers, burn everything, if he spoke to me in that manner.' His voice dropped to a whisper again. 'The next day, when I came to my office, everything was gone.'

'I don't understand.'

'Gone!' He looked up angrily. 'You don't understand what I am telling you? My filing cabinets, my research, all my papers, they were gone! He had taken them. He said they could not be returned to me. They were taken from my office because they were his property. But they were not! They were mine! He told me that I had no right to question him; that the papers – my papers! – were the property of the British government!' He sat in a chair for a moment, his hand covering his eyes. 'And then, the other man called me.'

'What other man?'

He took off his glasses, pressing a thumb and index finger in the corners of his eyes. 'He did not tell me his name. He called me at my apartment late one night. We only spoke for a few minutes.'

'What did he want?'

Glantz's voice was low. 'He said that he had information to suggest that I had made some important discoveries. He told me that I must give what I knew to him, or I would be in very great danger. I don't know who he was, or why he knew what I had been working on. I have suspicions – nothing definite.' He continued, almost as if talking to himself. 'There was an assistant at the laboratory that I dismissed a month earlier. I never liked him. I did not trust him. He could have talked. I don't know. It is too difficult to know what happened. I was working, and I did not think about him.'

'And did you tell Willis about this call you received?'

'Who?' Glantz was distracted. 'Willis? Yes, I told him. He laughed! He said there was nothing to give! Any final calculation that I could give to this man would be . . .' He reached for the word. 'Gibberish? Yes, gibberish, without the rest of the information.'

'Was that true?'

'Yes, without everything that preceded it, what I was working on would have very little meaning.'

'Did this other man call again?'

'Only once. I told him the truth: that I no longer had any documents. That they had been taken away from me. I don't think he believed me, even though it was the truth.'

'What did he say?'

Glantz closed his eyes. 'He said that I was in trouble. Just that – trouble! He rang off, without speaking again. I told Herr Willis. He was very pleased. He said that I should not be bothered again. He wanted me to work on the final stages of my calculations. I told him that I would not, that he must return everything to me, and leave me alone, and he began to threaten me.'

Mark nodded. It had a familiar Willis touch. 'What did he say?'

Glantz spoke calmly, without expression. 'He was always polite. Herr Willis is always polite, making little jokes while he talks. Each time he called, he made little hints, but they were threats! He said that Suchim would be very surprised to learn that I had passed all this information to him. But I did nothing! He had taken it from me! He said that, without a position at Suchim, the Swiss government would question my right of residence in Switzerland. Each day, he added a little more. He said that, when they learned what I had been doing, the Swiss government would revoke my passport, and that I would not be permitted to remain. He said that, if I continued to refuse to collaborate with the British government, I would be returned to East Germany, to face charges of treason and spying. I am not a spy, Herr Holland. I am a scientist!' He looked at his hands. 'Besides, it was important that I should finish my work.'

'So you continued to work willingly?'

'I continued to work, for myself, not for him. Not for that man! I knew he wanted the rest of it; the parts he had not stolen already! Yes, I continued to work.'

'Why?'

'I am a scientist, Herr Holland. I work to solve problems. I had still enough information in my laboratory to go on working. I had been studying the same problem for six years – changing, experimenting, reconsidering each step of the way. I had lived with it for six years. And there were computers, which had stored all the results. I still had the computer information.'

'And you finished?' There was a long silence.

'Finished? No. In science, Herr Holland, you never finish. You reach the end of a series of studies, but that opens the door to new studies, new problems.' He laughed, wryly. 'The final part was an accident. I had miscalculated, and I went back to correct the error, and I made a second error. It was when I made this miscalculation that I found what I had been looking for! It was an accident that I found it at all! Six years of work solved by an accident!'

Mark nodded silently. So that was what Willis meant by 'stumbling on an interesting theory'. It was hardly in the same category as Madame Curie discovering radium.

'What happened then? Did Willis know about it?'

'He knew, yes. I tried to disguise the truth, but he guessed that I had found the answers. He wanted to know more, but I gave the excuse that I was working on an important side effect, and was needed in the laboratory. He did not call back that afternoon, and I went home. The following morning, the bomb exploded in my apartment. It missed me by only minutes.'

Mark sat in a chair, watching his face in profile. 'What do you want to do?'

Glantz was silent for a long time. When he spoke, he looked up, staring at the empty television screen. 'I cannot go back. He has destroyed everything that I had in Geneva. I cannot return there. I cannot go anywhere unless I agree to his conditions.' When he faced Mark, his eyes were brimming with tears. 'They tried to kill me.'

'Yes.'

'The bomb was in my house. They put it there. A few minutes later, and I would have been blown to pieces! They warned me!'

'Are you sure of that?'

He stood up angrily. 'Sure? I just told you! I have been running away ever since. I cannot sleep for more than a few hours. I cannot stay anywhere for very long, before it is time to move; before they find me.'

'Why didn't you go to London?'

'It was not safe. It was the first place they would look for me. They would watch the airport, the boats.'

'Then why not let Willis come to you?'

'It was not safe either. They could be watching him. I have never seen him. I do not know what he looks like. And he would not come. He said that I must come to him, and bring the final equations.'

'These final equations, can you memorise them?'

Glantz laughed. 'I use the term very loosely, for a scientist. It is possible to learn them, I suppose, but it would take a long time. It takes over half an hour even to speak them.'

'I see. May I ask you a question?' Glantz nodded. 'You knew what you were working on, from the beginning?'

'Of course.'

'Why did you do it?'

Glantz looked at him with an expression of surprise. 'Why? Because I am a scientist. Why do I do anything? A scientist asks the question "why?" every day of his life. It was a problem to be solved. Scientists solve problems. That is their work.'

'But have you considered the consequences of this work? Willis has told me enough about it . . .'

Glantz returned his gaze to the television screen. His voice was cold. 'I am not concerned with consequences. My work as a scientist is to solve problems. It is not your concern, either.'

'But you were concerned that Willis should have the papers.'

'I am concerned that he should take them, without my permission, without my agreement. They are mine!' He began to tremble violently. 'He had no right! Now, he will take the rest, and the others will kill me!'

'What do you want to do?'

'I have been thinking about it. I have had a great amount of time to think in the past days, Herr Holland. I have spoken to nobody for a week: just waiters, shops, hotels, airline people.'

'Is there anyone in Geneva?'

'No. There is no-one. I live alone. I have always lived alone.'

'Your friends?'

'I have colleagues at the office. My private life concerns no-one.'

Mark wondered whether he was trying to protect anyone in Geneva. Probably not. He was a man on the run. His consolation seemed to lie in pornographic films. When Helga betrayed him all those years ago, it could have done more damage than he realised. 'Don't you have a friend of some sort? A girlfriend for example?'

Glantz spoke angrily. 'There are no women in my life! I told you. I live alone.' He became calmer. 'Willis must help me.'

'How?'

'He has taken everything. I am in danger. He must give me money.'

'Perhaps. What do you want?'

'Cash. Dollars. He owes me that.'

'Where will you go?'

'I have thought about that for some years, Herr Holland. I have considered it for a long time.' He faced Mark again. 'I did not always enjoy my life in Switzerland. There was only work. Now that is finished too, I want money.'

'But where will you take it?'

'There are countries – South America – Brazil. I speak Portuguese, did you know? For three years, I studied the language. I had made plans before.' His anger had spent, and he spoke like a man daydreaming. 'There was a time, a few years ago, when my work began to displease me. Perhaps you will call it a period of conscience. But then, I thought I had found a breakthrough to a problem, and I set aside such plans for the moment. Brazil could wait another year. There is already some money in a bank. It is not very much, not enough.'

'What will you do there?'

'I can work. I am a pharmacist, Herr Holland. I have a pharmaceutical degree. I do not wish to continue in research work. With a little money, I could establish myself in a modest fashion in Brazil, out of the mainstream, where I will not be bothered further.' His voice hardened. 'Herr Willis owes it to me. He must pay me!'

'And in return?'

He sighed. 'I will give him the equations he wants.'

'You have them with you?'

He shook his head. 'They are in a safe place.'

'I see.' Mark paused. 'How much?'

Glantz drew a deep breath. 'One hundred thousand dollars in cash. No bank transfers, no credit notes. Cash.'

Mark hesitated. It was not an enormous amount. It all depended how anxious Willis was to purchase.

'Can we telephone from here?'

Glantz thought for a moment. 'Yes. I have a number. Do you think he will agree?' His voice was almost pleading.

'I don't know.'

'But you will ask him for me?'

'Why don't you ask him yourself?'

'He told me that I must negotiate with you. He was not prepared to talk about money.'

'Then let's try and talk to him.'

'Very well, I will call you when I am connected. You must wait here, please.' Glantz went into the bedroom, and closed the door. Mark could hear him speaking to an operator, but his words were too indistinct to identify the number he was requesting. At length, he appeared in the doorway, beckoning. Willis was on the line.

'I gather you've been having a nice little chat with our friend?'

'Cut the small talk, Willis. He wants to sell.'

'How much?'

'A hundred thousand dollars, in cash.'

'I see.' There was a momentary pause. When he spoke again, Willis was brisk. 'Very well. We'll pay him in Paris.'

'Why Paris? Why not here?'

128

'I prefer Paris. Has he the papers?'

'He says they are in a safe place. I don't think they are in the apartment.'

'Then it's more likely that they'll be in Paris or nearby. He must have had them when he left Geneva. If he hasn't got them now, they must be there.'

'Or somewhere between Geneva and Paris.'

'Doubtful, but possible. Tell him to meet us at the Queen Elizabeth on Tuesday at twelve. If he's hidden them somewhere else, he has enough time to retrieve them.'

'I'll tell him.' Willis hung up.

Glantz was waiting outside the door. He had probably been listening. 'Well?'

'He agrees. One hundred thousand in cash. He'll make the trade in Paris.'

Glantz blinked. 'But I thought you could pay me here.'

'No. He won't pay here. You don't have the papers with you, anyway, do you?'

Glantz shook his head silently.

'Then you have until Tuesday midday to bring them. Do you know a hotel called the Queen Elizabeth, in Paris?'

'I do not think so.'

'It's on the Avenue Pierre Premier de Serbie, round the corner from the Hotel George Cinq, near the Champs Elysées.'

'I can find it.'

'Can you deliver the papers by Tuesday at twelve noon?'

'I can make them available to you, yes. They are safe.'

Mark went to put on his raincoat, which he had thrown over the back of a chair. 'Why did you ask for me, Herr Glantz?'

'I trust you. You saved my life.'

'That was a very long time ago.'

'Nobody else has ever done such a thing for me. You were wounded. I thought you had been killed. We were running, and I saw you fall. They fired at you, and it gave me a chance to escape.'

'It was my job to help you escape. It still doesn't explain why you asked for me.'

'Because I trust you. I explained that. And I know what you look like. Will you bring the money to Paris? I do not trust anyone else.'

'I suppose I can.'

'Then please do so.' His voice was calmer. 'I have never thanked you. I saw you in Geneva, but you did not recognise me. I was going to speak to you, but there was no opportunity. Then, when Willis started to call me, I thought perhaps that you were working for him, and I was afraid. But I have learned that you work with musicians. You are a fortunate man, Herr Holland. I also love music.'

'Willis told me.'

'Perhaps I should have called you, but it was too late. They were already after me, and I had to escape.'

'Yes. Have they tried to contact you since then?'

'Since the bomb explosion? No. I have hidden, and they have not found me. Why do you ask?'

'They must have known that you escaped with your life. They would have checked.'

'Of course, but by that time, I was gone. My greatest risk has been in meeting you. If you are being followed, they will know where to find me.'

'Then why not meet someone else? A stranger?'

'No. There is too much risk. How would I know it was someone I could trust?'

Mark felt a sudden pity. The poor bastard! Knowing how Willis operated, he could just as easily have been hired to kill Glantz, but the man had an almost childlike faith in him. He still clung to the memory of a night in Berlin, fifteen years earlier, when Mark had heaved him over a wall because he was too inept to do it alone. He paused in the foyer. Glantz was fiddling with the television set.

'I shall leave you then, Herr Glantz. Is there anything else you need at this time?'

'No. I thank you for saving my life a second time. I will fly to Paris tomorrow morning. Perhaps I will wait until the evening flight and travel overnight. I do not want to spend more time than is necessary in Europe.'

'Well, if you have the stamina, there are flights from Paris to Rio. You could leave almost immediately.'

'I do not know. I may not fly directly. I think it may be

better to take a more indirect route.'

There was nothing further to be said. Mark could see Glantz look towards the vacant television screen, like an alcoholic watching a bottle. All for the second-hand thrill of watching two actresses imitate the act of love. He stood at the front door, waiting for Glantz to open it, and they shook hands silently, like conspirators. His palm was soft and wet, but his fingers were strong, biting into the back of Mark's hand. The door closed behind him, and he could hear a bolt being drawn. He knew that, if he lingered by the door, he would hear the sounds coming from the television set again.

The snow was still falling heavily. There were few cars, and those which were moving slid cautiously along the silent street. Mark made his way to Park Avenue, hoping to find more traffic in the main thoroughfare. Snow settled on his hair and shoulders. As he stepped off the pavement, his foot sank into a puddle of icy water that had not escaped through the drainage gratings. He swore softly, but continued walking, feeling the cuff of his trouser clinging to his leg. On Park Avenue he was lucky, finding an empty cab, its light shining like a beacon through the heavy flakes, staggering northward up the hill. The driver was an elderly black.

'I'm on my way home, mister. I can take you north, if you're going that direction.'

'I'm trying to get to the Mayflower on Central Park West.'

'Sorry, mister.' He started to move again, accelerating slowly against the snowy surface.

'Wait. Could you take me some of the way? I'll make it worth your while.' The man hesitated, and Mark opened the door of the cab and sat down, if only to seek momentary shelter.

'I got to get home, but if you like, I'll take you down Fifth as far as the Plaza. It's not such a long walk across Fifty-ninth street.'

'It's a deal. Thanks!'

'You're welcome.' He drove slowly, in silence, stopping the cab opposite the Plaza Hotel. Mark handed him a ten-dollar

131

bill. 'Well, thank you sir, I'm much obliged. I'm sorry I can't take you all the way, but I'm more than two hours late already.'

Mark walked the length of Central Park South in about twenty minutes, keeping wherever possible to the sidewalks on the south side of the street, where tall buildings protected him from the snow and where ill-tempered doormen swept snow from their entrance paths every few minutes. The quietness of the normally busy street was strange. By the time he had reached the hotel, he felt almost light-headed. He was too cold and wet to worry further. All that remained was to get in as quickly as possible, and the thought of a hot bath urged him on. Under other circumstances, it was almost fun.

When he reached the hotel and its welcoming blast of tropical air, he stood under the awning for a moment, brushing his shoulders and shaking his head like a dog emerging from a swim. His face tingled from the cold. The doorman, resplendent in a clean uniform and with an umbrella at hand, eyed him coolly. The front desk had no further messages, and he made his way slowly to the elevator.

The 'Do Not Disturb' sign had not been moved, but a thin sliver of paper was lying on the floor. The door had been opened. He hesitated. It was possible that a housemaid, delivering fresh towels, had knocked and, hearing no answer, had entered. But it was unlikely. The sign, hanging from the handle, carried a clear instruction. He inserted a key in the door, and opened it quickly. It may have been his imagination, but he thought he heard an inside door close as he walked forward, turning on the light. The room was empty, apparently undisturbed. His eye sought the foot of the door to the walk-in closet. Lying clearly on the carpet was the other piece of paper.

Mark moved swiftly. He walked across the room and lifted the telephone. He placed the receiver on the bed, and spoke aloud to the room.

'Hello. Operator? This is six-oh-one A. Are there any messages for me? OK, I'll hold.'

It was unlikely that anyone planning to attack him would do so while he was apparently speaking to the hotel operator. Even as he began speaking, his hands were working quickly, removing the outer casing of the camera. Within seconds, the barrel and firing assembly had snapped quietly into place, and he had unrolled the plastic pouch. Leaving it as long as he dared, he finally spoke again.

'Yes. Who did you say? Just a minute please, while I write that down.'

The silencer was screwed into position, the trigger inserted and, almost immediately, the cartridge clip clicked into its niche. The whole operation had taken a little over a minute, even though it had felt like an eternity. Cradling the gun in his right hand, he said: 'Thank you, operator – goodnight.' He replaced the receiver rather noisily.

The door of the closet had not moved and, walking quietly, he switched on all the lights in the room. If someone was in the closet, standing in the dark, it would give Mark a second's advantage as his eyes became accustomed to the brightness of the room. He turned on the television set, with the sound quite high. Appropriately, two detectives were shooting it out with gangsters on a Hollywood set. Moving to the door of the closet, he lay full length along the floor, his body curved along the wall, so that only his head and shoulders were in the doorway. He cocked the gun in his right hand and, holding his breath, pushed the closet door wide open with his left.

A man was standing in the centre of the tiny cubicle, a gun in his right hand. It was a heavy automatic, with a long, blue steel silencer attached to the muzzle. As the door of the closet swung open, switching on the light bulb over his head, he blinked in the sudden brightness, raising the gun to fire straight ahead. From his unexpected position at floor level, Mark fired a single shot. The gun gave a muffled report, drowned by the gun shots on the television set, and the bullet hit the man square in the chest, close to the heart. The force of it threw him against the back wall of the closet, where he rested for a moment before sliding down the wall. By the time the seat of his trousers touched the floor, he was dead, a look of faint surprise on his face.

Mark rested on the floor, his eyes closed, a feeling of sickness in his throat. Then he stood slowly, looking down at the body. The man was nondescript: heavily built, wearing a cheap grey suit. Mark put him in his middle thirties. He had dark hair, receding at the temples, and brown eyes, which now stared vacantly, glazed by death. His shoes were cheap plastic, with rubber soles, badly worn at the heels. Mark reached down, fighting the gall in his throat, and searched his pockets. As he expected, there was nothing to identify the man. Apart from an imitation leather wallet containing a few dollars, a comb and a ball-point pen, his pockets were empty. Standing again, Mark walked to the bathroom. There was blood on his fingers, and he washed them under the tap, not wiping them on a towel until they were completely clean. He wet a cloth and placed it over his face, waiting for the shock of cold water to calm his trembling. When he looked up at the mirror, his face was expressionless. He dried himself carefully, and walked back into the room.

The man was now lying, tipped over to one side, at the back of the closet, his eyes still staring blindly. Mark closed the door of the closet and turned off the television set. The room was suddenly very silent.

Going to the telephone, he asked the operator for Quentin's number in London. It was four o'clock in the morning, London time, and he could hear the phone ringing steadily. When Quentin answered, his voice was alert.

'Sharpe.'

'Quentin, this is your friend in New York.'

'I recognise your voice. Good morning. I heard you met our mutual acquaintance. Is anything wrong?'

'Yes.'

'Can you talk?'

'Yes. There was company, waiting for me at the hotel.'

'Really?' He paused. 'Were you able to look after it?'

'Yes, but I need some removals – quickly.'

'I see. Who is it?'

'I don't know. Just one of those hired hands you find. Medium height, dark hair, brown eyes. It doesn't really matter a lot, does it?'

'No, I suppose not. Where are you?'

'In my room. The company was waiting in the walk-in closet.'

'I see.'

134

'I would appreciate some rather fast action on your part. They know me very well at this hotel. I stay here frequently.'

'Yes, of course. How long can you hang on?'

'Until tomorrow morning, if necessary.'

'He may have a friend who'll miss him.'

'The thought occurred to me, too.'

'What's the room number?'

'Six-oh-one A. There's a "Do Not Disturb" sign hanging on the door. That could be good until midday or later tomorrow.'

'We can look after it much sooner than that.'

'It's snowing pretty heavily outside.'

'No problem. Can you get out of the room tonight?'

'I don't know. Let me think about it for a moment.' He paused, and an idea struck him. 'Yes, I think I can. How long do you need?'

'Twenty minutes or so. You can stay if you want to. I thought you'd probably prefer to be elsewhere.'

'Yes, I would. Thanks.'

'It's up to you. Does the place need tidying up?'

'Not really. The wall at the back of the closet might need cleaning and, depending on how long it takes your people, there could be some marks on the floor of the closet as well.'

'Understood. There's no problem. It will all be looked after during the night. How are you?'

'A little shaken. I'm out of practice.'

'You seem to be managing very well. It's just not your line any more, is it?'

'No, thank God!'

'When are you leaving?'

'I was expecting to check out tomorrow morning. I'll take an early plane.'

'Good. HW thinks you should come to London *en route*.'

'Why?'

'He'd like to discuss it before we set out across the channel. See if you agree with his ideas.'

'All right. Where do you want to meet?'

'We're supposed to go to a gala at the Festival Hall. How about backstage? If you take the first plane, you should be able to do it comfortably. You might run into a few old friends.'

'If I took the Concorde, I could do it in style.'

'Not on our budget, you couldn't!'

'I suppose not. I'll be coming in from the artists' entrance. Hang on for me.'

'We'll be somewhere backstage. It's a big concert, so there will be a crowd. If you're early, check into one of the airport hotels, like the Post House. It's quicker in the morning.'

'I will, and thanks for the help.'

He placed his hand over the cradle, to discontinue the call. Returning to the bathroom, he washed again, thoroughly. His hands felt dirty, and he did not look up at his face in the mirror. In the bedroom, he dialled the operator, asking for Bianca's room.

'Are you staying at the hotel, sir?'

'Yes.'

'In that case, you can dial it direct.' She gave him the number.

Bianca sounded sleepy.

'I promised I would call you.'

'Marco, darling! I had almost given up hope.' Her drowsiness had disappeared.

'I hope it's not too late.'

'Don't be silly, darling. Why don't you come and talk to me? I'm very lonely.'

He hesitated. 'I think that would be fun.'

'So do I.' She giggled. 'Give me five minutes, so I can make myself presentable for you. I need to look special.'

'Bianca, you always look special.'

He waited ten minutes before arriving at the door of her suite. The lights in the living room were turned to their lowest. In the background, a radio was playing softly. Bianca was dressed in a pale silk peignoir, loosely held together at the waist by a cord. Her perfume was sensuous and overpoweringly strong. The peignoir was translucent, and Mark could see that she was wearing nothing beneath it. She stepped back, allowing him to enter the room, then closed her arms about his neck, kissing him on each cheek in the correct Italian style, but letting her lips brush across his face, so that they paused momentarily against his. She stepped back, surprised.

136

'But Marco, darling, you are all cold and wet!'

'Yes. I'm sorry. I got caught out in the snowstorm. I had to tramp for miles.'

'Come with me, darling.' She took him by the hand, leading him through to the bedroom. For a moment, he thought she wanted him to take a hot bath. Standing next to the bed, she turned towards him, smiling happily.

'You poor darling!' She shook her shoulders gently, and the peignoir fell to her feet. The magnificent Morini body was much more beautiful than legend had suggested. Her smile broadened. 'Why don't you get out of those wet clothes,' her hands reached out, 'and into something warm!'

He left her at seven the next morning. Bianca was still sleeping, a serene smile on her face, the cream skin of her arm encircling a pillow. Gathering his clothes, he dressed quickly in the living room, while the radio droned on, still playing sentimental canned music. As he closed the door, he remembered to hang a 'Do Not Disturb' sign outside.

His own room was undisturbed, the lights still blazing, the bed unused. Hesitating for a moment, he stood before the closet door. Then, steeling himself, pushed it open. It was empty, except for his damaged jacket and raincoat. His travelling bag sat, as before, in the corner. He knelt on the floor of the closet. The carpet was slightly damp to the touch, and there was a damp patch on the plaster of the rear wall, as though it had been cleaned recently with a wet cloth. Quentin's removal men had done an efficient job. In a busy New York hotel, nobody took any notice of a couple of men in overalls with a laundry trolley.

He showered, letting the hot water beat against him. Even as he dried himself, he could feel Bianca's perfume still clinging to his face and body. Within minutes, his clothes were packed, and he took the elevator to the lobby. At that hour, there was little activity. A few early risers were in the breakfast room, and one of the cleaners was hoovering the carpet. From the street outside, he could hear the sound of shovels removing snow from the sidewalks.

He checked out, paying by credit card and, moments later, was standing under the awning in the street. The sun was shining brilliantly, and, following the snow, the temperature had risen considerably. The doorman greeted him with a friendly salute.

'Can I get you a cab, sir? Where to?'

'Thank you. Kennedy Airport.'

'JFK coming up.'

A cruising cab screeched to a halt. The doorman held the door for him and, as he entered, Mark gave the man a five-dollar bill. He looked at it, and his face lit up.

'Thank *you*, sir. You be sure to come visit us again. Have a nice day!'

London

The plane was already circling Heathrow, preparing to land. The sun had set, leaving a faint grey trace in the overcast sky, and the lights of the city spread as far as the eye could see. Sometimes in the past, when he had arrived at night, he had tried to identify the unlighted patches – the reservoirs and parks – but it was impossible. Every city looked the same at night. The only variation was the area.

Strapped to his seat, and forbidden to smoke until he was in the terminal building, Mark wriggled uncomfortably in an effort to stretch aching muscles. When he had first begun flying, in the pre-jet era, every journey had seemed like an adventure. Despite the discomforts of those days – the constant throbbing of the engines, the bumpy ride when cloud cover exceeded the aircraft's ceiling, the long hours of the Atlantic crossing, the red-eyed stopovers for refuelling – it had seemed a more elegant way to travel. Service had been first-class standard for the humblest tourist passenger. He could remember a journey across East Africa where the pilot put his DC–3 on automatic and sat with the passengers, advising them of the best shops and hotels in the next town. In those days, the planes had landed by three o'clock in the afternoon because the hot air rising from the land made flying uncomfortable for the passengers, and the price of a ticket included an overnight stop in a hotel. Today, it was polite but impersonal, with a friendly farewell at the exit door that was as automatic and insincere as the perennial American 'You're welcome' response to a word of thanks. It was just a reflex action. Passengers were herded in and out of jets as efficiently as possible: nuisances to be fed, distracted and entertained for a requisite number of hours. On one occasion, when an important engagement made it impossible to travel any other way, he had taken the Concorde to New

York. The service and the food had been excellent and, for the first time since the pre-jet era, there was something of the old spirit, coupled with the exclusivity of a gentlemen's club, an élitist atmosphere that only a British airline could maintain. The advantage of the flight had been its brevity, for he was convinced that jet-lag stemmed not so much from change of time zone as from the constant vibration and rocking for an extended period. The greatest disappointment was the supersonic part. It felt no different. There had been a slight sense of acceleration, a pushing in the small of the back that one felt during any take-off. The Mach recorders, displaying the air speed on the bulkhead of each cabin, had dutifully mounted to 2.2, but there was no immediate sensation of change. It was all over quickly, the hostesses almost running to clear away the last vestiges of the meal before the aircraft landed again.

Mark recalled the days when New York to London included a fuel stopover at Shannon Airport. One emerged, sandy-eyed and stiff, into the soft, dewy greenness of Ireland, where a great shed housed duty-free flotsam from around the world and, next to it, a restaurant offered plates piled high with freshly cooked bacon and eggs. In the toilets, white-coated Irishmen, standing stiffly to attention like batmen in the Guards Regiment, handed over fresh razors and shaving soap to wash away the rigours of the journey, with bottles of eau-de-cologne and after-shave to refresh prickly skin. The best one could find today was an occasional hot towel or, more frequently, a metal packet containing a piece of strong-smelling wet paper. 'Oh Lord,' he thought, 'I must be getting old!'

His companion stirred in the seat beside him, a woman in her mid-thirties, wearing a tee-shirt and jeans. She worked in a New York advertising agency, and planned to combine several days of work with some holiday sight-seeing. As a seasoned traveller, she dressed comfortably, eyeing his creased pin-stripe suit with the superiority of an old hand. Mark was impressed with her knowledge of the sights she planned to see, from Dr Johnson's house in Gough Square to the Toy Museum in Scala Street. As a Londoner, he had not seen either of them. He had been less impressed with the blow-by-blow descriptions of her battles with the marketing director in her office.

140

From verbal sparring matches to acid-laden departmental memoranda, it appeared that she had triumphed in a battle royal that had lasted for about eighteen months. The vice president of her department, he learned, had finally adjudged her the winner of the contest, and one of the many rewards in such a victory included the present trip to London. Why was it that Americans always unloaded their innermost thoughts on early acquaintance? Was it really that they were open, 'out-going' and friendly, or was it a soaring egotistical self-preoccupation? Her general opinions, offered liberally on every subject from world politics to literature, were seemingly impeccable, gleaned from *Time, Newsweek, People, New York Magazine* and the Sunday supplements. Fortunately, she had treated herself generously to the free wine served in Club Class and had, when the film was shown, quietly passed out.

During the long, sleepless hours of fitful dozing Mark's thoughts had strayed between events. When he slept for a few minutes, he had seen visions of Glantz and Willis, merging together like separate photographs projected on to a single screen, the blank white reflection of their glasses providing a central point of focus. He could still sense, rather than taste, Bianca's heavy perfume, could still hear the hoarse, whispered encouragements that seemed to come from the base of her throat, as she alternately laughed and cried out with passion. It had been exciting and repellent at the same time, lacking any sense of tender intimacy: a fierce, selfish coupling, as remorselessly solitary as the performances on Glantz's television screen.

He had forgotten to call Anne-Marie before leaving New York. Perhaps it was better that he had. It would be difficult to explain the stopover in Paris. Once he had told her everything, she would understand. The haste of his departure from the hotel had made him overlook a number of details, but there had been time to call Abe from the airport. He was not surprised by Mark's sudden return to Europe. He lived in a world of last-minute changes and cancellations. Alvin's review in the *New York Times* had been good but not outstanding. The critic had enjoyed the Scarlatti and Prokofiev, but had found the Chopin 'slightly introvert, with too much emphasis on the left hand'. Abe was satisfied. There were several quotes that could be reprinted in his next brochure, and he had no wish that his protégé, with the début behind him, should want to embark immediately on a major career.

The girl at Mark's side nudged him. 'What do you do?'

For a moment, he did not understand the question; then remembered that it was considered polite to ask even the most searching questions.

He smiled. 'I manage classical musicians.'

'That must be interesting. You meet people all the time?'

'Yes, I suppose I do.'

'I'd like that.' Her voice was wistful. 'My world is all advertising. I never seem to meet anyone outside the business.'

She busied herself with a lipstick, and Mark did not reply. How strange that she should feel isolated by the ever-gregarious advertising industry! But then, he had spent all his working life, both 'careers', in an enclosed world. During the years in the Department, it was important not to mix with the 'civilians' in the outside world, where anonymity was an asset. It was probably because music had kept him sane during the last years that he had left to enter a musical career. It was the only other career for which he felt equipped, unless he had become an honest mercenary, on hire to whichever group needed a well-trained assassin. At least they had no problems of conscience with which to struggle.

But he loved musicians. Their dedication to their work, their constant, narcissistic struggle for perfection, had something in common with religious fanaticism. It was a totally absorbing life, ignorant of the outside, 'real' world. If World War Three had started, Konstantin Steigel – whom he must remember to call! – would remain unaware of it, buried in a Mahler score, or puzzling how to reduce the thickness of the low strings in a Brahms symphony. He would only know about it when circumstances created the cancellation of a concert or changed an itinerary. He was one of the fortunate innocents, insulated from the ugliness of reality in a cocoon soundproofed by the harmonies of Beethoven and Mozart. During the Second World War, he had lived quietly in Switzerland, with only inept Zurich musicians to swear at until it was over. When age finally prevented him from conducting any more, he would probably return there, to dream of Schumann symphonies or cast an ideal *Don Giovanni* from the long list of singers with whom he had worked for more than half a century. Mark knew this was an exaggerated, idealised view, but the life was enviable. Perhaps everyone lived in an enclosed community of his own making, from insurance salesmen to milkmen, but musicians always lived in the shadow of greatness, avoiding the sordid little daily dishonesties.

The flight was half an hour late, but he still had plenty of time and passed quickly through the airport, this time remembering to cash money at the bank, checking into the Post House hotel, a useful stopover point on the perimeter of Heathrow, next to the motorway. Quentin had already made a reservation. The air was mild and damp, pleasantly fresh after New York.

From his room, he called Anne-Marie. The line was bad, and her voice was distant.

'Are you leaving soon?'

'I'm already in London. I still have a couple of details to work out, but they won't take me very long. I'll be in Geneva by tomorrow evening.' He felt that he was shouting.

'I'm so glad. I know it is only a few days, but it feels as though you have been away for a very long time.'

'For me, too. How were things at the office? Did you still have the same strange feelings?'

'No. Talking to you drove them away.' She laughed. 'You're very good for me, and very patient.'

'And very much in love. Any news?'

'Not really. Oh, yes! Heidi Steigel called. Did you hear what happened?'

'No.' He felt a tenseness in his chest.

'A man died during the concert. He was sitting in her box. You must have met him.'

'Do you mean Herr Krebs, the television director?'

'Yes. It seems that he had a heart attack during the concert. Heidi said that you had already left, and when she turned to speak to him, he just fell at her feet.'

'Good Lord! Was she very upset?'

'Not very, but she said it shocked her for a moment. The

place was full of policemen and ambulancemen, appearing from nowhere, all arguing about who should take charge, and she was trying to get to the dressing room for Konstantin. You know how carefully she likes to look after him. I'm surprised you didn't know about it.'

'I left early, to meet Werner and his wife, and I've been out of touch for the past few days. Poor Heidi! I had warned her I couldn't stay until the end. It must have been a dreadful shock.'

'She was quite cheerful. He wasn't a close friend of theirs. I think when you reach her age you accept the idea of dying more calmly.' 'Perhaps,' he thought. 'How like a musician's wife, to be more concerned that her husband had a dry shirt and a towel after the performance!'

Aloud, he said: 'I'm sorry about Krebs. He looked healthy enough. He was complaining of jet-lag. Poor devil!'

'Yes, it was sad.' There was a long pause. 'Mark, when you called me before, you said that you wanted to have a long talk.'

'Yes. I still do.'

'I just wanted to tell you that you do not have to talk about the past if you do not want to.'

'But I do want to. I've been thinking about it throughout this trip, darling. There are things that I should tell you, that I want to tell you, but not on the telephone. When I'm home, and we have time.'

'Then I want you to.' She paused again. Her voice was barely audible. 'I think Myra is right.'

'Myra?'

'Yes. If we are going to start a family for her, it would be better that we are married.'

'You mean it?' His heart leapt.

'Yes, I mean it. I'm sorry it took so long to make up my mind, but it was a big decision for me.'

'I'm so happy, darling. You'll see that it won't change anything between us, except maybe to make it better.'

'I think so. I am happy too, now that I have decided.' She was momentarily distracted. 'Mark, I have to go. Madame Renaud is at the door.'

'Madame Renaud again?'

'Yes, I foolishly agreed to hear a young pianist she is developing.'

'I'll have to teach you how to side-step the Madame Renauds of the world!'

'You can teach me everything.'

'I love you.'

'And I love you. I'm sorry to have to go. I will see you tomorrow, and we will have all the time we need.'

'Yes. Goodnight.'

He arrived at the artists' entrance of the Royal Festival Hall at ten o'clock. The concert had ended a few minutes earlier, and the audience was already streaming out of the exits, past the drab, moulded concrete structures of the South Bank complex, with their strangely incomplete appearance. They always looked as though they still awaited a final plaster and a coat of paint. The heavy service lift disgorged the first of the musicians, still dressed for the stage. This was their 'rush hour', and they were hurrying home, pushing quickly past the strolling concert-goers who were still savouring the final bars of the music.

The Green Room, next to the conductor's dressing room, was crowded with the usual assortment of backstage Londoners. There were little girls in party frocks, excited to be included in the evening's entertainment, and slightly overawed by the surroundings; students in roll-neck sweaters, their hair flowing copiously, with battered miniature scores clutched tightly; elderly couples, shabbily dressed, who spoke with middle-European accents and greeted the Hungarian conductor with streams of unintelligible dialect; visiting American tourists in plaid trousers, who had heard the maestro in Cincinnati or Detroit; nervous concert-goers, earnestly holding pens and programmes at the ready for a precious autograph; hopeful musicians, friends, well-wishers, distant relatives. Slightly apart, and circling the outer edges of the room, were the professionals: managers, like Mark, dressed in quiet suits, exchanging friendly greetings and smiling while their eyes constantly surveyed the room to catch sight of any important visitors; and record company executives, present either for pleasure or for obligatory attendance, and determined to be seen to be present.

Along the corridor outside the Green Room, at the far end, the soloist held court in his dressing room, politely accepting congratulations from the circulating visitors, while the centre of the corridor was occupied by the wives of the managers, the record executives and the orchestra management, congregating together like members of a club, and wondering how long the evening's celebrations must continue before they could make a cheerful but hasty exit. Mark watched them all with affection, smiling in the direction of a familiar face, or shaking hands with an old colleague. He would like to have told them all that Anne-Marie had just said 'yes', but they would not have understood. It was the end of a long journey – did one still call it a courtship? – and it seemed to him to signal the second beginning of his new life. Within twenty-four hours, Willis, Glantz and the others would be in the past.

He found Willis and Quentin Sharpe in the soloist's dressing room. They were crushed together on a couch at the back of the room, watching as the soloist, a handsome young émigré Russian violinist with long, dark hair almost touching his shoulders, received his guests. Willis, his puffy face yellowish under the dressing room lights, waved a languid hand in Mark's direction, and rose to greet him.

'Mark, my dear boy, this is a nice surprise! Let me introduce you to our brilliant young soloist. Volodya, I don't think you've met Mark Holland from Geneva, who came all the way to hear you.' Turning to Mark, he added: 'And wasn't he just splendid?'

Ignoring Willis, Mark shook hands with the Russian and said: 'Congratulations, I enjoyed it very much.' The Russian bowed from the waist, his head almost touching Mark's outstretched hand, and said: 'Very pleased to meet' in a clipped accent which suggested that it was the extent of his English vocabulary. All the signs backstage at the Festival Hall were in English, French, German and, oddly, Russian. It occurred to Mark that this might be one of the rare occasions when it would be useful.

146

From his corner of the couch, Quentin raised his eyebrows and gazed at the ceiling. There were further introductions before they could escape, and they finally pushed their way through a new batch of guests, mainly students from the end of the line, to make an exit down the side stairs of the hall. Willis waddled in front of them towards the Charing Cross footbridge.

'Why don't we walk over to the other side? We'll never find a taxi over here, and it's a pleasant evening.'

Strolling over the bridge behind Willis and Quentin, Mark looked eastward to St Paul's Cathedral, set above the river and floodlit against the night sky. The graceful arches of Waterloo Bridge were reflected in the dark waters of the Thames, and he felt a sense of peace and security. No wonder Wordsworth was so moved!

They found a taxi on the Thames Embankment, and Willis gave the address of a small French restaurant in Charlotte Street. In the cab, Mark asked: 'How was the concert?'

Willis made a face. 'Pretty dreadful stuff! A new piece by some Pole, that horrid Berg concerto, and some very noisy Bartók. I really think concert promoters should have a little more respect for public taste. No wonder they have to find commercial sponsorship for every concert they give!'

'They have to do that even when it's a full house.'

'Well, it would certainly be fuller if they chose something a little more attractive. People don't want to pay to be educated.' He sniffed.

Mark smiled. He was feeling too contented to start a fight with Willis. 'A lot of people pay to hear Berg and Bartók.'

'I can't understand why.'

From the folding seat, Quentin laughed. 'You only went to ogle Volodya. You were asleep in the second half!'

'Well,' Willis bridled, 'at least he's worth looking at. It's an awfully long wait to hear one snippet of Bach, I must say!'

They rode in silence to the restaurant, where a waiter showed them downstairs. The room was almost deserted. Willis ordered a bottle of wine, explaining that they had eaten before the concert, and Mark declined any food. He was still digesting the day's plastic. At length, Willis put his arms on the table, leaning forward, his circular face staring in Mark's direction.

'What happened in New York?'

Mark spoke slowly, describing his meeting with Glantz in detail. As he talked, he pictured the man, sitting before his television set, waiting pitifully to escape from the nightmare that followed him. His earlier mood darkened, and he felt anger rise. The white-faced Slug who sat opposite, calmly absorbing the information, had created this nightmare without conscience or reservation. It was just another project, a further move in the deadly chess game. He shifted his gaze to Quentin, who sat further back in his chair, impassive. When he ended, Willis spoke first.

'Well now, how would you describe his mental state?'

'Terrified. What did you expect?'

Willis nodded silently. He seemed pleased. 'Do you think he'll keep his appointment with us?'

'He has no alternative. He has nowhere else to go. He can't go back to Geneva. He's even frightened of going to Paris.' Mark's voice was bitter. 'You've done your usual, efficient job, Willis. You've destroyed him. I hope you're proud of your handiwork.'

Willis blinked. 'I'm simply ensuring that he returns some valuable property to us.'

'Valuable property! When we talked in Vienna, you neglected to mention the regular phone calls, the daily threats, each one a little more frightening than its predecessor. As for his "accidental" discovery, you knew damn well what he was working on, what he'd been working on for six years. The only "accident" that occurred was the method by which he came up with some of the final answers. He would never have started the whole despicable project if he had known it was for you.'

'All that may be true, my dear Mark, but he did begin it, and now he's finished it, and it's his job to hand it over to us. You and I are just middle men in the enterprise from here on.'

'Middle men! My God, Willis, a generation ago, you would have been standing before a tribunal, looking innocent and saying "I was only obeying instructions"!'

'No, a generation ago I was working in the London office,

trying to make sure that there would never be another group of innocent-looking men claiming they were only obeying instructions. I've been doing so ever since.'

'At what cost, Willis? How many people have you trampled on, destroyed, thrown away, in this noble pursuit?'

Willis remained calm. 'As many as I considered necessary. Don't be so pious, Mark. I'm not trying to excuse my work, and I don't apologise for it. It sometimes has its unpleasant consequences, but somebody has to do it. Very well, we will meet Glantz tomorrow, give him his hundred thousand dollars, and go our several ways. You fly to Paris by the first plane tomorrow morning. There's a room booked in your name at the Queen Elizabeth.'

'And the money?'

'We'll be bringing it.'

'Glantz asked me to bring it to him.'

He waved a hand. 'It's a minor detail. We can bring it just as well as you. His chief concern is that he gets it.'

'Will you be flying with me?'

'No. We'll be using our own aircraft.'

'Why?'

Willis permitted himself an exasperated frown. 'First, because we choose to. Secondly, because we don't like the way you've been attracting so much inquisitive attention. We'll get back to that in a minute. Thirdly, because we don't normally carry attaché cases stuffed with dollar bills on commercial airlines, no matter what you see on television; and fourthly, because we don't wish our presence in France to be a matter of general interest. The French government extends us certain minor privileges, which we reciprocate, including a landing strip at Le Bourget, where a member of their Security Service looks after our needs. You are not a member of the Department any more, Mark, so it will be necessary for you to make the normal journey via Charles de Gaulle.' He took a deep breath, but smiled. 'Satisfied?'

'I suppose so.'

Willis continued. 'To return to what I was saying, we are also very interested in what has been happening to you.'

'That's very thoughtful of you!'

'I don't like the fact that they're sticking so close to you. What happened at the hotel in New York?'

Mark described his return to the Mayflower. Neither Willis nor Quentin asked where his gun had come from, or where he had eventually spent the night, and he did not offer the information. When he had finished, Quentin took over.

'Our people checked your visitor when they took him out of the hotel. They haven't come up with anything except that they are sure he's a European, or has spent a lot of time in Europe. It's related to dental treatment he has had in the recent past. They say no American dentist would use the same materials, or do the work in the same way.'

'What does that suggest?'

'Probably that they were watching for you at Heathrow, when you left. He could have taken the same flight, or followed in a later one. It wouldn't have taken them long to find you at the Mayflower, if that's where you always stay. You might have done better to stay somewhere different.'

'Probably. You seem to forget that I don't do this sort of thing for a living any more. It's a long time since I've had to act like a criminal on the run!'

Quentin ignored the remark. 'Our other concern is that you might have been followed when you went to see Glantz at his apartment. We haven't spoken to him since you were there. We have no reason to hear from him before tomorrow. On the other hand, at the time you went to see him, you didn't suspect you were being watched.'

'The snowstorm may have saved me. There was no traffic to speak of, and very few cabs. I did share mine across the town with another man, but he was continuing on, and I watched the cab leave before I went into the building. It was still snowing when I came out, and I had to walk some of the way back. The man was already waiting in my room when I got there. Unless he had an accomplice, he would have had to move extraordinarily fast.'

Quentin nodded. 'In that case, Glantz is in the clear. We won't know until he shows up in Paris. I believe he will. What is of concern to us is that they should have been watching you so closely.'

150

'In view of the calls Glantz received in Geneva, I'm not surprised. You said in Vienna that you suspected they thought I was still working for the Department, watching Glantz.'

'You're probably right. What will you do when this is finished? Go back to Geneva?'

'Of course, as soon as I can!'

'They may still come after you.'

'You're forgetting our agreement. The first part involves your making it very clear to them that you've collected everything you need from Glantz.'

Willis interrupted. 'That can take time to filter through.'

'Bullshit! Willis, don't treat me like a beginner! You know the names and you know the people. You can make a direct phone call, if you choose, and tell them the whole lousy story. It's the least you could do, for Christ's sake!'

Quentin said: 'I agree. Mark's out of it.'

Willis sighed. 'I don't like to lose points with them, but you're right. Very well, since you've been such a good, co-operative boy, it's as good as done.'

'Don't forget the second part.' Quentin's eyebrows raised, and Mark turned to Willis. 'The agreement we reached only two days ago. How the time flies when you're having fun! Sally Faulkner.'

Turning to Quentin, Willis said: 'He's right. I did promise. When Mark agreed to continue on to New York, despite his wounds, I offered to erase all references to him from the computers.'

'Where does Sally come in?'

Willis sighed, as though speaking patiently to a child. 'Mark doesn't like us very much, you may remember, and he doesn't trust us.'

Quentin smiled. 'Surprise!'

'So,' he continued, 'since he does trust Sally, who is an old friend of his . . .' He sniggered. ' . . . I guaranteed that Sally would confirm our actions. She knows how the computers work, and she'll confirm to Mark that we've done what we said we would do.'

'That's reasonable. If and when she shows up, I'll let her see. She can do it herself if she wants. It's quite easy.'

Mark sat forward. 'If and when? Is Sally away?'

'We haven't spoken to her since Friday evening. She was supposed to come in for a Sunday briefing this weekend, but she didn't show up. She probably forgot. And she wasn't in today. I'll see her when we get back from Paris.'

Mark sipped his wine. 'Does she usually take a lot of time off?'

'No more than anyone else. She probably has a cold.'

'Well.' Willis looked at his watch. 'It's getting late, and we all have an early start in the morning. If there's nothing else, I suggest we get a good night's rest.' He turned to Quentin, reproachfully. 'I may have snoozed for a minute or two during the Bartók, but the music was much too unpleasant and noisy to allow me to do anything more.'

Quentin giggled. 'Yes.'

'Mark, I assume you'll take a taxi out to your hotel? We're paying for it.'

'You certainly are, not to mention several air tickets, a new jacket and shirt, as well as daily expenses which I haven't worked out.'

'A jacket?'

'There's a nasty hole in the arm, where a bullet went through it.'

Willis was long-suffering. 'Very well.'

They parted company outside the restaurant, Willis and Quentin sharing the first taxi. A second cab was cruising in Mark's direction. He hailed it, and was about to as for the Post House. On a sudden impulse, he asked instead for Chalcot Crescent. Sally's keys were in his pocket. He wanted to see her one more time, to thank her and return the keys. Perhaps it was a sense of guilt, a need for forgiveness, so that the past could finally be laid to rest. They had been lovers, and he had shared her bed, explored her body, revealed his own naked needs. And, when the pressures from Willis and the Department had become too much for him – the deceptions and the double-crossing, the calculated destruction and extermination – he had deserted her, punishing her for the crimes she had never committed. He knew that he had walked out, callously and without warning, because he had needed to punish some-

152

one, take his revenge on a life he hated and had grown to despise. Why Sally? Because, at the time, she was the only person vulnerable enough to be wounded. Now, he had to see her once more. His thanks for the help, for the sweetness and the forgiveness she had already given, no matter what reason she searched for in her letter, were an excuse. He needed to expiate the guilt he had denied admitting for the past seven years. Sally had been treated cruelly because Willis was untouchable. He was a man who did not understand guilt or repentance. His justification was 'duty'. He had never 'obeyed instructions'; he gave them.

Mark settled back in the seat of the cab as it trundled through the late evening traffic by Warren Street tube station, past the mirrored glass building on the right, which reflected lights at strange, unpredictable angles. After tomorrow, when Glantz had collected his blood money and crept into obscurity in some Latin American back street, living out his fantasies on an electronic screen, when Willis and Quentin had closed the file on Suchim, adding it to an arsenal of dirty weapons for future use, if necessary, he would never have to see them again. His life would complete a full circle to the innocent, uncomplicated years before the Department. Anne-Marie would be there to share it, her cool beauty to ease the guilt and erase the past. She had joked about children. Was she saying it for Myra's benefit, or was it a way of telling him how she felt? It did not matter either way. Why not plan a simple, normal future, with children and mortgages and everyday domestic crises? It seemed to him that Sally's forgiveness represented a benediction on his future with Anne-Marie.

The taxi reached Chalcot Crescent, and the driver pulled back the glass screen of the cab.

'What number, guvnor?'

He could not remember – it was like a blind spot in his memory – but he recognised the house.

'This will do, thanks.'

The cab stopped, and he paid, tipping more than he should. The street was deserted, his footsteps reverberating against darkened windows as he walked to the front door. It was not very late, about eleven-thirty. As he approached he could see, through a parting in the curtains, that the living room lights were still on. He pressed the bell, and heard it ringing, but there was no response. Remembering the last time, he pressed again, holding his finger on the bell push for a long time. The house remained silent. Uneasiness overtook him and, reaching into his pocket, he took out the keys she had given him. It was the larger of the two that fitted the front door.

The inside hall was dark, vaguely lit by the street lamp filtering through the fanlight over the front door. Pushing the second key into the door of the flat, he wondered whether she might not have fallen asleep, leaving the lights on. In the past she had done that, and he had teased her about the electricity bills. He hoped she would not be startled, or angry, because of his unexpected arrival. He should have telephoned first, but he had forgotten to write down her number. Another blind spot.

The living room was empty, the lights still burning. On the turntable, a record was turning, the pick-up apparently stuck in the final groove before it automatically lifted. It made an uneven hissing sound. He called her name aloud, keeping his voice low, so that he would not frighten her, but the flat was silent. As he walked along the little corridor to the bedroom, he sensed a strange odour, which he could not identify: an acrid, unpleasant smell. The bedroom was empty and in disarray, the bed unmade, with the duvet kicked to the end. On the flowered sheet, her handbag had been emptied of its contents: purse, powder compact and lipstick, a key ring, an old comb and a crumpled Kleenex. The bag was lying on the floor, next to the bed. His heart began beating faster, and he spoke her name agan, calling louder.

He found her in the kitchen. She was seated on one of the straight-back chairs, by the little dining table. Her back was to the door, and her hands had been roughly bound together behind the chair. A piece of electric wiring cut deep into her wrists. He ran forward, calling her name. Even in death, her staring, agonised eyes revealed her suffering. Blood ran from the side of her mouth, and a darkened, swollen cheek was ridged and cracked. Her mouth was partly opened, as though she had been caught in mid-sentence, screaming with anger. The top of her pyjamas had been torn from her shoulders, and

154

lay in rags on her lap. On her neck, and her arms, and her breasts, there were dark, ugly weals where the burn marks had sunk deep below the outer surface of the skin. There were more than a dozen of them, randomly placed, like insane tattoos on her body. Another piece of plastic-coated electrical wire encircled her neck, and it had been pulled so tightly that it almost disappeared beneath a fold of skin. At that moment, he became aware of the intense, feral stench in the room. His stomach heaved, cold sweat upon his face, and he ran to the bathroom, vomiting. He did not know how long he remained there, kneeling over the lavatory like some pagan worshipper before an altar, retching and spitting spleen. At length, he sat back on his haunches, tears streaming from his eyes, howling with pain and anger. Then, mercifully, he blacked out.

He regained consciousness a few minutes later, lying on the narrow, tiled floor of the bathroom, his face against the cold, gritty surface. Very slowly, he lifted himself to his feet, pulling himself to a standing position by holding the edge of the hand-basin. He ran the cold tap into the bowl, filling it, then plunged his face into the chilled water, holding his breath for as long as he could bear. Emerging, he gulped air, then plunged downward again. He repeated this half a dozen times, water splashing on his clothes and spilling on to the floor, until the throbbing in his head had reduced to a dull pain. Still gasping, he threw a towel over his face, drying the excess water that ran down his neck. The smell had followed him into the room, and he ran quickly to the kitchen, holding his breath, and threw open a window. He returned to the corridor, closing the door behind him. He had not looked again at the figure in the chair.

He dialled Quentin's number. Each ring of the phone reflected his heartbeat. The nausea returned, and he was about to throw the receiver down, when he heard Quentin's voice.

'Quentin, for God's sake, get here quickly!' His voice was cracked and hoarse. He did not recognise it.

Quentin was alarmed. 'Mark, is that you? Where are you calling from?'

'Sally's. She's dead. Murdered. Tortured.' For a moment, he saw the anguished eyes, the mutilated body.

'Oh God!' It was a whisper.

'Please, Quentin, as quickly as you can!'

'I can be there in a few minutes. For God's sake, what happened?'

'They tied her to a chair, burned her! She's dead – they strangled her! Quentin, don't talk! Just get here!'

'Oh God! I'm leaving now. Listen, don't touch anything.'

'I haven't, except the bathroom. No, wait a minute, I opened the kitchen window. The smell . . .' He could not continue.

Quentin sounded frightened. 'Can you hang on there?'

'Yes, I think so. But for God's sake hurry, damn you!'

'I'll be there in about fifteen minutes, but I've got to call Willis first. Can you manage that long?'

'Yes. I'm all right.' The calmness was beginning to return, like a cold numbness.

'I'll be as quick as I can. Please try to hold on, and avoid moving anything, if you can.'

He sat on the edge of the bed, not moving, trying to make his mind blank. In the living room, next door, he heard the carriage clock chime twelve times. He leaned forwards, his face in his hands, his eyes screwed tightly shut, trying to erase the image that hovered before him. In the silence, his breathing was uneven and broken.

When the front door bell rang, it was as though he was awoken from a deep sleep. Movement helped, and he walked stiffly to the door. Quentin was accompanied by another man, who hovered in the shadows behind him. Mark did not speak, avoiding the other's eyes, but turned and walked into the flat. They followed him to the door of the kitchen, where he stood aside to let them pass. A few moments later, Quentin came out, white-faced, and went into the bathroom, shutting the door. The other man remained in the kitchen, and Mark returned to the living room. The bottle of brandy was still there, and he poured half a glass, drinking it in a single swallow. Quentin joined him, silently pouring a second glass, and sat in one of the armchairs. His voice was low.

156

'Willis will be here in a few minutes.'

Mark looked at him with hate. 'To admire his handiwork?'

Quentin looked up angrily. 'Oh, for Christ's sake, Mark! Don't try and blame Willis for this. He didn't involve her. You came here. You brought her into it. She didn't have anything to do with it. Don't try and salve your conscience by blaming Willis!'

'Thanks very much!'

'Well think about it, for God's sake, before you start slashing at the nearest person. Sally didn't work for us. You brought her into it.'

'You're right. I'm sorry.'

Quentin stood for a moment. 'I'm sorry too. It must have been horrible.'

The other man appeared in the doorway. He sounded apologetic. 'I called for some more help. They'll have to go over the place. I don't know what they'll find. Poor girl, she must have gone through hell. How can people behave like that?' He saw Mark's face. 'I'm sorry. It's a nasty business – very nasty! I'll wait outside for the others to get here.' He looked at the two of them, and withdrew.

Quentin said: 'I wish to God he'd get here!'

Mark nodded. 'I'm sorry I went for Willis. You're right. This time, it had nothing to do with him. I came here because I couldn't think of anywhere else to go. I lived here at one time. Did you know?'

'Yes.'

'It was before I – disappeared.'

'Yes.'

'She was very good: understanding. When I came back, last Friday, she was angry, but she let me stay. She looked after my arm, cleaned it and bandaged it. She didn't ask questions. We talked for a while.' He looked at the bookcase. 'She told me about Tony. I don't know what his last name was. He sounded like a good person. He looked after her, made her feel good.' He buried his face in his hands. 'Oh God, poor Sally!'

Quentin said nothing.

At length, the front door bell sounded again, and Quentin answered it. He re-entered the room with Willis, who said nothing, but followed him to the bedroom. Mark could hear them speaking in low voices, but he did not try to hear what they said. It reminded him of a time when, as a child, he had contracted chickenpox. Lying in the bedroom, slightly dizzy from a high temperature, he had heard his parents' voices drifting towards him but their words had been too indistinct to follow. Everyone had smiled whenever they looked in to see how he was feeling, but their eyes were nervous, uneasy. He had wondered whether he, too, should share this malaise, but the fever sapped his energy, making him sleepy. Now, strangely, he felt the same torpor.

Willis and Quentin returned and sat down, watching Mark. In the silence, he was conscious of the pick-up, still scraping on the surface of the record, and he crossed to it. Taking a hand-kerchief in his fingers, he lifted the arm gently off the record. There might be fingerprints. Quentin said: 'Leave it. They'll look after it later', but Willis raised a hand to silence him. His face was grey, and his voice little more than a whisper.

'Mark, I'm very sorry – truly.' Mark did not reply. 'We think they must have been trying to find out where you had gone.'

'She didn't know. I didn't tell her. I didn't even know myself. I didn't see her in the morning. She left before I woke, before your call. She couldn't have told them anything.' He looked at Willis. 'I would rather that she had.'

'Yes. I understand.'

'I only came here because you were both still away when I arrived in London.' He moved his hands in a gesture of help-lessness. 'There was nowhere else I could go.' He was silent again.

Willis clasped his hands over his knees. 'It's a tragic business. We thought that, once you had gone, there would be no further danger to her. We should have left someone to watch the house longer.'

Mark looked up. 'When did they . . .' He could not bring himself to use the words.

Quentin said: 'It's not possible to tell, at the moment. From a preliminary look, it could have been Saturday night. The lights had been left on, and she had been in bed. We'll know a little more when the others get here.'

158

'But why? Why Sally? And why like that? God, there are supposed to be drugs . . .' He gestured helplessly again. 'Why like that? Animals!'

Quentin continued. 'It looks like an amateur job. They obviously made use of whatever they could find lying around in the flat. They were in a hurry, and they didn't have time to get hold of something more . . . efficient.'

Willis silenced him with a stare. Turning again to Mark, he said: 'I'm sorry, Mark. This is a dreadful business. That poor child! I can promise you that we'll do everything in our power to find out who did this. They'll pay for it! In the meantime, I think we should leave. There's no reason to stay here, and there are people who will look after her.'

Mark looked up at Willis, feeling his anger returning, but stopped. Quentin had been right. It wasn't Willis's fault this time. He was looking for someone to blame. Instead, he nodded silently, returning his eyes to the floor.

'She was a fine person.' Willis spoke again. 'She didn't deserve this.'

Mark spoke quietly. 'Do any of us deserve this, Willis? This, or anything like it?'

'I don't know. I hope not. There are times when none of it makes sense any more.'

'But it goes on, and keeps going on, doesn't it?'

Willis was very calm. 'Yes. Once it starts, Mark, it goes on, with the inevitablity of a Greek tragedy. There isn't any way of picking up a phone and calling them and telling them to stop, because you've had enough. They wouldn't understand that kind of behaviour any more than we would. They'd think it was some kind of trick, and so would we. Once it begins, it must continue, and the rules become more and more vicious.' He sighed. 'In a little while, it will no longer be my responsibility, thank God.' Mark looked at him, and he gave a sad smile. 'I retire at the end of next month, Mark. I'll be sixty-five. It's a Civil Service department, just like any other. Retirement is mandatory.'

'What will you do?' He could not keep the bitterness out of his voice. 'Write your memoirs?'

Willis shook his head, ignoring the sarcasm. 'No. I have no

talent for writing, and there's very little that I would want to write about, even if it were permitted. My mother left me a little house in Dorset, not far from Bridport. I sometimes go there for the weekend. I shall move there permanently, when I finish up. It has a garden, with flowers. I like to grow flowers. I've discovered I love gardening. I suppose it seems a strange occupation for someone like me.'

'Not so strange. It allows you to go on playing God!'

Willis stood. 'I don't want to play at being God, Mark. I want to retire. I've had a long innings, and I'm tired. In a few weeks from now, someone else can have the responsibilities. I don't want them any more. I'm tired.' He walked slowly to the door. 'Quentin has offered to drive you home. I think you should go.' Lines of disappointment were deeply etched on his face. 'There's nothing more for you here, Mark, and in a little while, a lot of other people will have to come in – forensic specialists, fingerprint men, others. I'd rather you didn't have to watch them take over. It's very dispassionate work. They're not involved with – anyone concerned. It is better not to have to watch them.'

Mark stood also. 'You're right. If it's all the same with you, Quentin, I'd rather go with someone else. I don't want to have to talk.'

Quentin said: 'Yes, of course. I'll tell one of the drivers to take you.' He was about to leave, when Mark called his name.

'Thanks for moving so quickly.'

He smiled nervously and went into the hall.

At the door, Willis stopped Mark for a moment. 'We still have to go through with tomorrow, Mark. I'm sorry, but it's too late to change.'

'I realise that.'

'We have no way of getting in touch with him at this point. He has always called us, and we'll miss him if you're not there. It's his only chance of escaping.'

'I'll be all right by tomorrow.'

'Yes, I know you will, but I'm still sorry we have to ask you to do it. And I will keep my word. After tomorrow, you can forget us altogether. We will never bother you again. It's finished.'

160

Mark nodded, and followed Willis into the hall.

There was a car at the front door, and a uniformed chauffeur opened the rear door for Mark to enter. He paused for a moment to speak to Quentin, then returned to the driver's seat. As the car pulled away, Mark did not look back.

The car drove swiftly and slently through the empty streets, pausing only for an occasional traffic light. Mark stared straight ahead at the neck of the driver. He willed his mind not to think, but the image of Sally persisted. They passed on to the motorway, and the lights from the streetlamps, which had been casting sudden flashes of yellow in the cabin of the car, were now diminished. A quarter of an hour later, the driver stopped at the front door of the hotel, jumping out to open the door for Mark. Mark nodded to him, saying nothing. He collected his key from the desk and asked for a wake-up call early enough to make the first Paris flight. The long corridors of the hotel were deserted, with a faint electrical hum of machinery. Once in his room, he took off his jacket and shoes and lay, still clothed, on top of the bed, remembering.

Paris

The last of a grey, unfriendly fog was hanging close to the ground as the aircraft touched down on the runway, reversed its jets, and taxied rapidly to Charles de Gaulle Airport. Glancing through the cabin window, Mark could scarcely see the drab, unchanging landscape. The little town of Roissy, which he had once driven through when an enterprising Parisian cab driver was avoiding a traffic jam of protesting farmers on the *autoroute*, was shrouded in the damp mist. The flat farmland, stretching to the horizon, was depressing. It always reminded him, incongruously, of Victor Hugo's 'L'Expiation': '*Waterloo, Waterloo, Waterloo, morne plaine...*' It would be hard to imagine a plain more *morne* than this.

He stood on the steeply sloping moving walkway that connected the *satellite* to the central terminal, with its ultra-modern plastic conveyer tubes that were already scratched and discoloured by constant use. For the first year, Charles De Gaulle Airport had been a striking modern example of adventurous design. Now, it looked tired and cheap, as though it had been constructed with inferior materials.

If London was his real home and Geneva his present place of residence, Paris had always, until now, been his spiritual home. He shared the Englishman's romantic illusions of the city, dazzled by its elegance – the gracious rows of buildings that looked as though they had all been designed by the same architect, the spaciousness of the Place de la Concorde and the Champs Elysées, the winding alleys of St Germain or Montmartre, the majestic old palaces overlooking the Seine. It was a jewel of a city, filled with deliciously alien sounds and smells – the Englishman's ideal of 'abroad' – and his childhood and teenage years had been coloured indelibly in his memory by this excitingly different milieu, in which the women were

162

exotic, sensuous, and the men blasé, world-weary, with an age-old knowledge of human foibles.

But, as he walked around the circular outer corridor in search of the taxi rank, his mind rejected the temptations and delights of the past. They had shared Paris, he and Sally, at the beginning of their short time together. They had already been out a few times when he was in London between assignments – concerts, a dinner, a theatre – and he had suggested, half joking, that she should come to Paris with him for the weekend. He had expected her to refuse, and was mildly surprised when she agreed, so much so that he asked whether he should book separate rooms at the hotel. Sally had laughed. 'Not unless you're proposing to invite a friend.' He had been embarrassed by her matter-of-fact honesty, but she had continued: 'I know what you mean, Mark, and I'd like to. Isn't Paris supposed to be the sort of romantic place where girls go for weekends? It's certainly one up on Maidenhead or Brighton! I have to warn you in advance that I'm a confirmed tourist. I'll want to do the whole tourist itinerary. Do you mind?'

He hadn't minded. They had enjoyed every moment. Mark knew the city well, and felt like a child inviting a new friend to his house for the first time, showing off all his toys. And they had behaved like the tourists they were supposed to be, walking up the Champs Elysées and exploring the new arcades, eating lunch in the Place du Tertre and fending off the Montmartre portrait artists. He had finally persuaded her to let a young man make her silhouette on black paper, cutting the shape incredibly nimbly with a pair of tiny nail scissors. The likeness had not been very good. They had walked, hand in hand, to the steps of the Sacré Coeur, viewing all Paris in the afternoon sunshine. She had clasped his hand a little tighter. In the evening, they had found a tiny restaurant on the Ile St Louis. They had been nervous as night approached, and drank too much wine. The bedroom of the hotel had been overheated, and they made love, sweating and slipping with such anxiety that they had both started to laugh, until desire had overtaken them again. The next day was for the Left Bank, visiting Notre Dame, and exploring the tiny streets of St Germain. Sally had invented one of those foolish games where

163

everything French was related to frogs, and they had giggled at suspicious waiters and behaved like children. Later, with the windows firmly opened, they had made love slowly and tenderly, giving and accepting. In the middle of the night, he had woken her and told her he loved her, and she had smiled and said: 'You don't, really, but thank you for saying it anyway.' There had been tears in her eyes.

He had been travelling frequently at that time, commuting between London and Hamburg, and, a month or so after Paris, when he was back for a long weekend, she had suggested quite casually that he should stay in the flat whenever he was in London. He remembered that she had given the same reason that he had offered Anne-Marie: that it would save the rent.

The taxi left the Boulevard Périphérique at the Porte d'Asnières, and headed up the Avenue de la Grande Armée towards the Arc de Triomphe. In the past, the sight had always pleased him. It was the tourist's landfall, the heart of Paris. He watched it draw close through sad eyes. Why did Willis have to choose Paris, of all cities?

They had changed the lobby of the hotel and, when he saw it, he wondered if he had entered the wrong building. The front desk had been moved, so that it faced the street. But the rooms were still comfortable, with their solid, old-fashioned furnishing. Willis had reserved two connecting rooms, which was surprisingly extravagant for him, and Mark wondered whether he planned to eavesdrop when Glantz arrived at noon. He thought of phoning Anne-Marie, but decided against it. In a few hours, he would be home, and the past week would be a bad memory, to be stored with all the others. It was only a little after eleven, and he was tense and ill at ease. Putting on his raincoat again, he went downstairs.

He chose a simple route, walking briskly up the Avenue George Cinq, past the fashionable hotels, to the Champs Elysées. The sun was beginning to break through the murky clouds, and a ray of light momentarily shone on the handsome, wide boulevard. It was extraordinary how the light transformed it, giving it the cheerful, open atmosphere that he had always associated with Paris. He walked towards the great arch at the top of the hill, pausing to look at the windows of Le

Drug Store, that favourite multiple boutique that attracted trendy young Parisians and tourists day and night. This was the branch that had burned down, but they had rebuilt an exact replica of the original. Standing before it, he wondered whether people could be reconstructed the same way.

He entered, and a blast of pop music bombarded him. It was the French variation on American rock and, although the rhythms and the howling guitars duplicated the original, they somehow managed to retain their Gallic identity. He had grown up on Charles Trenet and, later, Jacques Brel, but the popular *chansons*, with their romantic visions of love and Paris in the spring, had been elbowed out by the pervasive teenage music. And yet, the French remained obstinately French, changing with the times, but never losing their individuality. There might be a sacrilegious Macdonalds on the Champs Elysées, but they would resist further Americanisation with an obstinacy that the Germans and the British lacked. Many years earlier, at the height of the hippie movement, he had watched two young Frenchmen, long-haired, bearded, barefoot and in rags. They looked like their counterparts in every other country but, being French, they shook hands on meeting with the solemnity of their conservative parents. Willis had summed it up best when he had sent Mark to a Paris meeting with the Deuxième Bureau: 'You'll find the French among the most co-operative people in the world. You simply have to do things their way.' The music in Le Drug Store was deafening, the overpriced electronic goods and novelty lighters were the same as those he had seen in every airport duty-free shop, and he left after a few minutes. He walked as far as the Avenue Marceau, continuing in a circuit back to the hotel. At the front desk, he advised the concierge that a Monsieur Glantz would be asking for him and that he would be in his room.

The minutes ticked slowly away. Time always passed slowly in a hotel. A little after twelve, the telephone rang, startling him although he had been waiting for it. It was Glantz, and he was on his way up.

The man looked better than he had expected. He had bought a new, military-style raincoat, which he left open, and was wearing a light sports jacket and slacks. He had shaved carefully and, although his skin retained its grey pallor, he looked more self-assured and alert. When Mark opened the door, he entered quickly, walking with a confident step. He ignored any formalities, standing in the centre of the room.

'You have brought the money, Herr Holland?'

'No.'

Glantz was surprised. 'But why? We arranged that you would pay me. What has gone wrong? Have they changed their minds? They do not want to pay me?'

'No. Willis insists on paying you himself.' He smiled apologetically. 'I don't think he wanted me to carry that much money around. He said he would bring it personally.'

Glantz began pacing nervously. 'But this is impossible! I trusted you. You said that you would bring the money . . .'

'I said I thought I could, but when I saw Willis in London yesterday evening, he didn't agree. Is it so important? They've agreed to pay what you ask, in cash. Why should you care who actually gives it to you?'

'You don't understand! You and I, we trust each other, Herr Holland. I can explain a situation to you, and you will understand me. I am a man of honour, and I am telling this to you as the man who saved my life. You trust me. You must trust me, as I trust you. I would not lie to a man who saved my life. They do not know me, and I do not trust them. They may not believe what I say.'

'But I assure you there's no problem. If you have something you want to say, we'd better talk about it quickly. They should be here any time now. Willis said they expected to be here by twelve.'

Glantz looked startled. 'They're coming now? That is impossible! I cannot see them.' He made for the door, but Mark took his arm, gently restraining him. At his touch, Glantz hesitated. He spoke quietly and urgently.

'I have an envelope with me, which I will hand to you—but only to you. Do you understand? And I will explain about the contents . . .'

'I don't want to know. I'd prefer not to. I'm simply here to complete the exchange.'

'But you don't understand me! I have to explain. The equa-

166

tions are quite safe. You do not have to worry about them.' He reached in his pocket, taking out a large brown manilla envelope, sealed with adhesive tape. From its bulk, Mark estimated that it contained a dozen sheets of paper, carefully folded. 'This envelope is for you to . . .'

At that moment the connecting door to the next room opened, and Willis, closely followed by Quentin, came into the room. Quentin was carrying a small, black attaché case, made of imitation leather, with aluminium edging. Looking beyond them, Mark could see two other men whom he did not recognise. Quentin closed the door, leaving them in the other room. At his side, Glantz quickly replaced the envelope in his pocket.

Willis blinked and smiled. 'Well, Mr Glantz. At last! It has taken a long time for us to find a way to meet. My name is Willis, and this is my young colleague, Mr Sharpe.' He did not offer to shake hands. Glantz remained silent, watching them. Mark had the impression of a small animal, hypnotised by a snake. When Glantz said nothing, Willis continued, his voice relaxed.

'You know, you've really put us to an enormous amount of trouble, Mr Glantz, particularly my friend Holland. He's been following you halfway round the globe and back!'

Glantz backed away to the window. His voice was a whisper. 'This is not part of our agreement. I arranged that Herr Holland would bring me the money.'

Willis smiled. 'My dear Mr Glantz, Mark wasn't authorised to make any such agreement.' He bowed his head slightly, peering over the tops of his glasses like a good-natured schoolmaster. 'When you asked for Mr Holland to act as intermediary in this exchange, I explained at the time that he was no longer working for my department. Nevertheless, with his kind co-operation, we were able to make him available. On the other hand . . .' He glanced at the attaché case. '. . . One hundred thousand dollars is a considerable sum of money to place in the keeping of an – outsider. It was hardly reasonable to ask him to take that sort of responsibility, was it? I'm sure you can understand our unwillingness, under the circumstances.'

Glantz's face was stubborn. 'That was my agreement. Herr

Holland was to bring me the money.'

Willis smiled patronisingly. 'Oh well, there's no real harm done, is there? The money's all here. You have the documents?'

'Yes. They are safe.'

'Excellent! Well now, why don't we make the exchange, and finish with this whole tiresome business?' He nodded to Mark with a smile. 'Would you like to do the honours?'

Feeling self-conscious, Mark walked over to Glantz, holding out his hand. The man hesitated for a moment, then reached again into his pocket and withdrew the manilla envelope. As he handed it to Mark, he spoke.

'This is a matter of trust. There are still things to be explained. I am prepared to wait . . .'

Willis interrupted. 'While we verify the information? Oh, I don't think that will be necessary, Mr Glantz. I have already seen some of the material, and there has to be a certain point of trust between honourable people, don't you think?' He nodded to Quentin, who snapped open the lid of the attaché case. Inside, there were stacks of hundred-dollar bills, carefully packed in tight rows.

For a moment, Glantz was distracted by the sight of the money, which Quentin displayed like a pedlar in an Eastern bazaar. He released the envelope into Mark's hand and stood, his arms hanging limply, as Mark walked back to Willis. When he spoke again, his voice was tense.

'You must explain to them, Herr Holland. We did not have a chance to speak properly before they arrived.'

It was an unexpected comment, but Mark smiled reassuringly. 'I'm sure Mr Willis will let us discuss it further, if you wish.'

Willis produced a small silver pencil, with which he slit the edge of the envelope. The three men watched in silence as he unfolded the sheets of paper, concentrating his attention on them. After a moment, a beatific smile spread across the little man's face.

'At last, the infamous Project L-Fourteen!' He read the first two pages carefully, then peered over the tops of his glasses at Glantz. 'I am sure you must be relieved to be parted with this,

Herr Glantz, especially for such a handsome fee.' He shook his head slowly. 'What a dreadful responsibility!' He smiled again, giving a barely discernible nod in the direction of Quentin.

Glantz became agitated again. 'But I must explain about the equations and the music. You see, I . . .'

There was a sudden, crisp report, not very loud, and a scarlet hole, an inch wide, appeared in Glantz's throat. His hands reached up to clasp at it, his eyes bulging. There was a second report, and a second bullet thudded into his chest, causing him to stagger backwards, falling across a chair. Mark watched in astonishment as he fell, seemingly in slow motion, bouncing off the chair and rolling on the floor. Glantz was dead. Looking round, Mark saw Quentin, the gun in his hand, watching the body. His face was impassive.

For a moment, he thought he had gone mad. Words formed, racing through his brain, but he could not force them through his mouth. He gave a howl of animal rage, his eyes closed, his fists clenched, as white anger seared him. He turned upon Willis, who had retreated to the door, and, still unable to speak, advanced towards him, hands outstretched, ready to tear him to pieces. Dropping the papers, Willis cowered, covering his face with his hands. With unexpected speed, Quentin leapt between them, arm outstretched, the silencer of the pistol touching Mark's forehead. He felt the metal against his skin and halted, waiting for the finger to move, curling against the trigger, and oblivion. Quentin gave a harsh command, and Mark backed away, watching the muzzle of the gun. He shouted: 'What the hell are you waiting for, you bastard? Go ahead! Shoot, and get it over with!', but Quentin did not move, pointing the gun with a steady hand. Behind him, Willis was recovering, adjusting his glasses and pulling at his jacket. The room was silent. Then Quentin stretched out his left hand, the gun still pointing. 'The papers, Mark. Put them together and pass them to me. Gently!' His voice was controlled.

Stooping, Mark shuffled the scattered papers together. For a moment, he considered trying to take Quentin, but the young man stepped back a pace and said: 'Gently! Don't try anything now, Mark. It's not worth it.' He gestured to a writing table at his side, moving out of reach. The gun in his hand never wavered.

Mark placed the papers on the table, and the tension left his body. He slumped into an armchair, conscious of the following movement of Quentin's gun. His voice was tired. 'Take them and finish the job.' He sat with his head bowed, ready to die. In the street outside, he could hear the sound of traffic. An irritated driver was sounding his horn repeatedly.

Willis was the first to speak. His voice was shaky, but he regained confidence with each word. 'We have no further quarrel with you, Mark, whatever you may think. We don't wish you any harm. You're not going to die.'

Mark looked up. Willis and Quentin were standing side by side, watching him cautiously. Quentin's right arm had fallen to his side, the gun still in his hand.

Willis said: 'It's all over, Mark. The job is done.'

When Mark spoke, his voice was low. 'You filthy, lying, double-crossing, dishonest bastards! Murderers!'

Willis shook his head sadly. 'We couldn't let him live, Mark. We couldn't afford to.'

'Animals!'

Willis continued as though Mark had not spoken. 'We really could not afford to let him live; not with the knowledge he possessed, Mark. Not with a power like that.'

'In God's name, why not?'

Willis did not reply to Mark's question. Nodding to Quentin he waited while the younger man opened the connecting door to the next room. The two other men entered and, moving quickly, they lifted Glantz between them, and carried him into the adjoining room. It all happened in silence, like a scene from an Elizabethan tragedy. Quentin waited, revolver in hand, until they had departed, then closed the door again, leaning against it.

Willis looked at Mark. 'He hated us, Mark, hated us for what we had done to him. Not just these past few days, but for the past fifteen years, for deceiving him into believing he was a free man and, before that, from the day he learned that his Helga had been working for us from the start.'

170

'But he was going, disappearing. All he wanted was to escape. He told me in New York. He planned to go to South America.'

Willis sat in a chair by a writing table. 'I know, Mark, but for how long? Until the money ran out? Or until he realised he could take his revenge? He's a scientist, Mark, a brilliant man. It wouldn't take him long to realise that he could take that information,' he glanced at the envelope, 'and pass it on to the other side.'

'But it represented years of research.'

'Only in the discovery. Once you've found the way, it doesn't take so long to retrace your steps. And with the right facilities at your disposal, you can cover fifteen years in a matter of months. Even if it took longer, why should he care? It would give him something to live for. You seem to have forgotten the people who have been following you, Mark. You were leading them closer and closer to him. We couldn't afford to let them catch up.'

'What makes you so sure that he was the only one? There were others working on the same project.'

'No. We never let him keep anyone for very long in the laboratory. You seem to forget that we were monitoring his progress from the beginning. It was basically a one-man operation anyway. That's why we removed all his research papers. The day he skipped the country, we removed the computer tapes as well. There's nothing left at Suchim.'

'And no doubt anyone involved has since mysteriously disappeared!'

Willis permitted himself a slight smile. 'You've been reading too many spy stories, Mark. The lab assistants involved didn't have enough information to put the pieces together.'

'Except one.'

'The phone calls? Yes, but he obviously didn't know enough. Otherwise, they wouldn't have started calling.'

Mark closed his eyes. 'You could have let him go. He didn't want any more of this. He just wanted to get out – disappear forever.'

'Perhaps, perhaps not. Think about it, Mark. In view of what he knew, what he had discovered, how could we take that chance? Forever is a long time. You spoke to him in New York. You saw what he was like.'

'He was terrified, frightened of his own shadow.'

'He was terrified, yes, because he was afraid for his safety. But he was an arrogant man too, Mark, a man who was proud of his work. Even when we first took his files, he went on working. He was angry because we took the papers away, because he thought they belonged to him. He wasn't concerned with the morality of the work, or the appalling consequences . . .'

'Nor were you.'

'Nor were we. You're right. But he was more angry than frightened at the time, because we were taking away his toys.'

Mark sat forward. 'Don't try to justify your actions, Willis. He went on working because you were blackmailing him, threatening to have him kicked out of the country, threatening to hand him back to the East Germans. You never would have, but he didn't know that.'

'That's not true, Mark. Think about it! He's a highly intelligent man. He could have stalled for years, pretending to search for the answers.' Willis spoke slowly. 'Mark, he didn't have to complete the project. He could have told us there was no such thing as a "final equation". We could never have disputed it. He went on working because he wanted to.'

'For God's sake, the man was a scientist! He didn't function that way. How can you assume that everybody is as devious and as dishonest as you are? I asked him the same question as you, Willis, but for a different reason. I said: "Why did you do it?", and he replied: "Because I am a scientist", and went on with some high-sounding talk about asking himself the question "Why?" every day. He had to go on, Willis. It was his work. He had given six years of his life to it.'

'All the more reason not to let him go, once he left our – protective custody.' Willis stood up. 'Mark, you've just given him the same death sentence, even if your reasons were different. I, we, the Department, by our very existence, gave him an incentive to go to work again, as long as it was against us.'

'But it wasn't like that! He talked about moving to Brazil. He'd taught himself Portuguese. He told me about it; said he was a qualified pharmacist.'

Willis walked to the window, looking out. 'You're wrong. He might have started that way, but he wouldn't have continued. He couldn't. He had too good a brain. And the people who were trailing him were catching up with him. If it hadn't been for the bomb, they might have reached him before we did.'

Mark sat very straight. 'If it hadn't been for... Oh, my God! You set off that bloody bomb! It was never intended to kill him! You were driving him out, waiting to catch the pieces!'

Neither Willis nor Quentin spoke, and Mark realised he had stumbled on the truth. He sat back. 'What a fool I've been! I should have guessed. It made no sense to kill him, until someone had the information. And the timing was just too convenient, close enough for him to see the explosion, but not close enough to hurt him! If anyone had wanted to kill him, knowing where he lived, they would have made sure.'

Quentin said: 'We wondered why it took you so long to come to that conclusion. We couldn't believe you'd accept their being that clumsy. Under any other circumstances, we might have told you in Vienna, but you were raising your own hornet's nest. For some reason, our friends were on to you, almost from the word go. They must have been watching you as well as Glantz. When he ran, it must have caught them unawares, so they stayed on top of you, hoping you'd lead them to him.'

'Then why try to kill me?'

'We still don't know. That's the part that doesn't make sense. Maybe they thought that by getting rid of you, they could flush him out. But it still doesn't make that much sense. When you first told us about the attack at the Musikverein, we thought they must have already found him, and simply wanted you out of the way.'

'No wonder you were so bloody shocked!'

Willis said: 'We had to wait and see if he would show up in London. We weren't sure that he would succeed. Then, when you came in on the Salzburg flight...'

'I didn't come in from Salzburg.'

'Didn't you? There was a direct flight on British Airways

that day.'

'I didn't take it. Didn't Sally tell you? I flew in from Zurich. I changed planes there.' Mark did not tell them his reasons. There was no need to tell them how he had smuggled the gun into London and New York.

'Oh well, no matter. When they picked you up again in London, it gave us a ray of hope. If they had already taken Glantz, there would have been no reason to go on following you.'

Mark looked at Willis with hate. 'My God, you were using me both ways at once, weren't you? If the others were following me, it meant that Glantz was still on the loose, and you needed me for Glantz because I was the only man that poor, hunted bastard could start to trust. What do you call those animals they use in abattoirs? A Judas goat – the one who runs in front, leading the others to their own slaughter. I was your Judas goat!'

He walked over to the attaché case that Quentin had left by the door, and opened it. Beneath each hundred-dollar bill there was a neatly stacked pile of white paper, cut to size. Mark looked at the two men. 'You would have agreed to any sum he asked for, wouldn't you? There was never any question of payment. And my contribution – my "service to my country" – was to set him up!'

Willis spoke quietly. 'We needed you, Mark. If we had told you why, would you have done it?'

'And that's your justification: you needed me! You're despicable! You cheat and blackmail, lie and murder, you deceive and destroy, and you do it calmly and coldly, without remorse or conscience, without a single grain of human compassion! How do you sleep at night, Willis, with that sort of blood on your hands? You destroyed Glantz from the moment you heard of him; destroyed the woman he loved, destroyed the pitiful illusion of freedom that you permitted him to have, destroyed any faith or hope or fantasy, and when you had finished with him and used his brains to create God knows what horror, you destroyed his body too – threw it away! What sort of people are you? And don't tell me you did it for Queen and Country or for the forces of good against evil. You wouldn't

174

know good from evil if they were staring you in the face. And you made me a party to your filth. Well, I've done my dirty job and, if I'm going to live, I want my thirty pieces of silver. You can keep your part of the agreement.' He pointed. 'There's a phone next door. Go and call your friend. Tell him to take his dogs off me, because there's no more Glantz to lead them to. You've destroyed him, once and for all.'

Willis said: 'Mark, you have to understand...', but Mark shouted: 'Just go! Do it! Finish the whole bloody business! I've delivered your bloody sacrificial lamb. Keep your part of the bargain, or shoot me. There's enough blood on your hands, so one more body shouldn't make you squeamish. Go!'

Willis turned, silently, and walked through to the adjoining room, closing the door behind him. In the ensuing silence, Mark could hear him speaking on the telephone. Quentin started to say something, but saw Mark's expression, and instead turned his attention to the papers on the table. He seemed engrossed in his reading, but Mark noted that he had left the gun close at hand. After ten minutes, Willis returned. His face was sombre.

'I've passed the message through, Mark. I told you I would keep my word. You have nothing further to fear.' He walked to Mark's chair, looking down at him. 'I suppose there's no point in my saying anything more?'

'No. You've said and done enough.'

'Very well.' He looked over to Quentin, but the young man concentrated his attention on the document he was reading. Mark noticed that Willis's hands were trembling slightly.

Willis spoke sadly. 'I'm sorry, Mark. We would have preferred never to have involved you in any of this. Glantz insisted on you, and that gave us no choice in the matter. As to the business last night, I know that you will always hold us responsible, but Sally Faulkner's death had no part in this affair. It was a tragic mistake.'

'It happened because of who you are, and what you are, and the kind of distorted world you live in. Don't tell me about...'

Quentin's voice cut across. 'Willis!'

They looked at him. His face was pale, and the papers in his hand were slipping from his grasp. They fell, lazily swooping, to the ground.

'There's nothing here! He's given us the first part of the project – the part we already have!'

Willis turned ashen. 'What are you talking about?'

Quentin's voice rose in pitch. 'I'm trying to tell you. This is the first part! It finishes at the same place! He's written on the last page: "Further documentation and calculations follow." He hasn't given us the rest of the project!'

For a moment, nobody spoke. Then Willis turned to Mark.

'What did Glantz say before we arrived?'

'Nothing. He was very upset when he heard you were coming. He'd only expected to see me.'

'But what did he say?' Willis was shouting.

'Very little. You both broke in within moments of his arrival. Let me think!' Mark closed his eyes. 'He asked if I had the money, and I said no. That upset him. He said he thought the arrangement was that I alone would negotiate the exchange. I said you wouldn't agree, and asked why it should be so important. Then he said that, because we trusted each other, he could explain the situation to me and that I would understand, even if you didn't believe him. I didn't know what he meant by that. Then he showed me the envelope, and said he wanted to hand it to me only.'

'That is what he did.'

'I know. Let me think a bit more. He started to tell me something, saying that he wanted to explain what was in the envelope. I thought he was going to boast about his bloody equations, and told him I didn't want to know, but he was still very agitated. He said the equations were "safe", but he didn't explain what that was supposed to mean. That was the point where you came in.'

Quentin said: 'Oh my God!'

'Wait!' It was Willis. Let's try to remember what happened after that. We argued about the money and who should have brought it. He said he was prepared to wait for something. I thought he was talking about verifying the material. Can you remember anything else?'

'No. He handed me the envelope, and said something about

still wanting to talk to me. You read the top pages, and he started to make some sort of comment about music. But at that moment . . .' Mark turned to look at Quentin, who was now sitting, white-faced.

Quentin looked from Mark to Willis. 'It's not my fault, for God's sake! I did what you told me to do!'

Willis nodded silently. He walked across the room without speaking, and stood with his back to the two men. At length, he turned to face them. 'I think it's reasonably clear what he was trying to say, but we weren't listening. He didn't have the equations on him. If you remember, he said they were "safe", which can only mean that he had hidden them somewhere else. They weren't in the laboratory, and we're almost certain he didn't have them at home. We checked both places very thoroughly. That's why we always assumed he kept them with him when he drove out of Geneva. But why an envelope with the papers we already have?'

Mark said: 'He was trying to tell me something before you walked in, but I wouldn't let him. It might have been where the other papers are. This envelope could have been for the benefit of any third party who watched the transaction. He only expected to meet me, and kept saying we trusted each other because of the past. He said he wouldn't lie to me because I had saved his life.' He looked at Quentin. 'He was starting to say something when you shot him.'

Quentin buried his face in his hands. 'It wasn't my fault! I did what you told me to do.'

Mark looked at Willis. 'He was only obeying instructions.' He started to laugh. The convulsions welled up inside him uncontrollably, and he laughed louder, hysterically, until tears began to run down his cheeks. Willis and Quentin stared at him. The laughter was painful, making him gasp for breath, his body bent double. At length, he gained control of himself, moving back to sit on a chair, and Willis and Quentin continued to watch as he sat, half laughing, half crying, rocking back and forth. Slowly the spasms ceased, and he settled back, his stomach muscles complaining.

'Well,' Willis said. 'That would appear to be that.'

'What are you going to do?'

'There's not a great deal we can do, for the moment. We'll pass what information we have to our top research men, and see whether they can come up with any answers for us. I don't hold much hope that they will. And, as far as Glantz is concerned, we'll check and recheck every place we know he visited in the past month. We'll watch the post, of course. There's a faint chance that he posted the material to himself, but it's probably sitting in some poste restante and will never be collected. There's an outside chance that he sent it to you, Mark, which means, I'm afraid, that we'll have to stay in touch just a little while longer. All we can do is follow the well-tried operational methods. There's nothing else we can do.'

'And if someone else finds them?'

'The chances are that they'll mean nothing at all – a few sheets of paper with mathematical or chemical formulae scribbled all over them. And even then, they are only the last part of a series of complicated calculations. I've seen the first part, not that they meant anything to me. Even a first-class scientist would have difficulty deciphering them without all the keys. You can't understand one without the other.'

Mark stood up. 'So you've lost. You've lost the whole bloody thing! You've blown it – sunk, scuttled, finished! I'm glad, Willis. I'm not even elated, or avenged, or triumphant. I'm just glad. They can all rest – Sally, Glantz, Krebs, the others. The whole stupid, ugly operation comes to nothing! Six years, fifteen years, a lifetime of work, wasted! And all I feel at this moment is relief. You don't get your bloody virus, and maybe a couple of unborn children somewhere are going to survive into a cleaner world. You can check my post for the next few days, Willis. I no longer care. Don't expect me to help you. I'm finished with the whole thing, thank God!'

Willis nodded. He smiled weakly. 'I rather believe you're right, my dear.' He sighed. 'Perhaps it's as well.'

'Perhaps? You wanted to add God knows what to an unspeakable arsenal of poisonous weapons. You fuck up the whole job, leave a trail of dead bodies like a slug leaving a trail of slime, and all you can say is that perhaps it's as well?'

'No.' Willis shook his head sadly. 'I was going to say perhaps it's as well that I'm retiring. I'm too careless. I don't belong in this department any more. I'm no use to it.'

'You never were, Willis. You took the rules and twisted them to suit your sick mind.'

He raised a hand. 'I know. I've heard it all before, Mark. You're repeating your old speech. I know all the words before you say them.' He looked around the room. 'There's nothing left for us to do here. We'd better go back to London.'

Quentin was at his side, still petulant. 'It wasn't my fault! I did exactly as you said. I waited for your signal, damn it!'

'I know, I know.' He spoke placatingly, like a father to a small boy. 'It looks as though Joachim had the last laugh, after all.'

Mark was puzzled. 'Joachim?'

'Joachim Weiner. That was his real name, before he left East Germany. Didn't we tell you? I suppose not. It's not very important. We changed his name for him when he came out. Eberhard was his father's name. He chose that. I don't remember his middle name. It was something very ordinary, like Albert.' Mark was silent. 'It seems a very small thing, I know, but a man ought to be allowed to die with his own name.' He laughed. 'I must be more sentimental than I thought!'

He walked slowly across the room, haltingly, like an old man. 'Maybe you're right, Mark. Perhaps the whole operation was pointless after all. But he was a brilliant man, in his own field. He wouldn't come over to us, but I can console myself that he wasn't working for them.'

Mark called from his chair. 'There's one more thing.' Willis stopped, without turning. 'The computers. My files. That was the other half of our agreement.'

Willis nodded, and Quentin said: 'I hadn't forgotten. I'll look after it tomorrow.' His voice was expressionless.

'All references to me, including Anne-Marie?'

'Yes. All references. I'll do it in the morning. You can call me whenever you want. It only takes a few minutes.' He bowed his head. 'I'm sorry you won't be able to verify them.'

Willis looked back. His face had regained some of his old spirit. 'Well, you'll just have to take our word for it, won't you?'

Mark stared him down. 'I'll call anyway.'

When they had gone, Mark walked to the window and stared out into the sunlight. It was hard to believe that it was really over and that, in an hour or two, he would be back in Geneva. He had only been away for a week. Just like any business trip for a busy artists' manager. No doubt, Frau Emmi would want the details of his expenses for the accountant. And Anne-Marie would be there, waiting for him, and he would start, yet again, to pick up the pieces of his life.

Geneva

Throughout the one-hour flight from Paris, he tried to fight against the memories. He had not telephoned Anne-Marie. It would be more fun to surprise her. Besides, he had been in no mood to call her from the hotel, and he prayed that seeing her again, making new plans for the future with her, would help to erase some of the past. He reached over with his left hand to rub his arm. The plaster needed changing, and his skin felt sore. If there was time, he would stop at his doctor's office on the way home. The cool, efficient physician from Zurich, who seldom spoke when he made an examination, would make no comment on the cause of the wound.

There was so much to tell Anne-Marie, so much of his past to explain away, that he had no idea how or where he would begin. He tried to rehearse speeches, but they sounded as false and premeditated as the lies he had told for the past seven days. There was no way of fabricating. It was a simple matter of starting from the beginning, and going on from there. Simple? In the old days, he had always been able to bury the past, forget the incidents, pretend they had never happened. But now, to force his memory back over the years, to relive the violence and the deaths, the everyday deceits of so many years, was a harder task than he had anticipated. Perhaps he should avoid telling her all of it, and explain only that he had worked for the Department under the cover of a government arts body, using the Official Secrets Act as a blanket under which to hide. It would certainly sound more glamorous. But would it satisfy her and, even more, was it what he really wanted? He was not looking for glamour. The last time they had spoken on the telephone, she had freed him of any responsibility, and told him that he did not have to say anything. That was not what he wanted. He realised that he had been searching for this personal moment of truth – and how false even a phrase like that sounded! – for someone who could understand what he had lived with for so many years. It was a confession that he needed to share. The truth was for himself.

How much, for example, could he explain of the past week? And would she be able to understand his motives, from the peace and security of Geneva? He had never talked about Sally Faulkner, never mentioned her name. Anne-Marie obviously realised that there had been women in his life before, but he was not sure whether she would understand why he went to the flat in Chalcot Crescent as soon as he returned to London. Hadn't Sally said that he would have managed somehow? All those lies: Werner the television director, Bianca's imaginary film career, the lunch with the non-existent sheikh at the Connaught. The only truth he had told her had been the names of the cities he was in, and the meeting with Abe and Myra. And, above all, that he loved her. He wondered whether he could ever explain how their telephone calls, however brief they had been, however false the stories, had been his one link with sanity over seven insane days.

The plane had left the mountains and was circling over the flat plain on the edge of Lac Léman. The late afternoon sunlight slanted over Geneva in the distance. Below, the neat squares of land, carefully tilled and tended, were coloured with the first greens of the spring crop. By the look of it, Geneva had enjoyed a beautiful day.

He had told her that Glantz was a German violinist, and had almost tripped over his own lies, saying that they had met before and then contradicting himself. It was a long way from Glantz the violinist to Weiner the scientist. Weiner the mad scientist, with an 'accidental' discovery that could destroy mankind! Glantz the violinist made more sense, yet he was asking her to believe him on trust, and accept that there really was a world that she had been brought up to believe existed only in the cinema. Their world, cloistered as it was, consisted of conductors and pianists and violinists and singers, with their everyday needs and minor temper tantrums. Violinists did not die under assumed names, dragged out of a hotel bedroom by silent henchmen, ignominiously to be disposed in some unmarked grave. They sought their epitaphs in musical dictionaries and record catalogues. 'Here lies Eberhard Glantz, born Joachim Weiner – the Unknown Violinist'! Joachim Albert Weiner, if Willis's vague memory had served him correctly. He was not even sure of that. The plane touched down, and Mark watched the dark green grass of the airport come into focus as the aircraft braked. Joachim Albert Weiner. But surely, if he was a German, it would be Joachim *Albrecht* Weiner. He started violently, leaning forward so suddenly that the man in the next seat put out a hand to restrain him, muttering something about adjusting his seat-belt. Mark thanked him with a nod. The names: Joachim Albrecht. He had heard them recently, he was certain, but in a different context.

The plane stopped, and the man next to him stood up, waiting impatiently for him to move into the aisle. Mark remained in his seat, frowning, concentrating on those two names. He tried to picture them in print, but that offered no clue. Then he spoke them to himself, but the sound seemed wrong in his mind. The man at his side continued to fidget, finally saying: 'Ah, monsieur! Are you not going to move? The seat-belt sign has been turned off!' Mark stood up, apologising, and collected his raincoat from the overhead rack. Walking down the aisle of the plane, he puzzled again over the names, then shook his head impatiently. It would come back to him. It was better not to concentrate his attention on them so carefully. The stewardess at the door smiled mechanically, and said 'Goodbye, monsieur.' She had a pronounced French accent, a little like Anne-Marie's. Mark stopped dead still as he passed her, so that his travelling companion, following closely behind him, had to stop suddenly to avoid walking into him. He made a further sound of Gallic exasperation, but Mark was now running forward down the steps to the terminal. He had remembered where he had heard the names before.

Outside, he found a taxi and gave the driver the address of his office on the Rue des Marbriers. The driver asked: 'Shall I go by the express road and along the lake shore? It's slightly farther, but it's quicker at this time of day.'

'Whichever is the fastest. I'm in a tremendous hurry.'

The driver nodded and accelerated.

'You'll be better off with my route. The rush-hour traffic's just beginning to start.'

As Mark entered the office, he found Frau Emmi standing at her desk, putting the cover on her typewriter for the evening. She looked, as always, slightly flustered.

'Good evening, Monsieur Holland. I did not expect to see you here today. Did you have a good trip?' She hesitated. 'Mademoiselle Anne-Marie is not here this afternoon. She has already left, to go to the hairdresser's, and she said she would be going to the dress shop. I was planning to leave a little early myself.' Frau Emmi blushed as she added: 'I think she said that this was going to be a very special evening.'

Mark scarcely heard her as he walked past, but he smiled and said: 'Good evening, Frau Emmi. Why don't you go ahead and leave? I just wanted to go through a few papers that I left in the office last week. I don't expect to be very long myself.'

'I will wait, if you like,' she said, uncertainly. She had already put on her hat and coat.

'No, please don't bother. I'll lock up when I leave.'

'Very good. Goodnight, Monsieur Holland – and welcome home!'

Mark closed the door to his office, and sat at his desk. In a tray, there was a small pile of correspondence awaiting him. Most of the letters had notes clipped to them, covered with Anne-Marie's neat handwriting. He searched towards the bottom of the pile, knowing what he was looking for.

It was almost at the bottom of the tray: a plastic tape cassette, held by a large paper-clip to a letter. He picked it up, and read the spine of the box. Printed in ink on the card was 'Joachim Albrecht – Pianist'. Anne-Marie had pinned a note to the letter.

Mark –
I have listened to some of this. He is quite awful! The tape is very amateur, which does not matter, but his playing is very bad, full of finger slips and other technical troubles. He seems to have some idea of what the music is about, but he

can't play it! Do you want to listen to any of it, or shall I send it back with the usual thanks and regrets?

A-M

The letter to which she had attached her note was typewritten.

Dear Mr Holland,
I would be very grateful if you would audition the enclosed piano tape. I will telephone your office in a few days to learn your opinion of it. Thank you very much for your kind consideration.

The signature at the bottom was illegible, and the return address was a local box number.

Mark took the cassette out of its plastic box. His hands were sweating, and the plastic felt unpleasantly slippery. Next to his desk there was a small, cheap record and cassette player, a 'music centre', as the manufacturers ambitiously described it, which he frequently used to audition tapes and discs sent in by hopeful musicians. He switched the machine on, inserting the cassette. After a moment, it began to play. The sound of the piano was tinny and uneven, with clicks and other extraneous noises. It was very amateur, and sounded as though someone had hung a microphone next to an out-of-tune upright piano. Somewhere in the background, he could hear a radio playing. His office sometimes received very clumsily prepared audition tapes such as this, often from hopeful students, but the quality of the tape was even worse than usual. He turned up the volume control slightly, and the distorted sounds filled the room. The pianist was playing Schumann: the *Etudes Symphoniques*. Anne-Marie's assessment was correct. He was not very good. Mark had the impression that he played with the confidence of an accomplished pianist who had not practised for a long time.

He felt a sense of anti-climax. 'Joachim Albrecht' turned out to be a coincidence. They were not, after all, very unusual names. He was about to turn the tape off, but was puzzled by a minor detail. The piano sound appeared to be coming only from the left speaker of his equipment. The radio and background noises were on the right. If the cassette was stereo, it was a very odd way to record. The playback equipment was not very sophisticated. There was a balance control knob, which could be turned from side to side, to compare the left channel with the right, but it was not very selective. When he turned it to the left, the piano certainly became a little clearer. Turning it to the right, the piano was considerably reduced, but still audible, and the radio, apparently a news broadcast, could be distinguished amid crackling and hiss. He stopped the machine, and pushed the 'Eject' button, removing the cassette.

He was about to return it to its plastic storage box when another thought occurred to him. In a drawer of his desk, he kept a Sony Walkman, a miniature portable cassette player with headphones. He often took it with him when he travelled on long air journeys. He would listen to a complete opera in peace, and he preferred his own selections to the one-hour packaged entertainment provided by most airlines. He inserted the cassette in the little machine and, after adjusting the headphones, switched it to the 'Play' position. One of the advantages of the cassette player was that, included in its gadgetry, there was a small panel with separate, sliding volume controls for left and right channels. As the tape began to play, he reduced the left channel control to zero, raising the right channel to full volume. The machine was very accurate.

And then, in the isolated world of his headphones, he heard the voice. It was Glantz, without question. He spoke in a cold, analytical manner, almost without inflection, but the timbre and the accent were unmistakable. Mark stopped the tape. His shirt was clinging damply to his body, and his small office, simply but comfortably furnished, felt as though it was airless and suffocating. He pushed the 'Reverse' button on the player, and the sound squealed and rattled in his right ear. When it reached the beginning, it stopped with a slight click, and he pushed the 'Start' button again. There was a momentary silence, followed by a hissing sound, indicating the beginning of the recorded tape. There was a further series of clicks, as a microphone was adjusted, and the voice of Glantz began to speak.

186

'Findings of Thursday, March eighth, nineteen eighty-four. The following is to be added consecutively to the information already documented in Project L-Fourteen, dated January and February of the same year. For the purpose of the first equation, the symbol Omega has been chosen to represent...' The voice droned on, calmly and unemotionally. Except for the accent, he might have been a news reader on the BBC, giving the daily shipping reports. Glantz had kept his word. He had delivered the equations.

Mark listened to the entire first side of the cassette, not understanding more than an occasional word. The clarity of the voice, its inflections and imperfections, were faithfully reproduced. He sat, picturing Glantz as he slowly fed his poisonous recipe into the machine, seldom pausing for more than a moment, and with an occasional click as he stopped and started the recording machine. It was frighteningly calm. At the end of the reel, there was a final click, followed by silence. The room was oppressively heavy. Mark removed the cassette and turned it over, replacing it in the machine. Glantz had been right. In New York, he had said that it took a little more than half an hour to speak the whole terrifying message. When it ended, there were no words of farewell, no suggestion of human emotion. He simply came to the end of a series of complicated equations and stopped. The tape hissed quietly, and the voice did not reappear.

Mark sat in silence, letting the machine play on. It was as though he willed Glantz to speak one more time, to offer some words of humanity, to give some reason for his hideous creation. There were none. When the side of the cassette ended, he removed it from the player, and left it sitting on the centre of his desk. He sat, motionless, for a long time.

In the outside office, there was a can of liquid lighter fuel, standing on one of the filing cabinets. He brought it into his own office and, taking a steel paper-knife from his desk, he prised open the plastic casing of the cassette. The two sides pulled apart with a snap of breaking plastic, and he reached inside, pulling the narrow tape loose from its careful mounting on the spindle inside. It pulled away, bending and stretching, and he unwound it until he had made a small mound of tape, which he placed in the centre of the heavy glass ashtray on his desk. He poured lighter fuel over the plastic, until it floated in a small pool of liquid. Then, taking his lighter, he set fire to it. Flames leapt into the air with an explosive thud, and the tape twisted and writhed like a medieval sinner, exorcised of demons, burning and melting in the conflagration. There was an acrid, burning smell in the air, and he wondered whether fire and brimstone gave off a similar stench. After a few minutes, when the fuel had burned itself out, there were only twisted ashes in the blackened glass bowl. He tipped them into his waste basket. In a few hours, the late-night cleaning staff, provided by the building, would be there to remove them.

It was time to go, and yet he still sat at his desk, unwilling to leave. In the morning, when he called Quentin for confirmation that his records had been removed from the computers, he would tell them what he had done. It was too late for them to do anything about it, and there would be no further reason for them ever to call again.

He had left the door of his room open, to let out the smoke and the smell of burning tape, and his eye travelled to the outer office. An airline had sent a colourful calendar, which Frau Emmi had pinned over her desk. It showed a picture of Salzburg at festival time, basking in glorious sunlight. He smiled wryly, remembering the clouds and sleet that had hidden the city from view a few days earlier. The previous year, there had been a British Airways calendar, with pictures from all sorts of exotic locations. 'Fly The Flag,' he thought. 'I'm sure Willis would have approved of that!' He had gone to the trouble of mentioning that Mark could have taken a BA flight in the morning from Salzburg to London that first day. How typical that a man totally devoid of conscience should pretend to a petty hypocrisy like patriotism. He probably landed at Heathrow describing himself as a Terminal One man! Then, with a shock, Mark sat forward, seeing the answer to a question that had been nagging at his brain for several days. And, as if he had suddenly found the key to a complicated code, all the answers became terribly clear.

188

As soon as he reached his apartment, he telephoned Anne-Marie. Her phone rang a few times before she answered, and her voice was slightly breathless, as though she had been hurrying up the stairs to her door.

'Anne-Marie? It's Mark.'

'Mark! Where are you? I was beginning to worry again.'

'I'm here, in Geneva.'

'Here? But you should have called me from London. I would have met you at the airport.'

'I wanted to surprise you.'

'Oh Mark!' Her pleasure was evident. 'I am surprised, and I am so happy that you are home at last. Are you in the apartment?'

'Yes.'

'I will be there in ten minutes.'

'Please hurry!'

She laughed happily. 'All right. If I run all the way, in seven minutes!'

'Then run!'

The air in the apartment felt stale, unused after seven days. Throwing his luggage into a corner of the bedroom, he opened the windows and the door leading to the little balcony. He stepped out on to the narrow shelf, breathing the cool night air and leaning down, his hands on the low cast-iron railing. Across the lake, the flickering neon signs and coloured lights that decorated the office buildings and waterfront shops in the centre of Geneva glittered and sparkled, their reflections dancing across the black water. High clouds screened the stars, and the moon had not yet risen. Looking slightly to the left, where the town ended, Mark could make out an occasional distant light, a solitary beacon in the darkness, like a fallen star. The busy traffic in the street below stopped and started with the changes of the traffic light, impatient to reach restaurants, concerts, cinemas, assignations. It was only when they drove that the civilised Swiss lost their habitual, good-humoured placidity. He stretched his arms, feeling the dull ache of a tiredness that had been accumulating for days.

Anne-Marie must have run from her apartment. Within the seven minutes promised, he heard her key turn in the front door lock and the tapping of her shoes on the parquet flooring of the living room. Her voice called his name, softly, and she entered the bedroom, smiling. She was wearing a dusty pink overcoat with a wide collar, one that he did not remember seeing before. Freed of her severe, 'office' look, her ash-blonde hair hung loosely to her shoulders, catching the light. He walked in from the balcony, and she gave a delighted laugh, running across the room to him. They did not speak or kiss. Instead, she clung tightly to him, her head pressed against his shoulder, her arms tightly folded around his neck, fingers lacing themselves in his hair. His hands held her waist, and she moved closer still, pressing against him so that he could feel the firm contours of her body. She turned her head so that her lips could brush against his throat.

'Oh my dear love! I have missed you so much. I feel so help-less when you are not here. I do not eat; I cannot sleep prop-erly. I have no concentration at the office. It is not fair!' She laughed. 'If I go on like this, I will make myself ill. You will have to marry me for the sake of my health!' Mark said noth-ing, holding her tightly, and she moved her torso gently, so that her body rubbed against his. It was a signal between them, when she wanted to make love. 'I behaved so childishly while you were away, imagining all sorts of foolish things at the office, going quite mad when you did not call me. I'm sure poor Frau Emmi is convinced by now that I am having a ner-vous breakdown!'

Moving backward, she held his hands in her own and stood at arm's length, looking at him. She moved again, drawing him towards the bed, but he stood, holding her hands and resisting the gentle pressure. For a moment, she looked puzzled.

'Mark, you look strange. Why don't you say anything?' She laughed uncertainly. 'You have not changed your mind about me, now that I have said yes? I have to warn you, my love, that I will not let you go!' When he still remained silent, a look of concern came over her face. 'What is it, Mark? Is something wrong?' He took out a cigarette, lighting it with cupped hands. The movement broke the physical contact between them, and she leaned forward, playfully taking the cigarette from him and placing it on an ashtray. He watched it, balanced on the edge of the bowl, a thin finger of smoke rising vertically from its tip.

Her voice was uneasy. 'Please, Mark, tell me what is wrong. Have I upset you in some way? What is it? Do you not like my new coat? It was very expensive, but I felt like celebrating.'

She swivelled slightly, modelling the coat, which flared out around her long, slim legs. Mark watched her. She was beautiful, achingly beautiful, with the light casting subtle shadows beneath her high cheek-bones and across the graceful curve of her throat.

'Glantz is dead.' He made the flat statement.

She stopped in mid-movement, drawing in her breath. In a small voice, she asked: 'Glantz? The violinist you talked about in Vienna?'

'No.' His eyes never left her face. 'Eberhard Glantz, the research scientist working for Suchim. Perhaps you know him better as Weiner – Joachim Albrecht Weiner. Haven't they passed the message on yet?' His voice was cool, unemotional.

Anne-Marie had turned very pale. There was still a smile on her lips, but her eyes were now wary.

'I don't know what you are talking about, Mark. I thought you said he was a violinist. What are you talking about?'

Mark stepped forward to take his cigarette from the ashtray. He moved quickly, to catch it before it fell from its precariously balanced position. Anne-Marie, misinterpreting, flinched, as though expecting him to strike her. As their eyes met again, she gave a forced smile.

'Please, Mark. You are behaving so strangely. Why are you . . . ?'

He turned away from her with an irritated gesture. 'Oh come on, Anne-Marie, stop playing games! You know exactly what I'm talking about. For God's sake, stop this charade!'

She sat on the edge of the bed, watching him. Mark drew on the cigarette, inhaling the smoke deep into his lungs. When he spoke, it was as though he was talking to himself.

'It had been bothering me for days. Something was wrong – a piece that didn't fit into a puzzle – but I couldn't remember what the hell it was. When that damned driver met me at

191

London Airport, something clicked in my mind, but I couldn't place it.'

'What driver? What are you talking about?' Her voice was frightened, but Mark almost ignored her.

'It was only when I was sitting in the office this evening, looking at the calendar and thinking about that bastard Willis, that it came to me. How did he know that I would be coming into Terminal Two? Not even Willis or Quentin knew that. They thought I had flown directly from Salzburg to London on the British Airways flight. If I'd done that, I would have come in through Terminal One. But he knew I was going to be on the Zurich flight.'

'Who are Willis and Quentin, and why are you talking about flights and terminals?' Anne-Marie began to cry. 'Why are you doing this?'

As though interrupted from a reverie, he looked at her. Her fist was at her mouth, her teeth pressing against white knuckles. He felt nothing.

'But the terminal building didn't matter. They could have had a man at every bloody terminal. It started the whole train of thought. That's what mattered. There was only one possible person who could have kept them so well informed of my movements, and could tell them every time exactly where to find me.' He stood over her. 'In Konstantin's box at the Musik-verein; then London. For a while, I wondered whether London might have been one of Willis's little tricks – something he dreamed up with that sick little chess player's brain of his. I knew it didn't make sense, but I also knew Willis. But he couldn't have planned it, because he thought I'd flown from Salzburg. He didn't know about Zurich. Sally had forgotten to tell him.'

Anne-Marie was crying, her face in her hands. She made soft, animal noises.

Mark continued: 'From there on, it was simple. What a bloody fool I was not to spot it immediately. Of course they knew where to find me in New York! You made the booking at the hotel. You probably arranged for my usual room, so that they would know exactly where to look. Wherever I was, for the past seven days, what was the first thing I did?' His voice was bitter. 'I called my dear, sweet, loving Anne-Marie, who was so worried every time she didn't hear from me, and told me to take great care of myself! My God, your people aren't very good! You set me up for three different kills, and they missed each time!'

She pulled her hands from her face, now streaked and discoloured by tears. Ugly black lines of mascara ran from the corners of her eyes.

'It wasn't like that, Mark; you must believe me. It wasn't supposed to be like that. They were told not to touch you. They weren't supposed to kill you! Krebs was a mistake! The man in Vienna misunderstood. He wasn't supposed to kill . . .' Her hand went to her mouth, her eyes wide with fear, but Mark did not react to her confession. He had realised the truth already.

'A mistake? Now I understand! That's the final question answered. We couldn't understand why they wanted me dead.' He stared at Anne-Marie. His voice was cold, expressionless. 'It was just a silly, stupid, unthinking, thoughtless little mistake!'

She nodded, unable to speak for the tears which ran down her face, mingling with the spittle at the corners of her mouth.

Mark kept his voice low. 'Just a stupid mistake! A man dies, for no reason, for no excuse, because somebody fucked up! My God, there's no end to it, on either side!'

He was silent, walking to the open French window and feeling the cool breeze on his face. Behind him, Anne-Marie continued to sob, the sounds unrhythmic as she gasped for air. When he turned to face her again, his voice was cold. 'You can tell them they've failed. They've all failed. Glantz is dead. I watched him die, shot down as he stood there, trying to tell me where he'd hidden the last instalment. They were so eager to get rid of him – they couldn't wait! – that they did it before he told them. They just shot him down like a sick animal, and bundled him out of the room. And, if it's of interest to you, I found the rest of the information. You want to know where it was, my love? It was sitting here, in Geneva, all the time. You heard it yourself.' Their eyes met for a moment. 'Joachim Albrecht, Anne-Marie, short for Joachim Albrecht Weiner –

his real name. He'd recorded it on that piano tape, but you didn't listen to it carefully enough. He read the entire formula on to one of the channels of the cassette and covered it over by playing Schumann badly on the other channel. It's been sitting on my desk the whole time. God! How you must have searched through my office, looking for clues. No wonder you had strange feelings about the place! What were you afraid of? That I would notice how you and your friends had turned the place upside down?'

Anne-Marie had stopped crying. From time to time, her body was convulsed as she strove for breath. She was shivering.

'The tape is gone, Anne-Marie. I destroyed it, burned it. Nothing can be recovered. Both it and Glantz have been erased. So nobody's won.'

Her voice was pleading. 'You don't understand. They only wanted to talk to you. Please, Mark! They weren't supposed to harm you. They needed to find Glantz, to talk to him, persuade him not to tell them what he had discovered. It was too dangerous. There must not be a weapon like that . . .'

'Unless, of course, it's for your side, for future reference, in case things start to go badly for them. What are you trying to suggest: a balance of power? An extension of nuclear parity?'

'No! They just wanted to talk to him, persuade him.'

'Persuade him? The same way that they persuaded Sally Faulkner? Let me tell you about Sally. I loved her once, Anne-Marie, loved her and destroyed her, and she never did anything except return my love and forgive me for what I had done to her. When you carefully asked for my phone number in London to pass it on to your friends so that they could find the address, they just wanted to talk to her, too. They wanted to know where I had gone and whether she knew how to find Glantz. Let me tell you how they asked their questions.'

He told her. He described the room, with Sally sitting in it, described how they had strapped her into a chair, described the bruises and the blood, described the burns disfiguring her tortured flesh, described the cheap electric wire that strangled her final, agonised breath, described the look in her sightless eyes, described the stink of death and charred skin. The images were vivid in his mind and, as he spoke, the tears formed in his eyes, running down his face, and his voice broke. Anne-Marie had listened silently, eyes closed, reacting physically as he described each new atrocity. She heard his voice break and looked up, seeing him standing by the window, unable to speak further. She ran to him, stumbling, her hands outstretched, but he struck her across the face, knocking her to the ground. She rose to her feet, her hand against her cheek, fear in her face, as he moved towards her.

'Don't touch me, you fucking little whore! You killed Sally. You murdered all of them, just as surely as if you'd done it with your own hands! What did you think? That you weren't doing any harm, that you weren't involved, safe here in sunny Switzerland, passing a few messages?'

He came closer to her, fists clenched, and she backed away from him, her hands outstretched, pleading. Tears had begun to course again down her face, and there was an ugly red mark on her cheek, where his hand had struck. Mark no longer saw her face. It was Sally's, bruised and broken, with Sally's eyes staring in pain and death. Fury grew inside him, and he took another step, ready to hit her again. She backed further away, stepping on to the little balcony, watching him like a frightened animal. Short, guttural groans came from her throat as she gasped for breath. She did not feel the low railing pressing against her, but kept her eyes on his face. He moved forward, and she backed again, trying to keep him away. The railing cut deep into the back of her legs, throwing her off balance, her back arched over empty space, and she threw her arms forward, reaching desperately towards him.

He might have saved her, but he did not. As her body slowly fell backwards and her eyes widened with horrified realisation, he stood, hands at his sides, watching her fall. She screamed and slipped further, her weight carrying her over until she lost her footing and her body tipped backward into the night. Mark remained immobile, staring. In the space she had occupied seconds before, there was only blackness and the occasional twinkling light reflected in the water beyond. For a moment, there was silence from the street below, then the sound of brakes screeching and running feet. Several car horns sounded, and he could hear voices shouting.

He turned and walked back into the room. He was calm, breathing slowly, and the pulse that had been beating in his temple ceased its hammering. He sat on the edge of the bed and reached for the telephone. It was time to call Quentin. He would want the information to feed into the computers. It would round out the story to its logical conclusion. Perhaps the computers had already assessed the possibility. They were such logical machines, silently feeding the electronic impulses on to the tape, accumulating and digesting the information. It would all make sense now, with the sort of irrefutable reasoning that proves the argument of a geometrical theorem. QED. It was almost like music, resolving all its harmonies for the final chords on the last page of the score.

The telephone rang, shockingly loud in the silence of the room. He stared at the instrument, unbelieving, transfixed by its insistent ringing. At length, he slowly lifted the receiver from its cradle.

'Yes.'

'Hello. Mark, is that you? I hope I'm not disturbing you. I was afraid I must have missed you.'

It was Konstantin Steigel. Without waiting for a reply, he continued: 'Listen, my dear, Heidi and I have been talking over this business of a Japanese tour, and I must tell you that we are not very happy about it.'

'Oh.'

'Of course, you know that I don't mind, my dear. I am a professional musician, and I can conduct just as well in Tokyo, if I have to, as anywhere else in the world.' He lowered his voice. 'I'm afraid it's Heidi. She doesn't like all this travelling. It makes her very tired.'

'Yes.'

'Anyway, I think we now have a better alternative. I received a call this afternoon from that nice man at Covent Garden. It seems they have changed their plans for next season, and he asked me whether I would like to take on a new production of *Parsifal* for them. Of course, I told them that they must talk to you about this, Mark, but it is better that you

196

should know that I would much prefer to do this, and Heidi would be happier. Hello. Hello! Mark? Are you hearing me?'

He had not really listened. He understood the words, but they seemed dissociated from reality, like a half-remembered dream. From outside, he could hear the siren of a police car approaching. In a few moments, they would be looking for him. Mark gripped the telephone tightly, closing his eyes and trying to concentrate. 'Maestro, I'm sorry, but I can't really talk to you at the moment. May I call you back?'

The conductor sounded a little put out. 'What? Yes, I suppose so, my dear. Perhaps tomorrow morning would be a better time?'

'I'm very sorry. There's something of a crisis here.'

Steigel's good humour returned. 'Always a crisis in the music world! Don't worry, my dear. You must forgive me for assuming that my crisis takes priority over yours. Is everything well with you?'

Mark relaxed. 'Yes, thank you. Everything's under control.'

'Good. Anyway, we have plenty of time to make the arrangements. I will leave them to you. You always know how to put everything back together again.'

'I suppose so.'

'Very good. We'll talk again tomorrow. You can call me when you have settled your crisis. Heidi sends you her love.' The line went dead.

Mark sat on the edge of the bed and lit a cigarette. In a moment, he would go downstairs and find the policemen. It was the sort of tragic accident that was easy to explain, easy to understand. Those low balcony railings invited danger.

And in the morning, he would call London and tell Quentin about the tape. It was one small final victory that Willis would not enjoy. And, after that, there were Konstantin's concerts to be rearranged, and the young Israeli violinist who was looking for a manager, and the meeting with La Suisse Romande, and all the other plans that had to be made . . .

Start again.